HEAD
OVER
HEELS

Also by Hannah Orenstein

Love at First Like
Playing with Matches

HEAD OVER HEELS

Hannah Orenstein

ATRIA PAPERBACK

New York   London   Toronto   Sydney   New Delhi

ATRIA
PAPERBACK

An Imprint of Simon & Schuster, Inc.
1230 Avenue of the Americas
New York, NY 10020

First Atria Paperback edition June 2020

ATRIA PAPERBACK and colophon are trademarks of Simon & Schuster, Inc.

For information about special discounts for bulk purchases, please contact Simon & Schuster Special Sales at 1-866-506-1949 or business@simonandschuster.com.

The Simon & Schuster Speakers Bureau can bring authors to your live event. For more information or to book an event, contact the Simon & Schuster Speakers Bureau at 1-866-248-3049 or visit our website at www.simonspeakers.com.

Interior design by Erika Genova

Manufactured in the United States of America

1   3   5   7   9   10   8   6   4   2

Library of Congress Cataloging-in-Publication Data
Names: Orenstein, Hannah, author.
Title: Head over heels / Hannah Orenstein.
Description: First Atria Paperback edition. | New York : Atria Paperback, 2020.
Identifiers: LCCN 2020005035 (print) | LCCN 2020005036 (ebook) | ISBN 9781982121471 (paperback) | ISBN 9781982121488 (ebook)
Subjects: GSAFD: Love stories.
Classification: LCC PS3615.R4645 H43 2020 (print) | LCC PS3615.R4645 (ebook) | DDC 813/.6—dc23
LC record available at https://lccn.loc.gov/2020005035
LC ebook record available at https://lccn.loc.gov/2020005036

ISBN 978-1-9821-2147-1
ISBN 978-1-9821-2148-8 (ebook)

To all the athletes who spoke up about the abuse in gymnastics,
I'm in awe of your strength, bravery, and perseverance.
Thank you for making this sport safer.

• AUTHOR'S NOTE •

Head Over Heels was inspired by my love for gymnastics. I spent fifteen years training as a gymnast and always knew I wanted to write about the sport someday. In August 2018, the idea for this novel hit me and I quickly emailed my agent. "What *perfect timing* for summer 2020!" she wrote back. I was thrilled my editor agreed: the book would come out just in time for the 2020 Olympic Games in Tokyo. It never crossed anyone's mind that the event wouldn't happen.

Two days after I finished the final page proof review of this novel, the International Olympic Committee announced the 2020 Olympics would be postponed by a year due to the coronavirus pandemic. Since the modern Olympic Games were founded in 1896, the competitions have only been canceled for World War One (in 1916) and World War Two (in 1940 and 1944). While a postponement was undoubtedly the safest choice, it's also a devastating one for some gymnasts. Athletes have a very narrow window of opportunity to compete at their prime, and delaying the Games by even a year could mark the end of some gymnasts' Olympic aspirations.

This is hardly the first blow elite gymnastics has suffered in recent years. In September 2016, the *Indianapolis Star* reported that two former gymnasts had accused Larry Nassar, the former USA Gymnastics (USAG) national team doctor and an osteopathic physician at Michigan State University, of sexual assault. Since then, more than 265 women have come forward with accusations dating back to 1992. In July 2017, Nassar was sentenced to sixty years in federal prison after pleading guilty to child pornography charges; in 2018, he received two additional sentences of 175 and 40 to 125 years in state prison for sexual assault charges. As of February 2020, the United States Olympic & Paralympic Committee have proposed a $215 million settlement to current and former athletes who survived Nassar's abuse, but some top gymnasts have noted the settlement would prevent further investigation into USAG's role in the scandal.

In *Head Over Heels,* both Avery and Hallie's lives are shaped by the pursuit of Olympic glory. This book is a work of fiction, but top gymnasts' dedication and sacrifice, even amid terrible suffering, are not. As the sexual abuse scandal continues to unfold and the coronavirus pandemic pushes the Olympics off schedule, my heart goes out to the real-life Averys and Hallies. I invite readers to escape into a world in which the coronavirus pandemic does not happen, the Olympics go on as planned, and gymnasts deserving of justice chase their dreams.

OCTOBER

2019

• CHAPTER 1 •

The flight attendant thrusts a box of snacks under my nose without hesitation. I dab at the half-dried tears on my cheeks with the crumpled-up tissue I've been clutching ever since we left Los Angeles an hour ago and peer at the options.

"Popchips, Sun Chips, Doritos, pretzels, or trail mix," she recites, snapping her gum.

Everything is processed and full of salt, sugar, or both. "Thanks, but I'm all set," I say.

"The beverage cart will be coming next," she says, ignoring my sleeping neighbor and swiveling to the passenger on the other side of the aisle.

The thirty-something woman next to me, whose iPhone lock screen is a selfie of her in Minnie Mouse ears kissing a man wearing Mickey ones at Disneyland, took an Ambien the moment she sat down. I'm grateful, because I'm not up for a conversation right now. It's been two days since Tyler broke up with me, and I don't want to talk to anyone, much less a stranger.

There was no question that I'd leave the apartment we shared.

The lease was in Tyler's name, and even though I had always promised that I'd be able to pay half the rent someday, I'd never been able to afford my share of the luxury high-rise condo. I didn't have any friends I felt comfortable crashing with while I waited out my two weeks' notice at work, which they didn't really need anyway. I coached a preteen girls' recreational gymnastics team only a few afternoons a week, mostly to have something to do while waiting for Tyler to return from football practice and games.

Packing was simple because Tyler owned almost everything: the gleaming set of pots and pans in the kitchen, the oversized flat-screen TV he liked to watch *SportsCenter* on, the sprawling sectional he'd bought under the guidance of the decorator he hired the first time he cashed an obscenely fat check and thought he had an image to uphold. I threw the remnants of my old life—clubbing dresses and stilettos collecting dust in the closet—into the trash, then stuffed the remaining T-shirts, leggings, and sneakers into two suitcases. I left pieces of me behind: my favorite dog-eared cookbook, the heating pad I used when my back pain flared up, a pair of silver earrings he had given me. Anything else I needed would be waiting for me at home in Greenwood, Massachusetts.

I don't know if "sad" is the right word to describe how I feel. Maybe more "dazed." Or "lost." Or *What the fuck do I do now?* I'm not devastated or even angry. I love Tyler—or loved him, I guess. At first, I loved learning his quirks: the way he'd look over his shoulder after running onto the field, searching for my face in the crowd; the goofy way he grinned after his third beer; the polite, Midwestern way he always called my parents Mr. and Mrs. Abrams instead of Bill and Michelle. I admired his ease and modesty in the spotlight, traits that came naturally to him but never felt within reach for me. But I don't know if I necessarily *love* him. Not anymore.

To say that I didn't see the breakup coming both is and isn't a lie.

I guess I didn't want to look hard enough at what our relationship had become, not until he forced the issue and announced we were done. Because that would have required examining all of it—everything that'd happened since that day in San Jose, California, when I was nineteen—and admit that Tyler has a life to move on toward, and I don't.

After what happened at the Olympic Trials seven years ago, it was too late for me to apply to any colleges for that fall. I spent a miserable "gap year" slumped on the couch in my parents' basement, "exploring" and "studying" the way the TV could slide from morning talk shows to daytime soaps to the six o'clock news to prime-time sitcoms to the worst dregs of late-night movies.

I worried that twenty was too old to start college, but I had been recruited to one of the country's top gymnastics programs at Los Angeles State University, and it seemed a waste not to go. I had assumed that my reputation would precede me, that I'd be the star of the team. But I had been out of practice for more than a year by that point, recovering from my injury. I was flabby and weak, soft both physically and mentally. The other girls kept their distance; at first, I think they were intimidated to talk to me, but by the time they realized I was no queen bee anymore, they had already formed their own cliques. Practice was lonely and humiliating as I struggled to whip myself back into shape without my coach, Dimitri's, help. His methods had been extreme—punishing exercises, a cold shoulder if you didn't perform your best, rage if you failed—but I found myself missing them. My new coach asked us to call her Miss Marge. She began each workout with a mandatory dance party to get our hearts racing, and ripped open bags of Twizzlers as parting gifts at the end of every practice. The other girls loved her. But none of them had what it took to be truly great. Without training under the intensity of a legendary coach, how were any of us supposed to become champions?

I wound up randomly assigned to live with a scarily peppy girl named Krista. She was an LA native who claimed to be "ob-*sessed*" with everything, including my near brush with fame as an almost Olympic gymnast. She begged me to join her at the campus gym, where she clutched three-pound dumbbells while strolling on the treadmill, and stocked our room regularly with boxes of Franzia Sunset Blush she bought with her fake ID. Krista walked in on me in the shower one day by accident; she's the first person who brought it to my attention that normal girls shaved their legs with their foot propped up on the ledge of the tub, not at eye level, pressed against the shower wall.

I floundered through Psych 101, Intro to Mass Communications, and Human Physiology before my GPA dipped low enough for me to get kicked off the team. I watched myself fail with a perverse sense of curiosity: I had pushed myself to superhuman lengths for years; I had never seen myself falter before. Letting go was easy when you didn't care.

With Krista by my side, I fell into the world of dorm parties, then house parties, then bacchanalian nights at clubs. I learned the hierarchy of low-cal cocktails (vodka-soda, then vodka-tonic, then sugary vodka-cran as a last resort), the way to convince a club promoter to let you past the red velvet ropes for free, and the art of determining which men were game to flirt and which only wanted to grind their sweaty bodies against yours on the dance floor. I had finally unlocked the way regular girls got to feel powerful, beautiful, and magnetic: buzzed, carefree, gussied up in black Lycra dresses with men's hungry eyes locked with yours, moving to the beat of a soaring pop remix. Here, in the normal world, I didn't need to stick the landing. I could stumble—out of a club, into a cab, under the covers.

When I failed out of school midway through sophomore year, I barely registered it, other than to note that I could finally stop

showing up hungover to my 12 p.m. lectures. I had some savings—
bat mitzvah money and birthday money I had been given over the
years and had never had time to spend—and so I rented a room in
a three-bedroom apartment in Westwood. I lined up a series of odd
jobs (dog-walking, babysitting) that supported my habit of ordering
flimsy minidresses from NastyGal.com, and kept faithfully showing
up at 1OAK, Argyle, Supperclub, or wherever my best club promoter,
Angelo, would have me.

That's how I met Tyler. The way ESPN later described it, our
encounter sounded like an athlete's happily-ever-after: a former elite
gymnast just so happened to meet a rising football star one twinkling night in Los Angeles. That's the romantic spin. Tyler and his
friends bought a table at 1OAK and Angelo brought me and two
other club rats over to sit with the guys. Tyler offered to pour me a
drink from the glass pitchers of vodka, cranberry juice, and orange
juice. Back then, Tyler was just a rookie—the backup quarterback for
the LA Rams; the life-changing season that catapulted him to real,
mainstream fame as a quarterback was still a year ahead of him—
but he probably expected me to be impressed. Instead, I volleyed
that I had been a top athlete, too, a few years back. We talked and
danced and made out in the club for hours. When it was closing
down for the night, he shyly invited me back to his place. On any
other night, I would've said yes. But something came over me; maybe
I recognized a kindred spirit, someone I could find common ground
and an equal playing field with. Instead, I gave him my number and
told him to text me if he wanted to go out sometime. Sure enough, he
texted the next morning and invited me out for dinner.

That was four years ago. Dinner turned into a string of dates,
which soon led to a bona fide relationship. We fell for each other
fast—it was giddy and disorienting in the best way possible. He
liked that I understood and supported his strict training regimen,

unlike other girls he had dated in the past. And with his encouragement, the messy pieces of my life took shape. The more time we spent together, the more my diet shifted from fruit-flavored vodka to real fruits and vegetables. I started working out again. Tyler was the one who suggested that I seek out a part-time coaching job. By our third month of dating, I was smitten. By our fourth, I was confident enough to say "I love you" out loud for the first time. He said it back.

Moving into his apartment was a no-brainer. We spent almost all of our free time together anyway. Growing up, I had never allowed myself to really dream past the podium stand; when you believe you're on the edge of Olympic history, fantasies about boyfriends seem frivolous. But there I was, twenty-three years old, playing house with a hunky football player, lingering just a little too long over a bridal magazine in the checkout line at the grocery store. I had found myself living a dream I'd never known I wanted.

The next season, he threw the winning pass in the Super Bowl, and he became a household name. But the cozy closeness of our relationship thinned. We saw each other less, and when we did, it was often squeezing a date night into a football banquet dinner or charity event. I saw for the first time up close what it meant to be a champion, and I hated having my nose pressed up against the glass like a dirty onlooker; I still wanted that glory for myself. I couldn't admit that to Tyler; that meant giving him unfettered access to the haunted way my brain still taunted me with the word "failure."

It would be easy, I think now, as the airplane cuts through a gloriously white cloud and descends into a fog, to leave the breakup at that. I'm flying to the other side of the country, where Tyler knows no one. I could pretend we broke up because he got caught up in his own fame, and I didn't want that kind of life. Nobody would know the difference. Nobody but me.

There was an afternoon a few months back when Tyler came

home unexpectedly early; he wasn't feeling well. It was around 3 p.m. on a Thursday, one of my days off from the gym, and I was sitting on the kitchen floor with my legs splayed out in a lazy straddle, organizing the new spice rack I had ordered online. Around me, there was a mess of little plastic bottles: saffron, nutmeg, coriander, star anise, red pepper flakes. I had accumulated so many, splurging on whatever I needed to make a recipe sing. I'd discovered, once I moved in with Tyler, that I liked to cook; the process kept my hands and mind busy. And after an adolescence of grilled chicken and microwaved Lean Cuisines, the rich flavors I created felt like a gift. So I alphabetized the spices, sipping a generous pour of sauvignon blanc.

"Oh, you're . . . still home?" Tyler had said, a note of surprise in his voice, taking in my ragged pajama pants and the afternoon glass of wine. He looked past my shoulder, toward the living room I had vacuumed, dusted, and straightened up earlier that day.

"Hi! I didn't know you'd be home so early," I chirped. I tilted my chin up so he could give me a kiss, but he didn't. "Do you want something to eat? I can whip something up really quickly if you're hungry."

Tyler shook his head and turned on *SportsCenter*. The open-floor-plan layout of the apartment meant I could stay in that same spot on the floor and see him on the couch in the living room. But a few seconds later, he turned off the TV.

"You don't want to, I don't know . . . *do* something?" he asked, voice dripping with disgust.

"I'm doing this," I said, gesturing to the spice rack.

"You're practically a housewife," he said. "Minus the husband and kids."

I gave him a sour look. We'd talked about marriage as a possibility someday, because it seemed impossible to be living together in a years-long relationship in your midtwenties and *not* talk about it.

"I work," I said evenly.

"Part-time," he clarified.

"You're the one who suggested it," I reminded him.

"I didn't think you'd be happy with that little to-do forever," he countered.

"So, what? What do you want me to do?" I asked, slumping against the refrigerator and resisting the urge to grab my wineglass, lest it make me look even more like some awful cliché.

He sighed. "I don't know, have a . . . passion? Have some kind of ambition?"

"You know I do. You know I *did*," I said defensively, thinking furiously: *How dare he.*

"It's been a long time, Avery." His words drip out carefully, like he's been churning over the best way to say this for a while.

I was tempted to rattle off all the things I do all day that I genuinely enjoy: cooking, coaching, trying new workouts with my ClassPass. But that wasn't what he meant.

"Is this about money?" I demanded. "Do you want me to pay more in rent? Because I can make it work if you want me to."

"It's not about the money." He sighed. "It's just . . ."

He trailed off and looked critically at my bedhead, my shrunken sleep shirt printed with the name of a gymnastics meet I competed in more than a decade ago, and the overhead kitchen cabinets I'd flung open without bothering to close.

"It's just I expected a different kind of life with you, that's all," he said quietly.

And then he turned the TV back on.

There were more fights like that in the months that followed. Sometimes, I'd be honest enough to admit that long ago, ambition was all I'd had. And when the one thing I had built my world around collapsed, I didn't know where else to turn—I didn't know *how* to turn. Maybe I never fully recovered from the depression that hit like a truck seven years ago. I never found a reason to.

The plane enters a rough patch of air and gives a sickening jolt. As the turbulence jostles us, a clear *ding* rings out through the cabin, and the pilot makes an announcement over the PA system. "At this time, we ask that you return to your seats and fasten your seat belts. Thank you." The neon seat belt sign flashes on; there's an uneasy groan from some of the passengers. While my neighbor continues to doze, the man across the aisle from me crosses himself and downs the remainder of the Johnnie Walker he's been nursing. In front of him, an infant starts to wail in her mother's lap.

The turbulence up here doesn't bother me much. I'm more afraid of whatever lies ahead, once the flight lands back at home.

• CHAPTER 2 •

Mom and Dad meet me at the arrivals gate at Logan airport with faces scrunched in concern.

"That's all you brought?" Dad asks, taking the two bags from me.

"Oh, honey," Mom says, pulling me in for a hug. She kisses my hair. "We'll get you fixed up."

I had returned home plenty of times since moving to LA, but this time, it has a sense of finality. I'm not here for a quick Thanksgiving visit—when Mom hits the clicker and rolls her Honda into the cold, musty garage, I'm returning for good. I take a suitcase in each hand and trace my old, familiar steps through the house.

A corner of the living room serves as a shrine to what once was. There's a life-sized cardboard cutout of me, frozen forever at seventeen years old, in a red-white-and-blue spangled leotard with chalky thighs and a pile of medals around my neck. Trophies, medals, and competition photos fill the floor-to-ceiling bookcase behind it. I heave my suitcases past the living room, up the stairs, and into my childhood bedroom. It's still painted a childish shade of pink, and there's a smattering of glow-in-the-dark stars stuck on the ceiling. Once-glossy posters of gymnastics greats like Nadia Comaneci, Mary Lou Retton, and Shannon Miller cling to the walls.

I flop on the bed. Compared to the king-sized one I shared with Tyler, this twin-sized mattress feels like a flimsy pool float. I'm no longer a hundred pounds of pure muscle; I don't fit here anymore. I look at my phone with a sigh, wishing desperately for any sort of distraction. I have no texts; barely anyone knows I've moved.

I open Twitter. At first, it's a mindless stream of news, memes, and snippy comments from people I can't remember following in the first place. I see missives about gratitude and accountability from Krista, my old college roommate; according to her tweets, she's been sober for a year now. But then a headline catches my attention. My heart lurches as I open the story on TMZ: *TYLER ETTINGER NEWLY SINGLE? SPOTTED COZYING UP TO A SWIMSUIT MODEL*.

I read it over—once, twice, three times—but the words seem to swim on the screen. Someone on Twitter recognized Tyler at Bootsy Bellows, a celeb-studded club in LA, and took a grainy video of him grinding up on a woman that TMZ identifies as model Brianna Kwan. She apparently had a four-page spread in the *Sports Illustrated* Swimsuit Issue this year. In a fit of self-loathing, I hit play on the video. He nuzzles her neck as his hand trails down the front of her dress; she tilts her head back to whisper something in his ear. Paparazzi caught them outside the club, too, striding hand in hand from the back door to a waiting black car. Tyler knows what he's doing—he knows better than that. He's the one who taught me how to ditch the paps or throw them off the trail: don't show affection or even walk within the same photo frame when photographers are around unless you want the attention. He never did. He said he didn't like too much publicity around his personal life, but now I just wonder if he didn't want it with me.

TMZ concludes that Tyler has likely split from Avery Abrams, his ex-gymnast girlfriend of four years. "Or if not, he's sure to hear from her soon . . ." the site snarked.

I shove my phone under my pillow and bury my face in it. While Tyler is moving on, I'm spiraling into the worst version of myself: lethargic, self-pitying, aimless. The same way I felt after Trials. The version of myself that he didn't want anymore. I want to scream. I feel full of bitter rage in a way that makes me tear up. I went so many years without crying: not when Dimitri assigned me triple sets of conditioning because I talked back one day; not when a fall off beam knocked the wind out of me; not when I developed a stress fracture in my spine at fourteen. The Olympic Trials failure opened up a floodgate I couldn't close. Ever since then, the littlest things set me off. It's embarrassing, how quickly hot tears spring to my eyes now.

This isn't little, though. I wish it were.

I pull up Tyler's Instagram on my phone and scroll down, scanning for the occasional photos he posted of me or of us together. There should be one from a month ago, when we attended his cousin's wedding together—but it's gone. So are the pictures from our anniversary getaway to San Francisco. It's like he's erased me. My stomach drops when I see he's unfollowed me, too. Worse, still, I see he just recently followed that swimsuit model.

I feel sick. I can't remember the last time Tyler touched me the way he touched Brianna in the club, like my skin gave off the oxygen he needed to breathe. I knew our relationship had its issues, but Tyler always said that if you love each other, you stick it out the whole time, no matter what. Nothing a person could say or do would push you away forever. I believed him, because he was the first guy I'd ever really dated, and he had had a serious girlfriend in college. He knew. He and Megan had the kind of relationship where they went on summer vacations with each other's families and talked about future baby names. It only dawned on me later that he eventually left Megan, too.

• • •

When the phone rings at dinner, I'm grateful for anything that cuts through the conversation. Mom plated an endive salad and asked probing questions about why I think Tyler broke up with me; she served grilled tilapia and suggested jobs I could apply for; she refilled our water glasses and peppered me with updates about childhood friends I haven't seen in fifteen years. She can't do silence or stillness. She picks up the call on its second ring.

"Abrams residence, Michelle speaking."

I push a bite of fish across my plate and try to shut out the unwanted image of Tyler's fingers snaking down Brianna's taut abs. Mom listens, draws out an elongated "ummm," and cocks her head toward me.

"Sure, I'll put her on." She covers the receiver with one hand. "Avery, phone for you."

I can't imagine who it is. Nobody knows that I'm here. I take the phone from Mom and wander into the living room.

"Hello?" I ask uncertainly.

"Avery, hi," a male voice says. "I'm sure you don't remember me. It's been a million years. This is Ryan Nicholson."

Of course I remember him. His name is seared into my memory; you never forget the name of your teenage crush. Ryan was a top gymnast around the same time that I was. He trained in Florida, and like me, he was homeschooled for most of his teenage years. Because we both competed on a national and international level, we crossed paths at meets a few times a year. When my best friend Jasmine and I made lists of the cutest boys we knew, his name was always on them. To be fair, we were both homeschooled and knew of just eight or ten boys who didn't sport rattails—an unfortunately popular fad among male gymnasts in the 2000s—but still. His thick, dark hair; chocolate-brown eyes; and nicely muscled arms and abs made a lasting impression. He went to the Olympics in both 2012 and 2016.

"Ryan! Hi. Wow. It's been a minute."

"It sure has been," he says.

"Um, so . . ." I say.

It's like all normal social niceties have completely fallen out of my brain.

"I hear you're in town again," he says.

"How?" I blurt out.

I wonder if he read the TMZ story and drew his own conclusions.

"Winnie told me she ran into your dad at the grocery store yesterday."

Now *that*'s a name I haven't heard in a long time. She's the office manager at my old gym, Summit. I loved her.

"Oh! Right," I say, relieved. "What have you been up to all these years?"

"Has it been that long?" he asks. "Wow. I mean, well, a lot of things. Training. I went to the University of Michigan for gymnastics, and competed in London and Rio. Did some traveling for a while. And I've been coaching, too. You?"

"Well, I just moved back to Greenwood," I say, hoping that covers it.

There's a beat of silence on the line.

"Uh, you're probably wondering why I'm calling," he says.

"Yeah," I admit.

Years ago, if Jasmine and I could've chosen a personal phone call from Ryan Nicholson or Ryan Gosling, we would've picked Nicholson every time. I pace the width of the living room and wind up face-to-face with my cardboard cutout. I swivel to dodge her.

"I'm working at Summit Gymnastics now," he says. "I know you trained there for years with Dimitri Federov before he left."

"I did."

Dimitri put Summit on the map in the 2000s by producing more Olympic gymnasts there than any other training facility in American history—Lindsay Tillerson, Jasmine, and plenty of others. But after 2012, he left Summit to found his own gym, Powerhouse. Summit was taken over by one of its own longtime coaches, Mary Li, but I haven't heard much about her. It sounds like she prefers to stay behind the scenes these days, running the business, rather than training athletes on her own.

"I'm training this girl Hallie for Tokyo," he explains, referring to the 2020 Olympics. "She's amazing, especially on bars. Hardworking and determined like you've never seen before, real natural talent, total star quality. Maybe you've heard of her?"

"Um, believe it or not, I haven't been keeping up much with the sport lately," I say.

The truth is that if 2012 had gone differently for me, I might not have the hard feelings that I do now.

"I'm optimistic about her chances," he says. "Bars is on lock. She's strong on vault and beam, too. But floor is a weak spot for her. Her routine has an impressively high level of difficulty, especially when it comes to tumbling, but she keeps getting dinged on execution. Her artistry could be better."

I know what he means. There are two types of gymnasts: the powerhouses who nail sky-high tumbling and have so much energy, they nearly bounce out of bounds, and the delicate dancers who captivate fans with beautiful choreography, but never attempt the toughest tricks. I was among the latter. You can't choose—you work with what comes naturally to you. At five-foot-three, I was relatively tall and elegant for a gymnast, and my flexibility put the famously bendy Russians to shame. Floor was where I shone—I had a sense of poise and presence to my artistry that's almost impossible to teach. You either have it or you don't.

"I'm looking for an assistant coach to come on board to lead her training on floor," Ryan continues. "There's only so much I can do to help her."

Gymnastics is split by gender: women and men compete on both floor exercise and vault, though women also do balance beam and uneven bars, while men do parallel bars, high bar, rings, and pommel horse. But even though Ryan and I both did floor, the event is drastically different for men and women. We both performed difficult and exciting skills, but his focused on brute strength while mine were interwoven with dynamic choreography. It doesn't matter that Ryan earned an Olympic gold team medal, a gold on high bar, and a bronze on parallel bars. His skills don't fully translate to women's gymnastics, although plenty of men coach women. That's how it's always been. The greatest coaches in the sport's history— like Igor Itzkovitz and, yes, Dimitri Federov—are all men.

"I'm wondering if you would want to come by the gym this week and meet Hallie," he says. "See if you'd want to work with me to train her."

I can't help it. I actually laugh.

"I'm serious," he presses.

"Ryan, I'm flattered, but this isn't a good time for me," I explain. "I just moved back, and I'm not really looking for coaching jobs. I mean, I've never coached at that level before."

"So you're not interested?" he asks. "I mean, Avery, we're talking about the Olympics. I promise you, this girl has what it takes. She just needs to be polished up a bit. That's where you'd come in."

I hesitate. It's dark outside now, and the row of gold trophies on the top shelf gleam menacingly in the living room window.

"I can't," I say.

He sighs heavily on the other end of the phone. "Why don't you take my number in case you change your mind?"

"Uh, sure," I say.

I add his number to my own phone, even though I know I won't use it.

"It's not like there are dozens of qualified coaches with Olympic experience running around this town," he jokes.

His words make me pause. It's like UCLA all over again, when my name was bigger than my actual achievements.

"Just Olympic Trials, actually," I say curtly. "I never made it any further. I have to go; my family's having dinner. Take care, okay?"

I say goodbye and hang up. When I turn back to face the kitchen, Mom and Dad's eager faces already look hungry for news.

"It was nothing," I say, taking my seat. "Just a call about whether I'm looking for a coaching job. I'm not interested right now. I just got back, you know."

They exchange glances.

"It could be a good opportunity," Dad ventures.

"And you should have something to do," Mom adds. "It'd be good for you to get out of the house."

They're eager because that's all they know. Gymnasts don't ascend the ranks to become Olympians unless the whole family is committed from the start. My ambition burned out, but theirs never did.

"It's really no big deal," I say. "Let's just eat."

• • •

That night, I can't sleep. The TMZ video loops cruelly in my head, interspersed with my most romantic moments with Tyler. I see him hand-delivering a bouquet of two dozen white roses and lilies, just because it was Wednesday and he missed me. I flash to his eyes shut tight, head bopping to the beat of the club's house music. I remember the sexy, sleepy way his hair stuck up in bed when he woke up on Sunday mornings, and the time he bought out an entire theater so I could see a showing of *Stick It* on my birthday. My brain cuts to the way he slipped his hand into Brianna's as they exited the club, heads ducked from the flashing cameras. And then there's Mom's voice: *You should have something to do.* Something other than this: lying sweaty in a twin-sized bed in a room decorated by an eight-year-old.

Fuck it. If Tyler can move on, so can I. I download a dating app and throw together the bare bones: a full-body photo from my skinny days before the Freshman 15 set in; a close-up from Tyler's cousin's wedding, when my hair and makeup looked good; and no bio at all, because what's there to say? I set my location radius to thirty miles. Even after all this time, my name is easy to recognize in this small town. People still think of me as that girl who almost made the Olympics.

It's past 11 p.m.—probably too late to swipe without looking like I'm only here for hookups. But I feel a morosely intoxicating combination of sadness and loneliness, so I swipe anyway. I reject the first seven men right off the bat because once you've dated a pro football player on *People's* 50 Most Beautiful list (number forty-one, but still), it's tough to recalibrate your standards. But I find a groove eventually, indicating interest in a local firefighter, an accountant, and a middle school math teacher I vaguely recognize as someone who grew up in Greenwood a couple years ahead of me. I match with the teacher—Lucas—and involuntarily shudder. He's not Tyler. It's disorienting to actively seek out other men. I don't know if I really feel ready for this.

hey, Lucas messages me. *what's up?*

Not much, I write back. *Just moved back here this week from LA, actually.*

You grew up here? he asks.

I hold my breath. *Yeah,* I write.

But miraculously, he doesn't seem to recognize me. Instead, he asks what I'm up to tomorrow. When I answer truthfully that I have nothing major going on, he invites me out for a drink tomorrow night. I hesitate, then swipe quickly through a few more potential matches. Nobody else stands out to me. So I say yes. It's not like I have anything better to do.

• • •

Jade Castle is a mediocre Chinese restaurant with one of the few liquor licenses in this formerly Puritan dry town. My family never came here; we always preferred to eat at Ming's House—not that I could ever have anything besides the steamed chicken and broccoli— because Jade Castle has always attracted a less family-friendly crowd. When I arrive at seven thirty tonight, I spot the father of one of my middle school classmates sitting at the bar with a girl half his age, and a large round table crowded with boys in matching lacrosse team jackets, probably using an expired ID swiped from an older brother. I take an empty bar stool; I'm not sure if Lucas intended for us to eat or not. When a bartender asks if she can get me a drink, I awkwardly decline. It's been a very long time since I've been on a first date, and it feels like the muscle has atrophied. I felt optimistic setting up the date on the app, but now my confidence has evaporated.

Lucas walks in at seven forty, when I'm on the verge of losing my nerve and leaving.

"Avery?" he asks, tilting his baseball cap up to reveal a baby face and a smattering of freckles. He has a narrower frame than I expected; a Boston Red Sox jersey hangs from his shoulders.

"Hi," I say, unsure whether to rise and hug him.

I make an attempt to stand, but my feet get tangled behind the leg of the bar stool. He slouches onto the seat next to me instead and leaves his phone faceup on the bar.

"You want a beer?" he asks, not quite making eye contact.

"Uh, sure," I offer.

When the bartender glances our way, he holds up two fingers, and mouths, "Two." I get the distinct sense that he's been here on plenty of dates. He drums his fingers on the bar in a staccato rhythm, then visibly relaxes once he sees her returning with our drinks.

"So, LA, huh?" he asks finally.

"Yeah."

"Why'd you move back?"

The question makes me frantic. "Uh, I just needed a change."

"Must be wicked nice out there," he comments. "Warm. Beautiful. You go to the beach a lot?"

I feel stupid telling him I spent six years in LA and can count my number of beach days on one hand because I wasn't confident enough to wear a bathing suit.

"Yeah, all the time," I lie.

It's obvious that this date is not off to a strong start. And what's worse, it's not a stretch to imagine my future as a string of evenings just like this one, probably at this exact bar, probably while Lucas conducts a similar string of dates a few bar stools down.

"So, you teach? What are the kids like?" I ask, turning the conversation to him.

"The kids are fine. Bunch of Goody Two-shoes, a couple of class clowns, mostly smart kids," he says. "You know how this town is."

I do. The suburb's strong public school system attracts a wildly overachieving, goal-oriented population. When I was in elementary school, nobody thought it was weird that I spent sixteen hours after school every week training in a gym because everyone else spent that amount of time on horseback riding lessons, piano lessons, theater classes, or all three.

I don't know what else to say, so I cast around for anything we might have in common.

"Is, god, what's her name? Mrs. Marcotti? Is she still teaching math these days?"

He nods and rolls his eyes. "Yep. With a stick up her ass."

"She was a tough teacher," I say, ignoring the rude comment.

"You had her?" he asks.

"Yeah, in seventh grade? Eighth, maybe?"

"Me, too. What year did you graduate?"

"Uh, 2010? I mean, technically. I was kind of homeschooled the last few years."

He cocks his head and really stares at me. For a few stretched-out seconds, neither of us speak.

"You're that girl," he says, squinting like he's trying to recall the details. "The gymnast."

"Yeah," I say quickly, sipping my beer in an attempt to shut down this line of conversation.

"You were that girl in that *video!*" His voice gets louder.

My blood runs cold. In my most pathetic moments, I've watched the damn video alone. But Lucas is jubilant, leaning in closer but talking louder than ever.

"I *knew* you looked familiar!" he says cheerfully.

I feel cornered. I shrug and try to cast around for another topic of conversation to distract him.

"So, do you ever—"

Lucas opens YouTube on his phone and starts to type in "worst gymnastics crashes." It doesn't take him long to zero in on the clip he's searching for. He gleefully hits play, and I hear the familiar roar of an athletic arena cut through the bar's din. I can hear the faint, singsongy chant of my name—"Let's go, A-ve-ry, let's go!" I don't need to watch; I know it by heart: me, nineteen years old, in a shimmering red leotard and a ponytail, performing the sharply sultry opening dance moves of my floor routine at the 2012 Olympic Trials. Even all these years later, the music stirs my muscles; *this* is where I pirouette; *this* is where I roll my hip. I ground myself back into reality on the bar stool, willing myself into stillness.

But I can't forget what I know is playing out on-screen: the younger version of me launching into my first tumbling pass. It's the most impressive one of my routine: round-off, back handspring, whip, back handspring, double-twisting, double back somersault. I had performed it a thousand times before. But this time, I under-rotated and came crashing down onto the blue spring floor while I was still spinning. There was a horrific shredding sensation in my knee before my hands even hit the ground.

"Gnarly," Lucas says emphatically, shaking his head at the screen. "I used to watch this all the time. Sick."

My floor music continues as the audience gasps. I scream. Lucas taps the screen to watch the crash over again, cutting short the moment when Dimitri rushed onto the floor to carry me away in his arms. My stomach lurches as I watch Lucas lean even closer to the video.

I clear my throat. "Please turn that off," I say.

"I can't believe this is you," he says, glancing from me to the screen. "You were so tiny back then."

He makes no move to stop the video.

"Can you—?" In a jolt of frustration, I grab the phone out of his hands and shut the video off, leaving the phone facedown on the bar.

I do my best attempt at a smile, but I can sense it comes out all thin and strained.

"Whoa," Lucas says, holding up his hands as if to prove he's harmless.

"I don't like to watch that," I try to explain as calmly as possible. I swallow. "That right there? That was the end of my gymnastics career. And a lot of stuff changed for me after that. It was hard, okay? So, please, let's stop watching it."

"No need to be so intense," Lucas says defensively. He slurps down his beer. "I got it."

Somehow, I have a hard time believing he's "got it." I had trained for that moment since the time I was four years old, when my ballet instructor complained I had too much energy for dance and suggested I switch to gymnastics instead. By age eight, I was practicing four times a week. At twelve, I sat in a straddle on my living room floor, transfixed as Lindsay Tillerson won the all-around gold—I knew I could follow in her footsteps. Two years later, I convinced my parents to let me drop out of school and study with a tutor so I could train full-time under the legendary coach Dimitri Federov. In this sport, it's outrageous for anyone to claim an easy path to Olympic glory. But everyone from Dimitri to Jasmine to the girls who sent me fan emails all said the same thing: I had a better chance than any other athlete out there.

I was furious that I'd just missed the cutoff to be eligible for the 2008 Olympics. Sixteen is the minimum age to compete, and my birthday fell just weeks after the Beijing games at the end of August. So I threw myself into the next four years of training, desperate because I had dreamed of this one moment for nearly my entire life.

The Olympic Trials for gymnastics are held just seven weeks before the actual Olympic Games. Trials and the Games are held closely together to limit the likelihood of anything disastrous happening in the middle; god forbid a gymnast sprain an ankle, or worse, develop. In 2012, fourteen athletes competed for just five spots on the team, plus three alternates. I performed beautifully all day long, and floor was my final event of the competition. I liked the idea of finishing on a high note.

And then I crashed. It was over. All of it. Gone. Recovering from surgery was tough because it seemed as if there was nothing to recover *for*. I was nineteen years old. Even if my knee healed well, I was too old to seriously consider the prospect of training for Rio in four years. The cruel reality of the sport is that you train your entire life for one event, and then the moment disappears in a flash. By twenty-one, twenty-two—forget about twenty-three—your body has taken beatings for too many years.

So, the same night my career ended, Jasmine's took off. She didn't just make the Olympic team—she became the star of it. While she competed in London, I watched the competition on the couch, recovering from knee surgery. In lulls between performances from the American gymnasts, the commentators noted that Avery Abrams, widely considered the front-runner, the shoo-in, hadn't made the team due to a last-minute injury. They rattled my name off like a fun fact, the same way they commented on the architecture of the stadium and the number of Swarovski crystals sewn onto competition leotards. Jasmine won a gold on bars, a silver on beam, and a gold team medal.

I had imagined that I'd return home from London as America's sweetheart. I'd model for Wheaties boxes, chat up talk show hosts, and land *Sports Illustrated* covers for a few months. Then, once the mainstream interest in my athletic prowess had died down, I'd enjoy a revered career within the world of gymnastics. I'd be a commentator on TV, design a collection of leotards for GK, and give motivational speeches to aspiring athletes across the country. There was no plan B.

Meanwhile, Jasmine was on the Wheaties box. She was on the cover of not only *Sports Illustrated*, but *People, Seventeen*, and *Essence*, too. She was invited to New York Fashion Week and the Grammys. She won *Dancing with the Stars* and seemed to be Ellen DeGeneres's new best friend. Little girls across the country did cartwheels in leotards she designed. We had been best friends, training side by side for six years. At first, she called often, asking sincere questions about my knee surgery and saying she wished I could be there with her. She even sent me a care package of souvenirs from London—British chocolate bars and a commemorative mug stamped with Prince William and Kate Middleton's wedding portrait, taken the year before. I could barely stand to reply, and I let our friendship wither to monthly texts. I saw her in person just once after the Olympics; it was her twentieth birthday dinner, and I couldn't come up with a plausible excuse to turn down the invitation. It felt like all the comfort had been sucked out of the air between us. She didn't bother texting at all after that.

Lucas makes a show of sliding his phone into his pocket. I don't know what the protocol is for ending a bad date early, but I sense with absolute clarity that I should leave. I saw a woman on TV once slap money on the bar and saunter away, which looked supremely classy, but I'm not carrying any cash. I don't want to leave Lucas—as awful as he is—with the bill, just on the matter of principle. Instead, before I lose my nerve, I clear my throat and tell Lucas I'm leaving.

"I'm going to head out, but have a good night," I say.

I signal the bartender. As I wait for her to come my way, I stare straight ahead, not brave enough to even glance at Lucas.

He sputters, "You're leaving? Now?"

I hand my credit card to the bartender. "Just for the one drink, please," I tell her. Then I turn to my date. "I'm sorry, yes, I'm leaving. It's been a long night."

I grab my purse and jacket and stride through Jade Castle to get to the parking lot. I've only had a few sips of beer; I should be fine to drive home. Before I back the car out of the spot, my fingers find the preset for the angriest indie rock channel on the radio. The presets haven't changed since I was in high school. I take the familiar turns through the town center, replaying Lucas's moronically cruel behavior on a loop in my head. If I had to venture a guess, this is not how Tyler felt after his first night out with Brianna.

When I reach my driveway a few minutes later, I'm still too angry to get out of the car. I know that when I walk into the house, Mom and Dad will probably pepper me with questions about how the night went, and I'm not ready to face that.

I look up Ryan's phone number in my contacts. The unfamiliar area code is proof that he's an outsider—a fresh start. He saw me in the context of the sport, where career-ending falls are unfortunately more common than you might think. They're par for the course, not a local tragedy. Unlike Lucas, Ryan—hopefully—doesn't look at me and think, *train wreck*. He's seen me draped in gold medals. And it's not like I have anything else going on. I dial his number.

"Avery?" he asks, sounding confused.

"I've thought about your offer," I say, voice shaking with remnants of anger. "I'd like to take you up on it."

• CHAPTER 3 •

Arriving at Summit hurls me back in time. On Thursday afternoon, I swing open the front door in a daze, but no one else seems fazed by my entrance. Moms congregate in the windowed lobby, watching their children's practice. The office is still home to racks of leotards with matching scrunchies and warm-up shorts available for purchase. The entire building has the mingled scents of chalk and sweat. The only clues to the passage of time are the selection of photos hung in the front hall. There used to be a larger-than-life print of me at a competition with my signature in black Sharpie. It's gone now, and in its stead are a series of framed team portraits. I recognize a few of the faces—the younger siblings of the girls in my age group. The last time I saw these kids, they were seven or eight years old. Now they're teenagers.

When I enter the locker room, I feel the acute sense of no longer belonging. The narrow space is crawling with skinny kids who don't yet know that the scrunched cotton underwear hanging out the sides of their leotards makes them look like amateurs. The middle of the room is occupied by stacks of cubbies stuffed with gym bags, grips, sweatpants, and Uggs. My usual one is occupied, so I find an empty spot to store my socks and sneakers. I tighten my ponytail and steel myself to find Ryan in the main training area.

I open the glass door that separates waiting parents from the gymnasts and coaches and scan the gym for Ryan. The room is thick with memories. Everywhere I look, I flash back to younger versions of myself: six and crying because I just straddled the beam when I was supposed to land a cartwheel; twelve and high on the adrenaline rush of my first giant on bars; eighteen and prepping my floor routine for Nationals. I spot Ryan and a girl I assume to be Hallie sequestered on a stretch of mats by a mirror. They're conditioning—the full-body work-out designed to build the strength necessary to perform. I used to do an hour a day of crunches, push-ups, squats, rope climbs, and more, just to stay in competitive shape. Ryan's in track pants and a T-shirt, holding a stopwatch as Hallie does V-ups with weights strapped to each ankle.

I call his name as I approach. He glances at me, then down at the stopwatch.

"Thirty more seconds, Hal," he says. She grunts in recognition and keeps working. "Welcome back, Avery," he says, giving a firm handshake.

"Thanks for having me," I say.

It's odd to see him all grown-up now, and I wonder if he feels the same way about me. In some ways, of course, he looks exactly the same: chocolate-brown eyes, high cheekbones, a dimple in his left cheek, a thin scar over his right eyebrow, an impressively strong physique. But his thick, dark hair is longer on top—I guess he can wear it like that, now that he's no longer competing—and there's a smattering of stubble on his sharp jaw. Up close, I can see a colorful sliver of a tattoo peeking out from the sleeve of his T-shirt. *Of course.* He has the Olympic rings, just like his teammates do. Just like I would have, if things had gone differently.

"What do you think of being back here again?" he asks.

I take in the view of the gym, catching sight of coaches I recognize from way back when. "It's weird," I admit. "But this place feels like home."

"That's one of the reasons I thought you'd be perfect for the job," he says, clearly pleased that I feel the same way. "I want to take today slowly. Get to know each other. Have you meet Hallie. See how it goes."

"You know, I don't know if you and I have ever really hung out," I say. I feel like one of us has to note that this is our first proper conversation—we've always been in each other's orbit, but that doesn't mean we actually know each other.

"I'm pretty sure I asked you for directions to the vending machine at some competition once," he says, shrugging like he's just taking a vague stab at a memory.

But he's not. Because I remember it, too.

He's talking about Nationals the year I was sixteen, when the competition was held at an arena in Houston, Texas. The space was large and confusingly laid out; I must have walked in circles for five minutes on my way to finding the bathroom. I was returning from the women's restroom when I spotted Ryan—or Cute Ryan, as Jasmine and I called him. We had seen each other around at other competitions before, but hadn't ever spoken. Still, I was pretty confident that he recognized me.

"Hey, Avery—it's Avery, right?" he had asked.

I was secretly thrilled that he knew my name.

"Yeah," I said, trying not to blush.

I wanted to project the façade that hot guys spoke to me all the time. Totally normal. Yawn.

"Any chance you know which way the vending machines are? This place is like a maze," he said.

Luckily, I had just walked past them. I pointed him in the right direction. I won the gold all-around medal later that day, cementing my status as a gymnast to watch. But when I think back to that competition, what stands out is the twinkling, giddy adrenaline rush from Cute Ryan knowing my name.

All these years later, I feel vindicated, knowing that I'm not the only one who remembers the interaction.

"You know there's a machine in the lobby here, right?" I tease.

"Yeah, this one, I got covered," he shoots back.

The stopwatch beeps. "Done!" he calls to Hallie. She collapses on the mat. "Come over, I'll introduce you," Ryan says.

Hallie sits up, clutches her stomach for a moment, and undoes the Velcro straps securing her ankle weights. I'm sure that whatever set of reps she just completed was no joke, but she leaps to her feet. Her auburn ponytail swings over her broad shoulders. She's muscular and compact; the rippled outline of a six-pack is visible through the fuchsia Lycra of her leotard.

"Hallie, this is Avery. She's going to be coaching with me today," he explains. "Avery, Hallie."

She gives me a shy smile. "Hi. I'm sure you don't remember me, but I was a level four when you were training here. I remember you." She must have been one of the skinny kids running around in the locker room years ago.

"Oh, really? Wow," I say, unsure what else to add. Back then, I was so focused on my own training, I barely noticed the kids.

"Your poster was in the lobby," she recalls. "I wanted to be just like you someday." Instantly, her cheeks—already pink from exertion—flush red.

"Well, I'm sure you can aspire to loftier goals," I say.

"No, you were great," Ryan says confidently.

I don't want to tarnish his perception of my life since then, so I let the subject drop. "What are you working on?" I ask brightly.

"Finishing up conditioning," Ryan says. "We have fifteen minutes left. Then we'll move onto floor, cool?"

"Cool," Hallie and I say in unison.

Ryan alternates between leading Hallie through her remaining reps and filling me in on the situation. Hallie is sixteen now; he moved here to coach her three years ago, not long after he competed in Rio. The Olympics are the long-term goal, of course, but the next hurdle is the World Championships, held later this month in Stuttgart, Germany. She's very strong on bars and vault, and pretty solid on beam. But she's feeling less confident when it comes to floor. He wants me to watch her routine and see how I can help her polish it.

"Warm up your tumbling," he instructs Hallie, once she finishes conditioning.

She refills her water bottle, takes a slurp, then trots to one corner of the blue spring floor to practice her tumbling passes. She's diligent, efficient, and polite; she bounces in diagonal lines from corner to corner, letting other, younger girls tumble across her in between passes while she catches her breath. The other gymnasts defer to her with an obvious sense of reverence. Hallie's skills are strong, and she moves with a powerful sense of energy. It's too powerful, in fact—at the end of each tumbling pass, she bobs and stumbles to control her motion.

Next, she warms up the other elements of her floor routine: leaps, jumps, pirouettes, smaller acrobatic elements. Here, I see why Ryan is concerned. She has talent in spades, but lacks poise. The one lesson coaches drill into gymnasts from the first lesson is to *always point your toes*. Hallie points hers—but not with the sharp lines or intense muscular focus that she should. Until you've felt your thighs quaking as your toes curl toward your heels, you haven't really pointed your toes.

The problem, I realize, is presentation. Her chin needs to be a fraction higher, her shoulders should pull back by two inches. Her posture is stiff and strong, lacking grace. She goes through the motions of each skill in a technically accurate way, but that's it. She's moving, not performing. If I could teach her how to do that, she could be a champion.

If. I don't know if I can. I don't know if anyone can. It's a lot of pressure.

"What do you think?" Ryan asks.

I get the sense he's been watching me take her in to gauge my reaction.

"She's good," I say truthfully. "Really good."

"But . . ." he prompts.

I hesitate. "She could be better," I admit.

He nods and silently watches his charge work. She squats with one leg extended, then winds up to perform a clunky pirouette with her foot maneuvering inches above the ground. It's an awkward spin—known as the wolf turn—but the Olympic code of points awards it an insanely high difficulty score, so almost every top gymnast attempts to squeeze it into their floor and beam routines these days. I'm glad the move wasn't in vogue when I was competing.

"How would you want to train her?" he asks.

"I'd want to see her perform a full routine first, just to get a better sense of where she's at," I say. "But already, I can say that she needs to focus on her performance. She's talented, and her skills are impressive, but she could look a lot more polished. And her tumbling needs to get under control—she needs to stick those landings."

Ryan nods in agreement, and that gives me the confidence to keep going.

"It all boils down to one problem, really," I explain. "She needs to be sharper. More in control. Clean lines, solid landings, more intentional movement—that's what's missing."

I pivot to face him, and I'm grateful to see a bemused expression on his face. "Maybe you're right," he says. He calls out across the gym, "Hallie, ready to run a routine? Let's show Avery here what you can do."

Ryan connects his phone to a stereo system and calls for the other gymnasts to clear the floor. They scatter, giving Hallie a wide berth as she makes her way to a spot a few feet from one corner of the floor. She freezes into a pose with her left leg extended and her right arm above her head. Then, a tinkling flute leads into a sweeping piano melody, and her body comes alive. The structure of her routine is familiar: a few brief dance steps, an impressive tumbling pass, followed by a series of hastily executed acrobatic movements and artistic elements designed to propel her into a new corner of the floor, where she launches into another tumbling pass. The structure repeats again, giving her exactly ninety seconds to pack a lifetime's worth of training into a single performance.

There's no denying it—it's a good routine. But it's not the kind of show that brings home Olympic medals. Here, too, her posture is rigid; her motions seem rote and uninspired. The elegant music she's chosen doesn't fit her style at all.

"How long has she been competing with this routine?" I ask Ryan.

"It's changed a bit over the years, but basically, she's been doing this for forever," he says.

I nod. "She needs an upgrade," I say.

"New music? New choreography?" he asks, looking concerned. "Now? With less than a year to go?" We both look back to the floor as Hallie lands her final tumbling pass, throws her arms into a dramatic flair, then sinks into her end pose. She holds it for a second, then flops down on her back, chest rising and falling hard with the intensity of her breath. Floor is an endurance test; the best gymnasts make it look effortless, but that's just an act.

"Yeah, now," I say. "This is okay, but it doesn't play to her strengths. And there's so much to refine. It could be better for her to start from scratch and learn something she loves, rather than beating a dead horse here."

Ryan grimaces and rolls his neck, letting the vertebrae crack. Reflexively, I rotate my wrists until they crunch and push each knuckle into a satisfying *pop*. The sport is brutal on our joints.

Hallie joins us by the stereo. She has her hands on her waist and she looks like she's trying not to appear out of breath.

"What'd you think?" she asks, biting her lip.

"Awesome," Ryan gushes. "Great height and rotation on the double Arabian; that's really come a long way. The wolf turn looks tighter today, too. Your left hip isn't dropping as much anymore."

His comments aren't the full picture. Of course her double Arabian had fantastic height—she excels at tumbling, even the forward-rotating flips requiring superhuman power like that one—and she knows it. Her wolf turn was passable, but that's hardly the most pressing item to critique. I don't know Ryan well enough to determine if he's a softy or if he just lacks the gimlet eye necessary to pick apart the subtleties of a women's floor routine. But either way, he's shortchanging Hallie. He's letting her slide by without the grueling feedback she needs. If Dimitri ever saw this routine, Hallie would never hear the end of it.

"Avery? How did I do?" Hallie asks.

She radiates desperate energy; I can feel how badly she craves my approval. I was just like her once.

"That was very good," I say honestly, steeling myself to be straight with her. "But there's room for improvement, and I'd love to work with you."

Her jaw sets with disappointment. "Yeah?" she asks.

She shifts her weight onto one hip and crosses her arms across her chest. The muscular curves of her triceps jut out proudly, and for a split second, a wave of doubt washes over me. My triceps are soft and flabby. Seven years ago, sure, I could do what Hallie just did. I could do it better. But now? Who am I to tell this lean, powerful dynamo how to improve?

Hallie's hazel eyes narrow, and in them, I recognize a self-conscious flicker. I see her swallow hard. If I'm guessing right, she's gifted, hardworking, but anxious. I bet she knows her natural talent and ambition can only take her so far. Ryan knows it, too. That's why I'm here. In my experience, a coach can't only be your friend—they have to push you, too. Ryan doesn't seem like the type to zero in on a gymnast's insecurities and manipulate them into motivation, the way Dimitri did. But if he's an effective coach on bars, beam, and vault, then maybe I could be the bad cop on floor. Gymnastics is classified as an individual sport, but it's not really. No gymnast can succeed without a coach shaping them into the best version of themselves.

"Yeah," I say, straightening up to my full height.

I take a deep breath and try to plaster on the front of calm confidence I used to wear in competitions. I'm out of practice.

"Don't get me wrong, you're incredible," I say. I explain what I've already told Ryan. "But your execution is sloppy and rushed. Your landings aren't clean. Your posture is stiff. Your toes aren't even one hundred percent pointed."

"I *point* my *toes*," she fires back. "I'm not a baby."

I'm stunned into silence. If I had given Dimitri so much sass, I would've suffered through an extra hour of conditioning alone.

"You have the skills of an Olympian, but you don't look like one," I sum up. I sound cold, but I don't care. She needs to hear it. "I'm being straight with you because I know how hard you've worked for god knows how many years, and I don't want that to be a waste. You have a shot. Let me help you get there."

She gapes a little and turns to Ryan. He shrugs and juts his chin out at me.

"Show her what you mean," he says. "Go ahead."

I think for a moment. I could run through feet stretches until she learned what it *really* means to point her toes, but that feels low-impact, unimpressive, and possibly a sore spot. Instead, I tell her to follow me to a mirrored wall along one side of the floor.

"Show me the very beginning of your routine," I instruct. "Just the dance elements before your first tumbling pass."

She gets into position, pauses, then launches into motion. Her arms swing, her legs bend, her head tilts. She pivots and shimmies into place. The entire thing takes five seconds. When she's done, she looks up at me with a flat, expectant look.

"Okay, no," I say. "The start of your routine is where you draw people in. It's an opportunity to showcase what you've got—not a time to rush through a few steps of choreography before getting to the big, flashy stuff. Instead of that, it could be this."

I copy her movements, but amp them up. Each arm movement ends in a sharp flick of my fingers. Each step is taken with perfectly pointed toes. I pivot with a dramatic bump of my hip. As I spin, I catch my reflection in the mirror, and feel another crashing wave of nostalgia.

"See? Your turn."

She resumes her position, then dives into the first step.

"No," I say, cutting her off.

I squat down next to her and push her foot into the arched position it needs to be. Her ankle stiffens at first, then reluctantly turns to putty.

"Like that," I say. "That's your first step. It's not just about moving your foot from point A to point B—it's about creating an intentional shape. Dance can be powerful, too."

"Like this?" she asks, rocking back and forth from her initial pose into the step.

She watches herself in the mirror and bends her knee experimentally.

"That's better," I say. "Again, from the top."

We work like this for ten minutes, dissecting each step of choreography until she understands exactly when and how to move each muscle in her body. I bet she'd rather be practicing a new skill or drilling tumbling passes until she can stick one perfectly, but she lets me train her. When I demonstrate a move for her, she studies me carefully. And when she regurgitates the choreography back at me, she attacks it with new energy. As she hones in on the right motions, she looks closer and closer to the way I would've performed this choreography when I was her age. It breaks my heart. But it's not my time anymore. The only way I can belong to elite gymnastics now is like this, as a mentor.

Ryan had been watching quietly from the sidelines, but now he steps in with a suggestion. "Try the whole routine again," he says. "Throw all that in there."

I'm skeptical—you don't relearn how to move your entire body after just ten minutes of instruction. You can't simply "throw all that in there" and expect real change. But Hallie takes her usual place on the floor and winds up for another routine.

When the opening notes of her music ring out, she flies into action. The first few steps of choreography are sharper now, but soon enough, her poise falters. Her shoulders slump forward, her chin drops, her toes go slack.

"Hip!" Ryan roars over the music, as she sinks down into a wolf turn.

In response, her body flinches into position. She pulls off the turn well and bounds into the home stretch. When the routine is finished, she walks back to us, panting.

"Better?" she asks.

"The beginning was much better," I admit.

"Looks great," Ryan says.

I wait for him to give her notes on the rest of her lackluster routine, but he doesn't. Instead, he claps her on the shoulder. This gymnast-coach dynamic is one hundred and eighty degrees opposite from what I was raised on—I'm not sure I understand it.

"Let's break on this for now. Grab your grips, and meet me at bars in five," he instructs.

"'Kay. Thanks, Avery! This was cool," she says, giving me an exhilarated high five.

It's not my place to argue coaching strategy in front of her. Ryan and I watch as she scampers away toward the locker room.

"Nice work today," Ryan says, turning toward me and shoving his hands in his pockets. "Thanks for coming in."

He catches me off guard. I didn't realize I'd be dismissed so quickly.

"Oh, that's it? That's— Oh. Thanks for having me."

He nods at the door leading out toward the lobby. "I'll walk you out," he says.

My chest tightens at the prospect of leaving behind this musty haven of adrenaline and ambition. I don't want to *leave*—I want to dangle from the bars, tiptoe across beam, and launch myself eight feet high above the white trampoline.

"So, I'll see you tomorrow?" I ask awkwardly. My cheeks flush.

His eyes stay glued to the floor. "I, uh, I don't know. To be honest, I'm interviewing another coach, too. We'll see how things go."

"Who?" I spit out.

"Does it matter?" he asks. He hesitates, then adds, "She wasn't ever at your level herself, but she has a decade more coaching experience than you do. I think she could be good for Hallie."

"I really feel like I can make a big difference here," I insist, pushing past the insistent lump that's beginning to form in my throat. "I know I can."

He doesn't respond. This is humiliating. I'm surprised at how bold I am with him, but I have nothing left to lose. I'm lucky enough that this gig fell into my lap; finding another one that would make me feel even a fraction as excited as I'd be coaching at Summit doesn't seem possible.

We're at the door now. Ryan places his hand on the handle. Parents lined up in gray plastic folding chairs peer at us through the waiting area window. Their passive boredom in Lululemon leggings and zip-ups is so familiar to me.

"Avery, I like you. I respect you. I want to be honest with you—I don't know if this is going to work," he says apologetically. "Worlds is so close, and then there are just a few more months until the Olympics. I don't know if your approach is the right one. I think she needs to polish what's she's got—not start over."

A mental image appears in a flash: me slipping underwater, slumped on the couch in my parents' basement, with nothing to look forward to tomorrow or the next day or any day at all. I don't have to imagine it; I know it intimately. This gym is the only place I've ever felt truly at home; this job feels like it should be mine. I can't fathom Ryan giving it to anyone else. But I don't know how to succinctly explain the territorial greed I feel for this coaching gig and how badly I need it without sounding desperate.

Ryan opens the door handle, and I mutter "Thanks" as I propel myself through the waiting area, down the hallway, and into the locker room, where Summit gymnasts who aren't quite good enough have always gone to break down into silent tears.

NOVEMBER

2019

• CHAPTER 4 •

A familiar voice blares from the TV. I crunch an apple noisily between my teeth to block out the sound. My parents are sprawled out on the couch in the living room with their feet kicked up on the ottoman, passing a single glass of red wine between them as they watch the World Championships on TV.

"Hon, you're sure you don't want to watch with us?" Mom calls from the room next door.

"It's Jasmine!" Dad adds. "She's doing great."

I groan.

"I'm fine in here!" I call back.

Jasmine has been a regular commentator for televised gymnastics competitions since the last Olympics. As jealous as I am, she does a fantastic job. Her deep knowledge of the sport, status as a household name, and pretty features make for good television.

It's been two weeks. Ryan never called. I assume he must have gone with the other coach. I bet the coach is even there with Ryan and Hallie in Stuttgart right now. Truly, I can't imagine a worse evening than watching a person who knocked me out of the running for a job while listening to commentary that—had life gone differently—I could be delivering instead.

I chomp on another bite of apple while swiping left on three more dating app profiles. I haven't been out with anyone since my Jade Castle date with Lucas. In fact, I've barely done anything at all. I've half-heartedly cobbled together a résumé and scanned job boards. I know I can't coast like this for much longer—my bank account is running low—but I can't get the thought of the Summit job out of my head. Nothing else compares. I've been slightly more proactive on the dating front; I have a handful of conversations going with different guys, though honestly, I'm too wary to meet up with any of them. Another profile pops up.

Cali > Mass, the profile reads. *Love football, hockey, and 420.*

I flick disinterestedly through the guy's photos, if only because we've made the same geographic move. In his third photo, he's wearing a Rams jersey with Tyler's name stamped across it. I swipe left and, in a fit of frustration, delete the dating app from my phone.

"Ave, you gotta come in here!" Mom shouts. "That girl from Summit is coming up next."

"And this coach, remind me, what's his name?" Dad asks.

I won't get any peace in here.

"Coming!" I shout back finally.

I trudge into the living room and perch on the arm of the couch. There's a glare on the TV from the overhead lights reflecting off the trophy case along one wall. I've told my parents to move them. Jasmine and a decorated male gymnast from the '90s are on-screen. In some ways, she looks the same: her eyes still sparkle with a hint of the glittery eyeliner she's always loved, and her warm, brown skin pops against a tight, long-sleeved, magenta top that looks vaguely reminiscent of a leotard. But now, dolled up for the cameras, she's wearing bright lipstick that matches her outfit, and her hair is smooth.

A banner running across the bottom of the screen lists the commentators' names: Barry McGuire and Jasmine Floyd-Federov. I always forget she works under her hyphenated married name. That was the other thing that happened during my downward spiral in LA: Jasmine and Dimitri. They got *together*. The news felt like the most violent hangover of my life. I turned down the invitation to their wedding, citing a family reunion that same weekend. It was a lie.

Nothing about it feels real. For starters, he's more than twenty years our senior. He called us each "girl" interchangeably, like it would've been too much effort to learn or use our names. And between me and Jasmine, he was always harder on her. When he mocked my vault, chided me for running like a girl, and made me do laps around the gym with weights strapped to my ankles, I could get through it. I knew his next compliment was just one good routine around the corner. But when Jasmine wobbled through a beam routine and he screamed that she was a "sloppy cow," everyone knew that he really meant it. His abrasive demeanor, stormy mood swings, cruel nicknames, and outsized punishments were intended to mold us into champions, but they left me with pure distaste for him. I can't fathom how Jasmine survived all that and could stomach marrying him. If we were still friends, maybe I could ask her. Maybe I'd see a different side to him. But my chance is long gone.

"Now, Hallie always has very strong showings on vault and bars, and today was no exception. Her beam routine was fairly decent, but floor hasn't historically been her strength," Jasmine explains. Her tone is authoritative but sympathetic—she knows exactly how it feels to be the underdog.

Barry tuts in agreement, launching into a list of her floor scores from the past year.

"But I hear she's been training hard on floor recently, so let's see how she does," Jasmine adds diplomatically.

She tucks her hair behind her ear, and I catch a flash of a diamond ring glinting on her left hand. I just can't fathom how or why she's with Dimitri. I certainly can't imagine her *loving* him.

The camera pans to Hallie lingering by the edge of the floor, awaiting her turn. She rolls her toes under her foot, bites her lip, and tugs on her ponytail to tighten it up. She's alone. Jasmine and I at least always had each other. Before every competition performance, we'd huddle up, arms looped around each other's shoulders. We'd chant something encouraging, like, "We got this," or, "You're gonna nail it." It made us feel confident, centered. And as we approached each performance, we'd call out the same singsongy chant for each other: "Let's go, Avery, let's go!" *Clap, clap.* "Let's go, Jasmine, let's go!" *Clap, clap.*

A high-pitched beep rings out across the arena, indicating that Hallie is permitted to start. She strides to her spot on the floor, settles into position, and waits for her music to begin. I watch carefully as she hits the opening steps of choreography. Her movements aren't quite as elegant as they should be, but at least her chin is lifted proudly and her toes reach toward a sharp point. Her first tumbling pass is sky-high, but there's too much power in her landing; she bobbles out of place, and then out of bounds. She takes three separate steps as she winces and struggles to slow her inertia. Not good.

Mom and Dad gasp and squint. Old habits die hard—they still get anxious and overly invested, even as unattached bystanders, rather than parents with skin in the game.

"Three steps, that's a three-tenths deduction," Jasmine notes.

Hallie slides down into a one-legged squat to wind up for her wolf turn, looking determined. She pushes off the ground into a hasty spin, but her left hip drops like usual, and her left heel drags across the floor—another deduction.

"Oof!" Barry says. "She's struggling."

Duh. I really could do better commentary than this.

I feel a prick of pain in my hand, and realize I'm biting my knuckle out of nerves. It's tough to watch her sloppy execution and stiff style while powerless, stuck here in my parents' musty living room.

Hallie drags herself through the rest of the routine and sheepishly salutes the judges before trotting off the floor. Ryan wraps his arm around her shoulders and walks with her quickly away from the cameras. He's muttering something under his breath.

"So, that routine probably knocks Hallie off the podium for all-around, but she still has a shot at medaling on individual events," Barry says.

"Let's go back to that gorgeous double Arabian, though," Jasmine suggests.

Sure enough, the channel plays back that impressive tumbling run. Jasmine walks the viewer through exactly what makes it so special to fill the time as the judges deliberate on Hallie's score. When it finally arrives—12.475—Hallie furrows her brow and looks away, dejected.

I feel myself tunneling back in time to every shaky routine I performed at a competition. I remember the raw horror that seized my nerves, the way my frenzied brain taunted me on a loop—*You're never going to make it. Just give up now.* Failure is inevitable in this sport; it happens to everyone at some point. But there's no room for failure, not if you want to make the Olympics. Not if you want to win. The paradox is crushing.

"Poor girl," Dad says. "She's talented, but that routine didn't do her any favors. What'd you think of her?"

I sigh and slide off the couch. "I think I'd do a better job coaching her than whoever Ryan hired."

• • •

I know Hallie and Ryan won't stay in Stuttgart for long. There are just eight precious months to go until Olympic Trials—no time for a European vacation. I figure they'll travel home on Sunday and start practice again on Monday. I give myself one extra day, just to be sure, and on Tuesday night, I drive to Summit. I back into a parking spot under a maple tree and stay in the driver's seat so I can watch the last few gymnasts stream out the front door. They have pink cheeks and messy buns, with bare legs stuffed into Uggs. I listen to Kiss 108, the Top 40 station, as I wait for Hallie to emerge.

I dressed carefully tonight: no-nonsense black leggings and white sneakers paired with the red, white, and blue hoodie every member of the US elite women's gymnastics team received during training in 2011. The once-bright cotton has faded, but my name is still embroidered on the sleeve—proof that I once belonged.

Sure enough, Hallie trudges out of the gym with a phone in one hand and an electric yellow bottle of Gatorade in another. A navy canvas gym bag hangs from one shoulder. She spots what must be her dad's car and makes her way toward it. I dip my head and pretend to fiddle with the radio dial; I don't think she sees me. Once she's buckled up and her dad has pulled out of the parking lot, I get out of my car and walk toward the gym before I can lose my nerve. It's dark, and a chill nips at my ankles.

Inside Summit, the fluorescent lights are still on in the lobby, but the parents have all cleared out. I take a deep breath and venture around the corner to the office. For a split second, the cozy familiarity of the charcoal-gray-flecked carpet and the neat rows of paper schedules thumbtacked to the wall make me slip back in time. I could be here to give Winnie my parents' check for the quarter, or to kill time before practice by flicking through rows of plush velvet and slick Lycra leotards. But it's late. Winnie's gone home for the night. Instead, Ryan is hunched behind the desk, one fist clenched tightly in his hair, the other propping up an iPhone, the sound turned all the way up.

"Yes!" he whispers. "*Yes!* No!"

Then, sensing my presence, he snaps his head up.

I give a belated knock on the door frame.

"Hi. Can I come in?" I ask.

He gives his phone screen a pained glance, then pauses the video he's watching.

"I wasn't expecting you," he says.

"I know."

I take a couple of hesitant steps toward him. There's nowhere convenient to sit, so I hover a few feet from the desk.

"Watching anything good?" I ask, nodding toward his phone.

"Football," he says, tapping the screen. "You a fan?"

"Not really," I say.

"I'm watching the Rams slaughter the Giants," he explains. "They have this quarterback—"

"Yeah, I know about their quarterback," I say curtly, cutting him off.

This feels like a sign that I shouldn't even be here at all. I wonder what Tyler would think if he knew I was returning to the gym to beg for a job. He'd probably nod encouragingly with puppy-dog eyes, like, *That's great, Ave!* and then go throw a winning pass or whatever. I clear my throat.

"I was hoping you'd be here tonight," I begin. "I watched Worlds, I saw Hallie . . . and Ryan, she's so close. She has so much potential, but she's not quite solid enough. I know she can do better. You know it, too—that's why you were looking for a new coach in the first place."

"Worlds was tough for her," he admits, looking away.

"Look, I don't even know who you hired. It's nothing personal. But watching her flounder like that on floor? It was painful."

"And you think you can do better?" he asks.

I nod. "I really respect you, Ryan. You're doing an amazing job with her. But she needs extra help on floor. Remember how quickly she picked up what I was teaching? What if we could do that every day? Just imagine how much we could accomplish together, you and me and her."

My heart is racing. Everything rests on his reaction. Ryan leans forward onto the desk and rests his chin on his interlaced knuckles. For a moment, he doesn't speak.

Then finally, he says, "It didn't work out."

"The other coach?" I ask.

He shakes his head. "Svetlana Morozova. You know her?"

"The name rings a bell," I say.

"Russian. She's, like, sixty, super old-school. She and Hallie didn't really click."

"Oh."

He lifts one dark eyebrow. "She likes you, though."

"I like her, too. I get her. I mean, I think I do," I admit.

"She kinda reminds me of you, way back when," he says. "Super determined, ambitious, follows every rule."

I laugh; I had no idea he knew me well enough to think of me in any particular way, much less like that. I could volley back a joke about how *that* didn't last so long, but it feels too sad, given the reason I spiraled out of control.

"She sounds easy to coach, then," I offer instead.

Ryan nods wordlessly. He holds my gaze for a beat longer than is comfortable. I want the job so badly.

"I can do it," I blurt out. "I was in Hallie's exact shoes seven years ago. I know what she's going through. I know how to take her to the next level. Floor was my thing—it's what I did better than almost anyone else in the world."

"I remember," he says, leaning back in his spinning chair and kicking his sneakers up onto the desk.

"If I trained Hallie, I'd go back to basics and focus on her poise and her posture. I'd find her new music and give her new chore- ography that plays to her strengths."

Pitching my plan to Ryan reminds me exactly how deeply I need this job. I'm on the verge of choking up, but I take a deep breath and force myself to hold it together.

"She's gonna shine—I know it. Just . . . please. Give me a chance."

Ryan runs a hand along his stubbled jaw and squints at me. I feel too exposed now; I curl my fingers around the sleeves of my hoodie and fold my arms tightly across my chest.

"I'll talk to Hallie's parents," he says finally. "If they sign off on you working with her, then the job will be yours."

I'm grinning so hard, my cheeks hurt. "Thank you," I say.

The gravity of Ryan's decision fills me with a giddy sort of delight; my mind glosses right over the fact that the Conway family has to approve of me first and skips straight toward a blur of practice, choreography, and chalk dust. I throw my arms around Ryan in a hug, and to my surprise, he actually hugs back. He promises he'll let me know when he's had a chance to speak with Hallie's parents. When I exit the gym, I don't even feel the crisp night air. I feel the way I felt about leaving practice a decade ago: pink-cheeked, high on adrenaline, blood running hot.

As I cross the parking lot, I feel this primal urge to cartwheel across the smooth pavement. I turn to check over both shoulders before letting my arms stretch down and my feet pinwheel over the top of my head. I feel weightless when I sink into the driver's seat of the car and turn up the radio. It's late, and the roads home are empty at this time of night. I wish I had somewhere to go or someone to tell about my exciting news, but my only real option is home. I drive a little faster than I should, and for the first time, the glittering green traffic lights in the town center and the dark pine trees along the back roads feel like exhilarating markers of what could be my new life, not dull reminders of my old one.

The house is quiet when I walk in. Mom's probably watching TV in bed, and Dad is probably reading in his office. I slump down on the couch in the living room, feeling restless but unsure what to do. That old life-sized cardboard cutout of me in a leotard is propped up against the mantel. There are visible shadows marking each individual ab and the muscular curve of my thighs, but even so, I'm slender and lithe. The cardboard version of me has one hand on my tight waist and the other casually holding the gold medal dangling from my neck. I don't want that old image of myself haunting me anymore. I get up from the couch and fold the cardboard stand in the back into the cutout. I pick it up and see a soft gray coat of dust on the floor. I carry the cutout to the garage and prop it up by the recycling bins, facing the wall. Then I grab the vacuum from the front hall closet and suck up a decade's worth of dust bunnies. I'm glad to see them go.

• CHAPTER 5 •

Two days later, Ryan arranges a meeting with Kim, Todd, and Hallie Conway before practice. I want Hallie to like me, of course, but I've already done my best to win her over. Now, it's crucial that I can convince Kim and Todd to trust me with their daughter's career. My nerves jangle with anticipation as I slog through rush-hour traffic in the town center. I used to dread being up this early, but today I'm wide-awake. This morning will make or break me.

Summit is still sleepy when I arrive. The practice space is empty; the fluorescent lights are off; there's no hum of Top 40 radio over the sounds of creaking bars and coaches' shouts. I meet Ryan and the Conway family in the office. Walking into that room makes my heart pound; I wish I had more professional experience to bolster my confidence.

"Hi, it's so nice to meet you," Kim says warmly, reaching to shake my hand.

She has bangs brushed across her forehead, and she's dressed casually in jeans and a faded, oversized button-down. I wonder if she still works, or if—like so many moms at this level—she quit her job to support her daughter's gymnastics career.

"Hi," Todd says, extending his hand, too.

Like his wife, he looks as if he's in his midforties. He's in a charcoal-gray suit, like he's heading straight to some office job after this meeting. Hallie gets her square face and hazel eyes from him.

I take the open seat between Ryan and Hallie.

"I'm sure you don't remember us, but I remember watching you train here years ago," Kim says.

"Oh, really?" I say, flustered.

"You were a beautiful gymnast," she says. "Really incredible to watch."

"Thank you," I say.

Kim's sunny demeanor turns slightly strained. She glances at her husband and continues, "Don't get me wrong, I'm excited to see that you're so passionate about helping Hallie here, but I also do want to know for sure that you're one hundred percent qualified to get her through 2020."

Hallie slumps back in her chair, like she's heard this complaint one too many times.

"Mom, I need help on floor," she mutters.

Todd clears his throat. "We'd like to hear more about your experience as a coach."

"It's not that we don't trust you," Kim rushes to add. "It's just, you know, Trials are only eight months away, and this is a once-in-a-lifetime shot."

"Of course, I understand," I say.

Families make enormous, life-changing sacrifices to give their kids a chance in this sport, and I don't fault them for wanting nothing less than the best for their daughter. Otherwise, those sacrifices aren't worth it.

"Hallie's sixteen now, and if we wait another four years, she'll be . . ." Kim makes a helpless gesture with her hands.

"Maybe too old," I offer.

"Twenty's not *old*," Hallie groans.

"In this sport? Honey, it's a long shot," Kim says, ruffling a hand through her bangs.

"Do you want to try for 2024?" I ask.

"That'll be where, Paris?" Todd asks.

Ryan nods.

"Of course!" Hallie says. "And then after that, college, maybe law school, who knows?"

It's impressive that she has the next dozen years of her life mapped out, but I'm not surprised. Since childhood, her entire life has revolved around a singular, far-off goal.

"But 2020 is your best shot," Kim reminds her gently. "And the Olympic team will be smaller and more selective than ever before."

She's right. In 1996, the US gymnastics delegation included seven athletes, nicknamed the Magnificent Seven. But the rules have changed over time. By 2012, the year I tried to make the Olympics, only five gymnasts competed, known as the Fierce Five. Another five girls, the Final Five, competed at the 2016 Olympics, but by that point, the Worldwide Organization of Gymnastics had already ruled that team sizes would dwindle to four spots each in 2020. Making the Olympic team this year will be harder than ever before.

"I'm very confident in Avery's abilities," Ryan says smoothly. "I wouldn't bring her in if she wasn't right for Hallie."

"Pardon my saying so, but that's exactly what happened last month," Todd counters.

I have a flash of Hallie's disastrous floor routine at Worlds.

"Mr. and Mrs. Conway . . ." I begin.

"Please, call us Kim and Todd," she offers.

I take a deep breath to steady my voice. "Kim and Todd, I coached gymnastics while living in LA, and before that, I was the

top gymnast in America when I was Hallie's age. Barring an injury, I would've made the Olympics, and I don't mean to brag, but I
would've medaled on floor. I know floor. I've watched your daughter
perform, and I have a good grasp on how to help her improve."

They lean forward hungrily. As much as Hallie has her eyes set
on the Olympics, so do they—maybe even more so.

"I'd like to choreograph a new routine for Hallie, one that plays
to her strengths," I explain. "It sounds like she's been performing the
same routine for years, and it isn't serving her well anymore. Once
she learns the new routine, it'll be a matter of finessing her performance: we'll work on controlling that extra power she gets on her
tumbling passes, sticking the landings, moving with more poise and
better posture, and polishing her dance elements. Her skills are all
there. But her execution could be more graceful and dynamic, and
that's where I can help."

Todd sits back in his seat. Kim bites her lip. They look at each
other.

"Hmm," Kim says.

I can't tell yet if they're fully convinced.

"If you're able to find another floor specialist who can work well
with Hallie with just eight months to go until Trials, by all means,
please do," I say. "But more than anyone else out there right now, I
get exactly what Hallie is going through and I know how to help her.
So, please. Let me help your daughter."

Todd rubs his jaw. Kim swallows. I feel the same way I did
during competitions, back when I had finished a routine I felt
unsure about and had to wait torturous minutes for the judges to
reveal my score.

"Mom, Dad, I really need help," Hallie adds. "Come on."

Her parents exchange glances.

"You really want this?" Todd asks.

She throws her arms up, exasperated. "I don't have time to waste. I'm going to go warm up."

Hallie heads to the locker room to drop off her bag.

"Let's give this a shot," Ryan says. "Trust me."

Kim sighs. "All right, but if the new routine doesn't come together soon . . . we'll have to have another conversation about what's next."

Todd gets up, closes the button on his suit jacket, then shakes hands with Ryan and me again.

"Let's make this work," he says.

I can't tell if that's a promise or a threat.

• • •

Kim and Todd leave, and Hallie and Ryan enter the gym. I tell them I'll join in just a minute, and make it to the bathroom just in time. Locked in a stall, I slump against the cool white tile wall, clap a hand over my mouth to muffle my sobs, and break down silently. I've never felt such intense relief in my life. I felt aimless in LA and completely lost back in Greenwood; once I had my heart set on this job, nothing else remotely measured up. I can't believe it's mine. The tears come in hot and fast. My shoulders shake. There is still so much of my life to figure out—I can't live in my childhood bedroom forever, and the loneliness I'm facing in the wake of my breakup is awfully isolating—but this is a start. This is good. I will be okay.

After wiping away my tears, I find Hallie warming up on floor, running through the same rote cardio exercises and stretches every gymnast has burned into their memory. Ryan flicks on the lights and the radio for her, then joins me to watch on the sidelines. I'm still buzzing with adrenaline.

"Nice speech in there," he says, clapping me on the shoulder. "You're good under pressure."

All gymnasts are.

"Thanks," I say.

"Her parents aren't really so bad," he says. "Todd's a little intense, but he just wants the best for her. They both do. Kim used to work in marketing, but now volunteers part-time at the library so she can mostly be around for Hallie."

Ryan pulls a three-ring binder from the shelf under the stereo. "I have her training mapped out for the next eight months, but I want to get your take on it," he says, taking a seat on the floor. "Sit. Let's look at this together while she finishes up."

We sit side by side. I try not to notice the way his white T-shirt stretches across his broad chest, though it's not easy. He flips through the stuffed binder, showing me the Code of Points, which assigns a different level of difficulty to each skill and changes every three years; a practice schedule; a list of goals; Hallie's emergency contacts and list of doctors. He finds the calendar section, outlined with what he and Hallie will be working on every month until Trials. It's crammed with his spiky handwriting—notes to himself.

"When it comes to vault, she's solid. She does an Amanar and a Mustafina," he explains.

Those are two of the most difficult vaults in the world, both named after the first gymnast to perform each, as is the sport's custom. The Amanar is a round-off, back handspring onto the board, with a two-and-a-half twisting back layout off, while the Mustafina is a round-off and half turn onto the board with a full-twisting front layout off.

"Her right ankle bothers her sometimes, so we've mostly been drilling them into the pit these days," Ryan continues. "I don't want to push her too hard on the landings. But the thing is, she gets a ton of power off the board, so she has a tough time sticking it. So one thing we're focusing on is keeping her ankle strong, so we can get those landings in consistently good shape."

"Got it. I'll be careful about her ankle."

"On bars, her routine is already excellent, but I'd like to upgrade it over the next few months," he says. "Like, right now, she does a Tkatchev into a giant into a Pak Salto, but she could cut the giant."

It's been a long time since I've spoken the language of gymnastics, and I'm relieved that it all comes flooding back: the Tkatchev involves flinging yourself up and over the high bar backward in a straddle position; a giant means swinging around the bar in a full circle with body outstretched; a Pak Salto is when you swing off the high bar, arch into an elegant back flip, and catch the low bar.

"Which means a higher difficulty value," I say, mentally mapping out the combination in my head.

Because the Tkatchev and the Pak Salto are both release moves, Hallie would earn more points for connecting them back-to-back, rather than separating them with a giant, which is considered an easier (and less risky) move.

"Exactly. We'll play around with it. And we're working on some other cool stuff. Have you ever heard of a Seitz?"

"Maybe?" I cock my head. I've been out of this world for a long time.

His eyes sparkle. "It's a transition move. Imagine a toe-on circle on the low bar with a full twist to catch the high bar."

"Wow."

"Yeah, *wow*," he says, exhaling. "That's our girl. We just gotta get her the recognition she deserves.

"She's not bad on beam. Her acrobatic skills are all there—a back handspring, back whip, back layout combo you could die for, a solid front aerial. But there are places she could tighten up, like that goddamn wolf turn."

"She does that on beam, too?"

"The way the Code of Points is these days, you basically have to. She does hers as a double, but I'm hoping we can get it to a two and a half."

"That'll be tough."

"Right." He closes the binder and drums his fingers on the cover. "And then there's floor. That's in your hands now."

"Thanks for letting me do this," I say.

Ryan smirks and taps on the binder again. "I mean, you gotta come up with a *plan*," he says.

I already know I want to choreograph a new floor routine for her, and that includes selecting new music for her to perform to. I know the rest will come in time.

The next hour of Hallie's workout slips away—for me, at least. I can tell *she* works hard. She doesn't skimp on tough ab work or mind-numbing reps, like some kids do. On the contrary, I get the sense she deepens her squats and tightens up her plank form when she notices me watching. I'm honored she considers me worthy enough to impress. When she's finished with conditioning, she takes a water break, then meets Ryan and me on floor. She places her hands on her hips and looks from him to me, waiting for instructions.

"I'm all yours," she says. "Put me to work."

"Trust me, I will," I say. "But first, we should talk."

I'm nervous, but know I have to drop the bomb anyway.

"Hear me out on this: your floor routine is good, but it doesn't play to your strengths. I would love to create a new routine for you—mostly the same tumbling, but new dance, new music, maybe some new skills."

She flinches and recoils, crossing her arms over her chest. "But—but we—there are—we have just eight months to go," she sputters.

"So why waste those months on a routine that's not working?" I shoot back.

"I've been using this routine forever. You want me to throw it away now? I'll never learn a new one in time."

"Of course you will. I see how hard you work. You got this."

"I'll be rushed, I'll forget the choreography, I'll mess it up—probably *in* competition, and then I'll fail out of gymnastics without even a high school diploma and I'll be stuck living at home with my parents forever."

I'm sure it's just a flippant comment, but the cruel reality of her words cuts me deep.

"Hallie . . ." Ryan admonishes.

"There's no need to be so dramatic," I say, breezing past her insult. "Please just trust me with this."

"I'm on board," Ryan tells her.

She bites her lip. For a moment, she's quiet, considering the prospect.

"Okay," she says finally. "Then so am I."

I pick up the binder and rifle through it until I find the section that lists every floor skill with value in the Code of Points. To test her capabilities, I rattle off different acrobatic and artistic elements and ask her to perform them, starting with tumbling. Her double Arabian is fantastic, but her triple twist isn't doing her any favors—that tumbling pass might work better as a double-twisting double back layout. Hallie diligently follows my instructions and swivels to gauge my level of approval after each tumbling pass—so she's sassy but ultimately obedient. I can work with that.

Fifteen minutes in, I notice her grimace and roll her right foot carefully from side to side.

"Ryan, hey," I say, catching his attention. He looks up from his phone. "It looks like her ankle is bothering her."

"Yeah, let's take a break," he says.

"Hey, hey, Hallie, stop," I call. "How's your ankle?"

She winces. "It's starting to hurt again," she admits. "It's really not that bad, though, promise. I'll keep going."

"No, let's rest for a sec. I'm going to grab you some ice, okay?"

She exhales, clearly frustrated with herself. "Fine. Thanks."

I retrieve an ice pack from the cooler and wrap it in a paper towel so it doesn't freeze-burn her skin. By the time I make it back to the floor, Ryan is already wrapping up her ankle with gauzy prewrap and white athletic tape to keep the joint stable.

"Thanks for the ice," Hallie says glumly.

"How long has this been going on?" I ask.

She sighs. "On and off for, like, two years."

"I think it's time to see that sports medicine doctor again," Ryan says.

"Dr. Kaminsky?" Hallie asks.

"Yeah."

She makes a face. "I'm fine."

Every gymnast racks up injuries like these, but they're nearly impossible to heal while actively training for competition. I pushed through my stress fracture at fourteen and wound up with back pain that flares up for weeks at a time, even more than a decade later. I sometimes wonder: if I could go back in time and make different choices, would I avoid a lifetime of pain? Even in my worst moments, I don't think I would. As debilitating as the flare-ups can be, what I gained from gymnastics—identity, discipline, commitment—is worth so much more. But just because I've made peace with that choice doesn't mean that Hallie needs to.

"A doctor might be able to really help," I say. "Why don't you go just once, just to check in?"

She juts out her chin like she's going to protest, but Ryan's reaction stops her.

"Hal, you don't want to mess around with an injury this year. Be smart about this."

"Fine. I'll go."

"Let's take it easy today," Ryan says. "After your break, we'll do bars. No dismounts, nothing crazy, just to play it safe."

She pouts. "But that's such a waste of a training day."

An idea hits me. "What about this—while you ice your ankle, why don't we listen to new floor music? Pick something out?"

Ryan backs me up, and Hallie reluctantly agrees. He steps out to grab some coffee, promising to be back in just a few minutes. This is the first time that Hallie and I have ever been alone, and I want to make the most of it. I need to get on her good side—and right now, that means finding the perfect song.

Floor music needs to be exactly ninety seconds long and contain no lyrics, so you can't use just anything. I start by rifling through the collection of CDs and cassette tapes still stacked under the stereo, but these have all been here since before even I was a gymnast. When my search turns up nothing fresh or interesting, I pull out my phone and Google new options.

"We need something powerful, something fun," I say, scrolling through a list of song titles. "Nothing dainty, nothing boring."

"Maybe . . . jazz?" Hallie asks. She looks up at me nervously.

"You like jazz?" I ask.

She shrugs. "Yeah, it seems fun to perform to."

"Jazz!" I practically yelp. "Let's find you something. You need something you'll *enjoy*, whatever that is."

For the next fifteen minutes, we listen to snippets of songs and debate their merits. When we land on a track packed with energetic trumpets, we know we've got it right. It's a big band number called "Jazz Fling." Hallie bops her head along to the melody. When Ryan returns, I play it back for him and watch his expression.

"You like it?" I ask hopefully.

He gives a bemused smile. "On floor, I defer to you. Do *you* like it?"

This is my first big decision as a coach. The right song can make or break a routine. I know the upbeat tempo and playful sound are a strong match for the powerful physicality of Hallie's movements. She has just enough bravado to pull it off.

"I do. Let's do it."

• • •

At noon, Kim returns to the gym to pick up her daughter for her midday break for lunch and homeschooling before she comes back for a second practice. It's completely unnecessary for Kim to actually walk into the gym and chat with us; Hallie could easily head out into the parking lot on her own. I get the sense that she's probing to see how well I'm doing. She instantly notices Hallie's taped ankle.

"What's going on here?" she asks.

"It's been an okay day, but I'd get that checked out soon," I suggest.

Kim sighs. "I'll make an appointment with Dr. Kaminsky."

"I'm *fine*, Mom," Hallie protests. "And hey, the other big news is that Avery is redoing my floor routine, and we picked new music. I'll play it for you in the car."

"See you this afternoon," Kim says, ushering her daughter toward the exit.

"Are you staying here or heading out?" Ryan asks me once they're gone.

It didn't actually occur to me that I'd need to figure out a way to spend the afternoon.

"I usually take my lunch in the office, help out around the gym, that kind of thing," Ryan offers.

I'd be happy to help other coaches with whatever they need, but the prospect of eating lunch alone with Ryan makes me nervous. Aside from Hallie, I'm not sure what we'd talk about. I grew up exclusively around fellow female gymnasts, gossiping about cute boys we saw at competitions, trading compliments on new leotards and scrunchies, and quoting *Stick It* to each other ("It's not called gym-*nice*-tics"). I've never had any platonic male friends; the only times I've ever hung out one-on-one with guys were dates. Freshly heartbroken or not, I still can't ignore that Ryan—formerly a cute boy—grew up into a highly attractive man. It's not smart for me to let this crush of mine fester. The last thing I need to do is let my feelings get in the way of this job or dump my broken heart on Ryan's plate.

"I, uh, I think I'm going to head home. But I'll be back later this afternoon, cool?"

Ryan fist-bumps me. "Cool, see ya."

I head into the parking lot and sit in the driver's seat, but don't want to go home just yet. Now that I'm alone, I can't help but dwell on Hallie's tossed-off comment from this morning—the one about failing out of gymnastics and being stuck living at home forever. Out of curiosity, I look at Craigslist for houses or apartments with spare rooms nearby. I've never looked for a place to live outside of LA before, and the tiny selection of results makes me nervous. There aren't that many people like me in Greenwood—the town is mostly filled with families raising kids in big, beautiful houses, not single people who need to rent out a spare bedroom. Rent here is more affordable than it was back in LA, but not by much. I'll need to work for a few months to save up enough money to move out. It's a daunting goal, but I know I can do it. I haven't had much faith in myself these past few years, but I have faith in this: my ability to work hard.

It's lunchtime. I could drive into the town center to pick up a sandwich or a salad. There's a new Italian place that opened up since I've last lived here that looks delicious. But that's money I don't need to spend. Instead, I drive back to my parents' house, thinking all the while about the day I'll call somewhere else home.

• CHAPTER 6 •

After practice ends that night, I get ready to leave the gym. But the prospect of heading home is unbelievably depressing—I love my parents, but moving back into what is essentially a shrine to my failed childhood dream is unbearable. They hover. They ask too many questions about my plans for the future. I'm grateful that they let me stay with them (rent-free, even), but I'd be fine spending as little time there as possible. So, halfway through crossing the gym's lobby, I turn around and head back onto the floor. It's late, and the gym is empty; this is a golden opportunity to start choreographing Hallie's new routine without gymnasts and other coaches gawking.

I choreographed all the girls' routines back in LA, but this is a different beast. With Hallie, there are no physical limits; anything I can dream up, she can do. That doesn't mean I have entirely free rein, though. The sport's scoring system is laughably complex. It used to be simple: a perfect performance earned a perfect ten. But now, according to rules instituted in the 2000s by the Worldwide Organization of Gymnastics, a routine's total score is made up of a difficulty score and an execution score. On floor, only the top five hardest tumbling skills and top three most challenging dance skills are allowed to count toward the difficulty score, though additional points can be earned by connecting multiple elements. Points are docked if you miss out on certain skills. I take Ryan's binder from the shelf under the stereo and flip through it until I find the section of the Code of Points that details the requirements: I'll need to include a leap or jump series, a front flip, a back flip, a flip with a full twist or more, a double flip, and a final tumbling pass with a difficulty value of at least a "D" (skills are ranked alphabetically, with the easiest ones labeled as "A"). In other words, choreographing a winning floor routine isn't just an art—it's a science, too.

I hook up my phone to the stereo system and roll my head and ankles out in a light stretch as I find "Jazz Fling," the piece of music we've chosen. I play the first ten seconds to jog my memory—*Dun dun dun . . . dun-dun-dun dun dun dun*—and experiment with movement on the floor. I could start with this pose, or that one. There could be a flashy kick, or a spin, or a flick of my wrists. I watch myself carefully in the mirror as I string together a sequence of dance, and try it out to the beat of the music. It's good. But what if I squeeze in a jump series before the first tumbling pass? I rework the choreography three different ways before I settle on a version I like. I try it out—and this time, I'm pleased.

The next section of the melody soars, and I make a mental note to reserve that for Hallie's first tumbling pass, the impressive double Arabian. I listen as the music unfurls and try to imagine what could come next. The song has flaring trumpets and a sassy beat. You don't just dance to this music—you strut. I pop my hip, flick my fingers, shimmy my shoulders. I let myself get lost in the song, leaping and pirouetting with abandon. It's been close to a decade since I've allowed myself to indulge in this way, and I can practically feel my heart glowing with joy.

That is, until I catch sight of the mirror across the floor, reflecting stiff joints that don't bend the way I envision. It's cringeworthy. I hear echoes of Dimitri's criticisms: the split in my leap isn't crisp enough; my Shushunova doesn't get enough height; the routine would really look better if my thighs were thinner. I thought I was done mourning the loss of my ability years ago, but fresh grief springs up again. It's overwhelmingly sad to know that no matter how hard I train, I can never regain the body I once took for granted.

I take a break, letting the music play out as I take an ice-cold slurp from the water fountain. Then I tighten my ponytail, take a deep breath, and queue up the beginning of "Jazz Fling" again.

Over the next hour, the bones of the routine begin to take shape. I'm reminded of one of the many things I loved about gymnastics: if you work hard, you can become a superhuman version of yourself, at least for a time. If I were in prime shape, I could spiral like a ballerina, contort myself like a circus performer, catapult myself like a soldier, and defy gravity like a goddess. There would be no limits on what I could do. Outside the gym, that's never been true for me—I couldn't make it through college, and I couldn't make Tyler stay in love with me. But here? This is my world. Or at least it was. Until I went to Trials.

I run through the light version of the choreography—I cartwheel across the floor where Hallie will tumble for real; I spin on my butt where she'll do a wolf turn. I don't want to overextend myself and trigger another flare-up of back pain, so I take it easy. Watching the choreography gel together is satisfying, and I get so lost in performing it that I don't hear the soft creak of the door on the other side of the gym. When the song finishes, there's a beat of silence, then the sound of applause.

I whip out of the dramatic final pose—chest thrust out, back arched, arms outstretched—and turn toward the noise. I'm mortified to see Ryan walking down the vault runway toward the floor.

"Impressive," he says.

I cross my arms over my chest, embarrassed. "I had no idea anyone was still here."

"I was in the office. So, will that be Hallie's floor routine, or are you just playing around?" He looks bemused.

"That depends," I say. "Do you really like it or are you just being nice?"

"Come on, Avery," he says with a smirk.

Ryan doesn't seem like the kind of guy who'd joke around when it comes to work. The stakes are too high. *I* genuinely like the routine: the choreography is playful, energetic, and suited to Hallie's strengths. But I'm not so brazenly confident to expect Ryan to like it right off the bat.

"It's great," he clarifies. "I love it."

"You know this isn't actually the real, final thing," I warn him. "I just can't perform at that level anymore. So Hallie will kick up the difficulty level by, like, five notches."

"Yeah, that's fine. I figured. Show me the beginning?" he asks. "I missed it."

I jog to the stereo to restart the song, then scamper into place for the opening steps of the routine. I'm terribly self-conscious of his gaze on my unmuscled arms and soft stomach, but that leaves me with only one choice: I *have* to throw myself into the choreography and perform it to the fullest extent, because otherwise it'll look lackluster. It's fine for him to think I'm out of shape—but he can't think I'm bad at my job.

"Nice, nice, nice," he calls over the music as I sashay through a section reserved for a tumbling pass. "I got it."

Relieved, I turn off the music.

"So?" I ask, trying not to let on that I'm close to panting.

He crosses the floor to join me near the stereo. "So! That's it."

I laugh. "No, I mean, do you have any notes? Suggestions?"

"Mmmm . . . no? Not now, at least? Let's see how Hallie does with it. Avery, you did an amazing job."

He shakes his head, grins, and looks away.

"What?" I ask, suddenly self-conscious.

Now that he's just two feet away from me, I realize he can probably see the sheen of sweat on my forehead and the halo of frizz that always escapes my ponytail when I dance.

"I just . . ." He trails off and laughs quietly. "Do you remember Worlds in 2010?"

"Yeah."

The memories of that weekend snap into focus. My scrunchie flew off my head during my bars routine. That was the first day I heard whispers about me as a likely contender for 2012. Jasmine cried that night in our shared hotel room when Dimitri pointed out that maybe the reason she slipped off beam was because her ever-expanding hips and ass threw her off balance.

"I'll never forget seeing your floor routine that day. I mean, I remember watching from the sidelines and thinking, *Damn, that girl is going places,*" he recalls. He gazes off into the distance, then snaps back toward me. "And now you're here."

The words should fall flat, but he says them with a sense of wonder. His face lights up. I don't know what to say.

"If I had known, all those years ago, that we'd end up working together, I think I'd be kinda starstruck," he adds.

I can feel my cheeks flush pink. "Starstruck?!" I yelp.

"Hundred percent," he says, nodding.

A panicked thought flashes by—is he *flirting* with me? Am I imagining the coy warmth behind his words? I take in his casual stance and the impressive curve of his biceps straining at the sleeves of his T-shirt. He looks good without trying.

"Well, I was pretty starstruck, myself, when you called," I admit. My voice is just a touch more honeyed than usual. "Olympians don't call me every day, you know."

I'd assumed my ability to flirt had dried up after I started dating Tyler, but I'm pleasantly surprised to find it's still there. My hands find my hips; I straighten up and suck in my stomach.

He waves away my comment. "You should've been one, too. It was just bad luck."

"Yeah," I say, shrugging. This isn't my favorite subject. I'd rather change it. "So, you spend all your evenings here?"

"Ouch, are you telling me to get a social life?" he shoots back.

"Hey, all I'm saying is that you spend an awful lot of time in a gym that smells like feet," I say, holding up my hands.

I briefly weigh the pros and cons of what I want to say next, and spurred by a rush of adrenaline, I toss it out there.

"What, no hot date tonight?" I tease.

A flicker of surprise crosses his face. He recovers by shoving his hands into his pockets and looking away, laughing.

"Not tonight," he says softly. "But I'll take that as my cue that you want the gym to yourself to finish choreographing."

He starts to walk away, but I realize I don't want him to.

"Wait!" I call. "I didn't mean it that way. Stay?"

He wavers. "You want me to?"

It takes me a split second to think of a plausible excuse. "I need someone to film what I've choreographed so far, right?"

He turns back toward me with a smile. He pulls his phone out of his pocket. "Let's do it."

DECEMBER

2019

• CHAPTER 7 •

By the time Hallie's ankle is strong enough for her to learn the new choreography, the radio plays holiday shopping jingles between every song. The town center is decked out in blue and white lights. I have to throw a parka on over my sweats just to make it from the parking lot to the gym. Christmas break is three weeks away, and most of the gymnasts and coaches are buzzing about holiday plans and winter vacation trips to visit grandparents in Florida. But not us. Ryan, Hallie, and I will spend the week between Christmas and New Year's here. There's no sense in wasting a week of prime training time. I have been practicing the routine every night after Hallie leaves practice, ensuring the choreography flows flawlessly and I've maximized every moment to squeeze out the highest possible difficulty score. I've been waiting until she's gone so she doesn't catch a glimpse of it until I'm satisfied it's perfect.

"Let me show it to you first before I teach it to you, okay?" I tell Hallie.

She's just finished warm-ups, stretching, and conditioning, and is happy to sit on the sidelines for a ninety-second break. I give her my phone so she can control the music.

"If you check out the Notes app, you'll see the entire breakdown of the choreography," I explain. "You can follow along, so you can see where, for example, I spin around on my butt, but you'll actually do a wolf turn."

"Got it," she says, peering at the screen.

"And when I do a switch leap with a full turn and it sucks, you'll do a switch leap with a full turn but make it look good," I say in the same matter-of-fact tone, hoping she'll laugh.

She snickers. "Understood."

I unzip my hoodie and kick off my sneakers. They'll only get in the way. I hear the bars creaking on the other side of the gym; Ryan is doing pull-ups. His muscles bulge cartoonishly. I force myself to look away.

"Ready?" she asks, once I've struck the starting pose on the floor.

"Ready!" I say.

"Jazz Fling" fills the room. To the extent that I can, I perform the hell out of the routine with the same passion and intensity I used to give the judges. I need to sell Hallie on this routine. It strikes me—while upside down, midway through a cartwheel we're all kindly pretending is Hallie's third tumbling pass—that the thrill of this performance isn't so far off from the adrenaline high I used to get from doing my own routine during competition. Maybe there can be real joy on the sidelines as a coach and a choreographer. When I'm finished, I retreat toward her, trying desperately to catch my breath.

"Okay, cool, teach me," Hallie says, bouncing up to her feet.

"You like it?" I ask.

"Well . . ." She fidgets, scratching the back of one calf with the other foot. She looks at me with a shy gaze. "It's different. I'll give it a try."

She's clearly skeptical, but not strong-willed enough to challenge my judgment. I'm relieved she doesn't reject the routine flat out, but I know I can't let my expression waver. The coach-gymnast relationship is sacred and built on a concrete foundation of respect and trust; she can't catch on to the fact that I'm anxious and have feelings that can be hurt, just like anyone else.

"Whew, okay. Let's break it down from the top. Start here, a couple feet out from this corner," I instruct, pointing to the spot in which she needs to stand.

From the other side of the floor, I see Ryan watching us with a smile.

I walk Hallie through the choreography step by step, focusing on teaching her the broad strokes of every move. We can sharpen each motion later on, once she's gotten the hang of the routine. She hasn't warmed up her tumbling yet, so she goes for lazy, easy passes, like a round-off, back handspring, back tuck instead of the real deal. With Hallie toning down her skills and me performing to the fullest extent of my abilities, the playing field is almost level.

She picks up the routine fairly quickly, delighting in the creative combinations I've thrown together for her. Not everything runs so smoothly, though. I planned a switch ring leap connected to a switch leap with a full turn. A switch leap involves scissoring your legs back and forth, so you hit both a left split and a right split in mid-air before landing; each variation is tricky on its own, but the two moves back-to-back are even more complicated. That's the point, of course—the more difficult the series is, the higher the payoff is from the judges. Hallie fumbles the combination three times in a row. It doesn't matter how powerful or energetic she is—the move requires an absurd amount of precision.

"You have to use your arms for momentum in between the two leaps so you can have enough height on the second to make the full rotation," I explain.

She exhales and tries it again. It's sloppy, and she knows it.

The moment her feet touch the floor, she shoots me a frustrated glance.

"More height," I remind her, demonstrating the way she needs to swing her arms. "Try it again."

She takes a few steps backward and screws up her face. I can tell she's trying to visualize the move in front of her. She sashays into the combination, but the series looks more like a jumble of flailing limbs than real gymnastics. If we had a stronger relationship at this point, I'd feel comfortable pushing her to work through it. But right now, I don't want to bring down her mood. Today, her confidence is worth more than the difficulty value of that leap series.

"Or maybe we put something else in that spot," I suggest. "Moving on . . ."

When we make it through the end of the routine, I give her a celebratory high five.

"Let's do it again," she says, bouncing up on her toes. "For real, this time, to music."

"You think you have all that memorized already?" I ask.

I know she's good, but she can't be *that* good.

"Not *all* of it, but most," she says proudly.

"Okay," I say, chuckling. "One more walk-through together, then you do it by yourself for real."

We repeat the choreography. This time, she deftly slides into most of the right moves, though she does spend half the routine with her neck craned toward me. Her switch leap series is a flop, but she pushes through to make it toward the final tumbling pass and the simple last bit of dance. (By the time you hit the fourth tumbling pass, you're flat-out exhausted. Even waving to a crowd cheering your name feels impossible. So I kept her last few motions easy.)

Ryan drops down from the bars. "How's it going over there?" he calls, wiping sweat from his brow.

"Good!" Hallie and I shout at the same time.

"Jinx, you owe me a soda," she says quickly. As Ryan approaches, she lowers her voice. "Not that I even drink soda, but, you know."

"I'll get you a Gatorade," I reply.

"Can I see how it's going?" Ryan asks.

"What do you think, Hallie? Are you ready for music?" I ask.

"Yeah," she says, jutting out her chin. "Let's do this."

She scrambles over to the starting spot, settles into the first pose, then peeks back at me, as if to ensure she's doing it right. I nod and turn on the music. On her own for the first time, her performance is rough and uneven. She nails certain sections of choreography, though I'd still like to tighten up the way she moves and performs; other bits, though, she stumbles through, or forgets entirely. I watch her face freeze when she realizes she has no idea how to transition from upright and standing to down on the floor for the wolf turn. She doesn't have enough time to figure it out; the music has already moved on. So she spasms and drops to the floor, shouting an apology as she goes.

"That's part of it?" Ryan deadpans.

"Yeah, doesn't it look great?" I joke back.

Hallie flits through the rest of the routine, shouting a dramatic "Ta-da!" as she hits the final pose.

"Needs some work," Ryan suggests kindly.

"But we're on the right track," I insist.

"I'll run through it twenty more times today," Hallie promises.

"That's not necessary," I say. "Let me buy you that Gatorade, and then we'll drill the choreography until it's muscle memory."

Hallie skips through the gym, leaning on one balance beam as she kicks up her feet and clicks her heels in midair, making her way toward the vending machine in the lobby.

"Motivating her with treats? Interesting coaching strategy," he points out.

"Effective coaching strategy," I correct him.

I head toward the lobby. Ryan makes a soft noise like he's clearing his throat, and when I look back toward him, his mouth is half-open, like he's about to say something.

"Yeah?" I ask.

He presses his lips together and dips his gaze away from mine. "Nothing," he says. "I was going to say something, but it's nothing."

I look at him curiously, but he just crosses his arms over his chest and nods toward the door of the gym.

"Go catch up with Hallie," he says.

• CHAPTER 8 •

I want to believe that I've grown up a lot since I was Hallie's age. It would be nice to think that I've blossomed into a mature, confident, graceful adult. But then Ryan will make a particularly charming joke or simply breathe in my direction, and I'm forced to remember that I've been harboring the same teenage crush for a full decade. So maybe not much has changed.

"Heading out?" Ryan asks.

It's a Wednesday in the middle of December; we've just wrapped up our morning practice, and we're scattering in different directions for our midday break. Kim picked up Hallie for lunch and homeschooling, Ryan is retreating into the office for a meal, and per usual, I'm on my way out. Even though I've worked at Summit for a month now, I've never quite been comfortable spending the lunch break hanging out with Ryan. I know he stays here. I don't want to intrude on his personal space—and if I'm really honest with myself, the prospect of regular alone time with him sounds like a nervous thrill. What would I say? So I typically eat at home.

"Yeah," I say, a little embarrassed.

He gives me a bemused smile. "You know, you're more than welcome to hang out here," he says. "Even when you're off the clock."

I look at the door, then back at Ryan. "Do you want company?" I ask.

"That'd be nice," he says. "Unless you have other plans."

That'd be nice, I replay in my head. Between clubbing in college and a high-profile relationship with a famous athlete in my twenties, I eventually got comfortable around men—even intimidating ones I was attracted to. I could flirt, banter, relax. But maybe because Ryan is from a completely different era of my life, back when the prospect of interacting with guys point-blank terrified me, I lose my cool around him.

It's time for that to change.

"Do you have food here?" I ask.

"I brought a ton of leftovers, if you want to share," he says. "It's just some chicken and rice and veggies."

The offer is very sweet. "Sure, why not? Thank you so much."

He heats up the leftovers in the office's microwave and clears space off the desk for us to sit and eat.

"Did you make this?" I ask.

The chicken is a little bland, but it's not bad.

"It's basically the one meal I know how to make, yeah," he says.

"I ate a version of this pretty much every single day back when I was training," I say. "It's like comfort food."

"Exactly, same," he says.

There's a moment where neither of us says anything. I could change the subject to something completely professional, like Hallie's floor routine—but I recognize it wouldn't hurt for Ryan and me to get to know each other on a friendlier, more personal level, too.

"I actually love to cook," I tell him. "My first few years in California, I lived in dorms or these tiny apartments with bad kitchens, but eventually, I moved into this place with a huge, awesome setup for cooking. For the first time in my life, it was like I had both the space and the lifestyle to actually enjoy food."

"Oh, wow," he says. He looks down and pokes a piece of chicken with his fork. "I wish I had known that before serving you *this*."

"No, no, don't worry, this is good," I lie. "And it's so nice of you to share. Maybe I'll cook something for you sometime."

I can't tell if I'm overstepping a boundary, but he doesn't seem to flinch.

"It's funny that you say that you could enjoy cooking more once you left gymnastics," he notes. "That's how I felt about working out."

"Yeah?"

"It turns out, once the pressure of winning medals isn't hanging over your head, you can chill out a little more," he says.

"No kidding," I deadpan.

"I used to get so bored with conditioning when I was a gymnast, but after I retired, I realized I missed that kind of workout. So that's why I started lifting weights just for me—not for the sake of the sport."

"Ha, see, I felt the opposite way. I've done enough conditioning for one lifetime," I say.

"Fair enough," he says.

"How'd you get into coaching?" I ask.

"Back in high school, I coached kids' classes, just to make a little money during the summers," he explains. "So I knew I liked it. And then around the time I was thinking of retiring, my old coach from Michigan connected me to Mary here at Summit. The timing was perfect, since Hallie was leveling up and wanted to work one-on-one with a coach. The Conways looked into Powerhouse, but Dimitri didn't have room for her at the time." He explains that Dimitri's hands were full with other gymnasts: Emma Perry, Skylar Hayashi,

Brit Almeda. "And the Conways were pretty reluctant to find another coach in another state because of Todd's career. So I was the best option—better than nothing."

"They took a pretty big chance on you," I say.

He knocks his knuckles against the wooden windowsill behind him. "Trust me, I'm grateful for that every single day."

He already knows that I coached a preteen girls' gymnastics team back in LA, and we trade coaching stories back and forth. He's had more than his fair share of dealing with sassy thirteen-year-old gymnasts and their uptight parents, but so have I. This is such a niche profession, it's rare that I meet someone else who understands it completely; even in the close-knit gymnastics circle, I don't know any other coaches around my own age. I'm glad I got over my nerves about eating lunch with Ryan at Summit. It's good for us to be friends.

• CHAPTER 9 •

While the rest of the world counts down to the clock striking midnight on New Year's Eve, or the ball dropping in Times Square, we're more focused in the gym. Chalk dust hangs in the air as Hallie Sharpies a red X over the day in the calendar in Ryan's training binder. There are 175 days to Trials.

Hallie's floor routine has been my singular obsession for most of the month. I sometimes catch myself tapping out the steps while rinsing my hair in the shower, or humming the music while I refill my water bottle. She has the choreography down pat by now, and we've settled on which tumbling passes go where. We still have a ways to go when it comes to her actual performance—but I know the nuanced details, like the sassy tilt of a head or the satisfying *thunk* of a cleanly stuck landing, take time to develop. She'll get there. I'm optimistic.

So, today, Ryan wants Hallie to prioritize bars and vault. He told me I could take the day off, but the prospect of a weekday stuck in the house with Mom and Dad was too dull to consider. Instead, I spend hours lolling about by the chalk bins between the bars, fluffing the dismount mats, sucking down water bottles while wielding a whistle and stopwatch through Hallie's conditioning reps.

When Hallie heads home for dinner at six thirty, the sliver of night sky I can see through the gym windows is navy blue and studded with stars. New England winter nights are frigid, and this one is no exception. I'm gathering my stuff by the stereo—phone, socks, hoodie—when Ryan sidles up and leans nonchalantly against the plastic shelves.

"Are you going out tonight?" he asks.

I have no plans. Three days ago, as I slathered peanut butter on a banana and slid out the side door to the garage, Mom and Dad suggested that we all watch the ball drop on TV, like we used to. That's how I spent almost every New Year's Eve as a teenager, back when I lived at home and had no social life outside of the gym. My new life mirrors my old one all too well. If I were still living in LA, I might try to slither into a sequined minidress, pulled down tight around my thighs, and dance while clutching an overfilled champagne flute as the clock struck midnight. I can't do that here. I have no clue if Boston even has clubs, and if it does, there's no way I want to brave the line outside with bare legs on a winter night.

"Uhhh . . ." I try to stretch out the word in order to buy myself time to generate a response that saves me from looking like a loser with no friends, but nothing comes to mind. "Well . . . not really?"

I'm grateful that his expression doesn't flicker with pity.

"My friend is having a party tonight," he says.

"Oh," I say, exhaling and feeling my cheeks flushing pink. "You don't have to invite me out just because I have nothing better to do."

"No, no, I'm saying . . ." He chuckles and looks down. "I'm saying you could come? If you want to."

The way his voice lilts, I get the sense that he's not just being nice. He sounds nervous, like he's actually hoping I say yes. I've never seen a hint of vulnerability from him before, but I like it. Part of me wants to spit out a reassuring answer quickly so he doesn't have to feel flustered; part of me marvels at seeing him like this.

"Or, you know, if you'd rather do something else, that's cool, too," he rushes to add.

It's funny, I guess, the way we've spent hundreds of hours together at this point, and yet we're still not quite comfortable around each other. Our lunch two weeks ago was a good step forward, but we have a ways to go.

"That sounds like fun," I say, aiming to sound cool and confident, instead of overly eager. I'm not sure I land the right effect. "I could swing by."

"Sweet," he says, knocking the side of the stereo with his fist. "I'll text you the details."

A million questions start to unfurl on my tongue: *What should I wear? Should I bring drinks? Who's your friend? Where's the party? . . . Is this a date?* But by the time I work up the courage to spit out even the most basic ones, Ryan is already straightening up and heading across the gym.

"See you tonight!" he calls, stretching up to slap the top of the door frame as he disappears into the lobby.

Once I'm sure he's gone, I turn to face the mirror that runs along one edge of the floor. I'm bare-faced, with a lifeless ponytail that probably should've been washed yesterday. Chalk dust and foam pit particles cling to my clothes. I have no idea what kind of party I'm in for, but I can guarantee that this look isn't going to cut it. I head home, checking my phone at each red light, waiting for Ryan's text.

• • •

There's a message on my phone when I step out of the shower. I wipe the fog from my screen against the blue terry cloth of my towel and read Ryan's text: a Somerville address I don't recognize, 10 p.m., BYOB. Many of my former classmates moved to Somerville after college, especially the ones who stayed local for school. From what I know of it, it's the kind of place with fixed-gear bikes and all-organic markets, not far from Harvard. It's just bustling enough to feel hip—I think. I've never actually been.

I clutch the towel to my chest, shivering a little at the shock of cold air outside the shower, and head into my bedroom to find something to wear. My flimsy clubbing dresses are gone, but any of them probably would've looked desperate and out of place, anyway. Instead, I find a pair of pleather leggings and a silky black cami. I hesitate, wondering if my black knit sweater would be more appropriate. I rummage through a dresser drawer until I find it. The fabric feels comfortably thick under my fingers. Ryan is my coworker. But arms are just arms, aren't they? And it's New Year's Eve. I push the sweater back into the drawer.

I blow-dry my hair, put on a tasteful layer of makeup, grab a bottle of wine from the liquor cabinet downstairs—though I need to blow a coat of dust off of it first—to stash in my purse, and then . . . wait for time to pass. It's barely after eight. There was a time in my life when going out before midnight seemed lame. Now, the prospect of even making it to midnight seems questionable. I pad into the kitchen to scrounge for leftovers.

"You're going out?" Dad asks, looking up over his glasses. He's eating a plate of pasta with one hand and reading a magazine in the other.

"Yeah, if that's . . . okay?" I ask tentatively.

He tilts his head. "I guess I can see how sitting around with your parents tonight probably isn't your idea of fun."

"Oh, come on, Dad," I say, trying to force a laugh.

He shrugs. "Pasta's in the fridge," he says.

I make myself a plate and pop it into the microwave, trying to figure out what to say to him as the appliance hums in the background.

"Ryan invited me to his friend's place in Somerville," I explain. "I'll take an Uber there."

Dad reaches for his wallet and fishes out two twenties.

"No, Dad," I say, laughing. "Uber doesn't take cash. But I got it. I'm good. I'm making money now, you know."

After Dad and I finish our pasta, we join Mom in the living room to watch TV. The crowd packed into Times Square looks miserable in tonight's frigid, slushy weather. Their "2020" glasses are a jarring reminder that the Olympics are just months away. Between the countdown clock in the corner of the TV screen, ticking away the minutes to midnight, and the uncomfortable sensation of my pleather waistband digging into my stomach when I normally sit here in sweats, it's impossible to forget that I have somewhere to go. I'm anxious to leave; I'm nervous about the prospect of heading into a party where I only know Ryan, and I'm curious to see how the night will unfold. The year ahead feels like a fresh start, and I want it to hurry up and arrive already.

Mom and Dad encourage me to leave at nine thirty, but I force myself to wait at least another twenty minutes before I dare call the Uber. I don't want to show up embarrassingly early. When my driver arrives, he grumbles about traffic but plays a comforting mix of pop hits from the '80s and '90s as the car whisks me through the suburbs and into the city. If I were meeting Tyler at a party, I'd text him a heads-up: *On my way.* But I don't know Ryan that well. My finger hovers over his name in my phone. I do my best to resist the urge.

Finally, at ten thirty, the car stops in front of a three-story house with a strip of a snowy front lawn. A group of people cluster in the wide bay window of the first-floor apartment; that must be it. I scurry up the front walk, climb the short set of stairs to the porch, and take a deep breath before ringing the buzzer.

A trim, dark-haired guy comes to the door a few seconds later. His mouth parts halfway, and he gives me a quizzical expression. "Hi?"

I glance past his shoulder to see if I can spot Ryan, but I'm not tall enough to see beyond this guy's bulky frame. "Hi, uh, Ryan invited me?"

"Oh, hey, c'mon inside," he says, stepping back to welcome me into the apartment. His expression softens. "I'm Goose. This is my place."

"Goose?" I ask.

"Mike Guzowski, but everyone calls me Goose," he explains, gesturing to the group of people gathered in his living room.

The room is dim, illuminated by a strip of lights along the window that emit a soft glow that rotates through the colors of the rainbow. There's a massive sectional along one wall where an assortment of thick-necked, muscled guys sit with their dates, facing the TV. The screen is turned to the countdown in Times Square, but mercifully, it's on mute. Instead, ambient electronic music floats through the room. The party is dominated by a dining room table set up for beer pong with teams of two facing off at each end. The kitchen island is entirely covered with empty beer bottles, flattened six-pack cartons, open bags of chips, and a Tupperware full of lopsided, homemade chocolate chip cookies.

Ryan is perched on the arm of the couch, sipping a beer. He pops up when he spots me.

"Hey, you made it," he says, approaching me and Goose.

He hesitates for a split second, then leans in for a hug. It's the first time we've ever been this close, and I can detect some kind of cologne. I lean into him for a brief moment, and his hand grazes the small of my back.

"Good to see you," I say.

Training was only a few hours earlier, but here, at the party, it feels like it could've been days ago. I unzip my black wool coat and shrug it off, tossing it on the pile of parkas and peacoats on the love seat.

"I brought, um, this," I say to Ryan, fishing the bottle of merlot out of my bag.

"Oh, sweet," he says, looking down at the label. "Thanks. Should we open it?"

The merlot seemed fine earlier that night, but now that I see everyone else nursing beers, it feels like an uncomfortably fussy choice.

"Maybe later?" I suggest. "I'll have one of whatever you're having."

Ryan grabs a beer from the fridge, scans the table for an opener, and snaps off the cap. We clink bottles ceremoniously.

"You look great," he offers sheepishly. "I've never seen you, you know . . ." He gestures to the slick pleather pants and looks like he's at a loss for words. "I've never seen you with your hair down before."

Was his comment flirty? It felt flirty—but maybe he only wanted to bring me along because the other guys here have dates.

"Oh, thanks, yeah. I figured, you know, I could look a little more presentable for a night out."

I don't know what else to say, so I mumble that he looks great, too. It's not a lie; he's in a charcoal-gray sweater that looks like cashmere and slim-fitting black pants. Away from the gym's harsh fluorescent lighting, dressed in real clothes, he looks more like a GQ model than any real person has a right to. He may be my boss, but I'm not immune to the fact that he's hot. I like that while he's tall for a gymnast, he's much closer to my height than, say, Tyler. It's nice not to have to crane my neck to have a conversation with him.

"So, uh, how do you know Goose and everyone?" I ask.

"Goose and I grew up together in Florida," he explains. "He's been in Boston since college, and half the reason I was psyched to take the coaching job at Summit is because it'd mean seeing him regularly again. And then a lot of these guys are buddies from the gym. Here, let me introduce you." He gestures for two people on the sprawling sectional to scoot apart and make room for us. "Move."

A space opens up, and we sit, our thighs bumping as we get comfortable on the couch.

"This is Avery, the other coach," Ryan tells the group.

He reels off their names, though there are too many for me to keep track of them. His friends nod at me in recognition, like they've heard of me already and knew to expect me tonight. People say hello, then return to a heated conversation about the Patriots' chances of making the Super Bowl. The last thing I want to do is talk about football with another guy.

"So, you must have been a gymnast, too?" Goose asks.

Next to him, his girlfriend, a blond girl with meticulous highlights dressed in a clingy, metallic sweater dress—Melissa, I think?—looks up.

"Yep," I say. "I retired after an injury about seven years ago, so I'm just into coaching these days."

"That's sick," he says, shaking his head.

"So cool," his girlfriend adds.

The attention makes me slightly anxious. I know the next logical question is if I was ever in the Olympics, like Ryan, and that's a rabbit hole I don't want to have to deal with. So I jump in with a question of my own to divert the conversation.

"What do you guys do?" I ask.

Goose works in sales for a tech start-up, and Melissa teaches fifth grade.

"It looks like they're finishing up," Goose says, nodding to the beer pong table. "Want to play next?"

"Yeah," Melissa says, leaning forward. She clutches my wrist. "Girls against guys?"

"Let's do us against them," Ryan says, claiming me on his team.

"Are you any good?" I ask.

He gives me a cocky look. "Two world-class athletes against these two? We got this."

We wait a minute for the game to wrap up, and then Goose sets up the table for another round. He throws the first ball and sinks it into a red Solo cup, but Ryan doesn't look worried at all. I expect him to step up to the table for the first throw from our side, but he encourages me to take the shot. I center myself against the table, focus on the exact spot I want the ball to land in, and steady myself. The precision reminds me of preparing for a vault—except here, my skills are shaky at best. Sure enough, my ball bounces off the rim of one cup and ricochets across the living room. I chase after it in a hurry before it disappears under the couch.

"Try a lighter touch next time," Ryan suggests when I return. He mimics the throw.

I chuckle. "Are you coaching me? You know, we're off the clock. This is just for fun."

He holds his hands up. "All right, you're right, I'm sorry."

"No, no, I don't mean you have to cut it out—I'm just teasing you. Show me how to make a shot."

Over the course of the game, between turns, he slowly but surely guides me. He's standing inches behind me when I finally land one, and he leans forward to wrap his arms over my shoulders in a celebratory hug.

"Yes!" he exclaims. "Great job."

When we win the entire game a few minutes later, it's all because of Ryan.

"Victory!" I cheer, throwing up both hands to punch the air.

"We're a great team," he counters.

"That one point I scored definitely helped," I say faux-seriously.

He doesn't argue with me.

We relinquish the table to the next group of players and get another round of beers from the fridge. The party has gotten crowded.

"So, Avery, beer pong champion," he begins, "I know we spend all this time together at work, but please don't take this the wrong way—can you tell me about yourself?"

I laugh. "Like, first date style?"

"First date style," he echoes.

"Is this a date?" I ask, suddenly feeling emboldened by the beer and the victory and the heady rush of New Year's Eve.

His shoulders creep toward his ears, his lips curl, and he cocks his head to one side. "Maybe?" he asks coyly, self-consciously, like my question caught him off guard. "If you want it to be."

Before I can formulate the right response—*do* I want it to be?— he clears his throat and rushes to add, "Or if you don't want it to be, that is absolutely okay, too."

"I wondered what you were thinking when you invited me out," I say, hedging my bets.

"I . . ." He falters. "I never heard you mention seeing anyone. Are you seeing anybody?"

"I'm not seeing anyone, no," I say. I hesitate, then decide to share a little more. "But that's kind of why I moved back to Greenwood. I was in a relationship in LA, and then it ended."

I consider telling him more about my breakup with Tyler, but decide against it. That conversation would require exposing too much of myself. I don't need Ryan to see the raw, messy bits of my life. It's better that he think of me only as a stellar coach or maybe even as someone he might start to like. There's no use ruining that impression.

Ryan nods and sips his beer. "I'm sorry to hear that."

Maybe I'm imagining it, but whatever glimmer of potential there was between us before, it's hardened now. His jaw sets a millimeter tighter than it did before. Is he calculating how long I've been back in town and how quickly a person can get over heartbreak?

"It was . . . it was for the best," I say. "It was time. We should've broken up long before we actually did."

I've never said that out loud, but it's the truth. I've always been conscious of the fact that Tyler pulled me out of a dangerous spiral; I know he was so damn good for me when we met. But we both changed. We grew apart. And just because I'm grateful for how he was back then doesn't mean I owe him forever. The idea is strangely energizing. I've been leaning one lazy hip against the kitchen counter, and I straighten up to my full height.

"You're a fighter," he says serenely. "You'll get back out there in no time."

A fighter. I can't remember the last time someone called me that. It's been ages since I deserved that compliment. It feels good to be seen that way.

"Yeah, I know," I say, testing out what it's like to accept praise. Not bad.

Ryan digs through an open bag of potato chips, and when he looks back up at me, he has a funny look on his face. His mouth twists to one side. I get the sense that he's weighing whether or not to say something, and I don't want to interrupt his train of thought. I pick lightly at the chips.

"For the record, I'm not seeing anyone, either," he says finally. "I haven't had anything serious for a while."

"Mmm."

I worry that if I say too much, I'll scare him into changing the subject—and I want to hear more.

"It was tough to date when I was training seriously, and then after, I jumped into a relationship, probably just to feel normal and fill all that time, you know? I figured, if I can't be a competitive gymnast anymore, maybe I could be someone's boyfriend."

I can't help but let out a short, harsh laugh. "Oh, I know that feeling. Maybe too well."

His face lights up. "It's weird, isn't it? Going from this thing that dominates your whole world to nothing at all. It's like, well, shit, can I even *be* anybody else?"

I exhale deeply. "I know what you mean."

"But anyway, that didn't pan out. Obviously."

"Obviously," I say.

He takes another chip and turns it over in his hand, considering it.

"So I guess what I'm saying is that, if this *were* a date, I wouldn't mind," he says.

I like the hopeful twinkle in his expression.

"Well, I—" I start to say.

"Hey, everyone!" Goose booms from the couch. "One minute to midnight. The countdown's coming."

He double-fists electronic devices, cutting off the music with his phone and using the TV remote to take the Times Square broadcast off mute. I hadn't even noticed Melissa bustling in the kitchen, but while Ryan and I had been talking, she must have poured champagne into two dozen plastic flutes lined up in rows on the counter.

"Here, help me pass these out," she instructs as she squeezes by me, clutching four to her chest.

I'm frustrated that my conversation with Ryan got interrupted. I grab as many flutes as I can carry and make my way into the crowd, passing them out. When I turn back to get more, Ryan is behind me, his gaze locked on the trembling, overly filled drinks. I hand three plastic flutes to strangers and keep a fourth for myself. I feel too self-conscious to take up prime real estate in a spot in front of the TV, so I move to the edge of the party, near the windows. There's a roaring, rhythmic cheer coming from the hordes of tourists in Times Square that signals the new year is mere seconds away. I wonder how many millions of people must be watching this same exact sight, and what unfathomable pressure that must place on whoever is responsible for lowering that massive crystal ball.

"Ten, nine, eight," the party chants.

I shrink closer to the windows, unsure whether or not to join in. They aren't my friends.

"Seven, six, five," they shout, growing louder.

Suddenly, Ryan slips between the couple to my left, and he's by my side.

"Hi," he breathes.

"Hi," I say, instantly feeling less alone here.

He places his hand on the small of my back.

"Four, three, two, one! Happy New Year!" everyone announces.

All around us, couples erupt in celebratory kisses. I turn to him just as he turns to me. A curious grin plays on his face. His fingers slide over my waist, keeping us close. I place my hand lightly on his chest, tilt my head up to look at him, and we kiss. I feel a giddy burst of adrenaline, and it's not only the festive energy radiating throughout the room. Despite harboring a crush on him for years, I never fathomed a world in which I stir up the same dizzying feelings that he creates in me. Ryan pulls back ever so slightly, and a smile curls on his lips.

"Happy New Year," I whisper.

"I think I like this year already," he says softly.

He rests his drink on the windowsill, then pulls me closer to him, sliding his hands over my hips. His embrace is warm and thrill-

ing. I feel confident enough to let my hand roam from his chest to
his shoulder to his neck, feeling the powerful muscles underneath
his sweater. My fingers brush the plush edge of his hair. He nuzzles
my cheek and trails kisses down the side of my neck. The sensation
is electrifying, and my eyes flutter open.

Most of the crowd has moved on from making out; the music is
back on. It suddenly hits me that I'm kissing *Ryan*—not just Cute
Ryan from my teenage dreams, but Ryan, the coach I work alongside
every day. The person who, like me, is responsible for molding an
Olympic champion, and probably shouldn't be distracted right now.
A thick blanket of self-consciousness settles over me, and I tense up.

"You okay?" Ryan asks, dropping his hands from my waist.

I stare out at the room of people. "I, uh, I . . . I'm sorry."

"For what?" he asks, looking concerned.

"Should we be doing this?" I ask, pushing my hair back from my
face.

Anxiety creeps into my chest.

"Is this too soon?" he says, inching away from me.

I take a deep breath. It's hard to face him.

"I like you, but I didn't expect to like you like this," I say, fum-
bling for the right words. I'm not brave enough to say what I really
mean, which is that I didn't expect to like him *this much*. Crushes
never really work out that way—just because you think someone is
attractive from afar doesn't mean shit when it comes to having a real
connection. "Should we maybe, I don't know, think about this? I
don't want to mess up what we have at work."

He rubs his jaw and doesn't look at me right away. "Sure thing."

"I should go," I say.

He doesn't protest.

The entire ride home to Greenwood, I replay that kiss in my
mind and regret leaving.

JANUARY

2020

• CHAPTER 10 •

Summit is closed on New Year's, but opens the following day. I pull into the parking lot with one minute until practice, although I don't get out of the car right away. Ryan's Subaru is parked, and I'm worried about entering the gym without Hallie as a buffer. I spent most of yesterday ping-ponging between desire and self-doubt; I want to let myself enjoy the memory of that tantalizing kiss, but I know I shouldn't. Without the heady buzz of the party clouding my judgment, it seems awfully stupid to jeopardize my professional relationship for the chance at anything romantic. We can't risk Hallie catching on; she's sheltered enough that a midnight kiss between her two coaches would sound scandalous, not festive. It would be a distraction she can't afford to indulge in right now. And beyond that, Ryan is the closest thing I have to a friend these days. I don't want to ruin that. The thought of explaining this tangle of emotions, responsibilities, and fears to Ryan makes me queasy—I'd rather simply pretend the kiss never happened. We were tipsy; I was lonely; that's that. So I wait until I see Hallie's mom drop her off before I dare get out of my car and enter the building.

Hallie is usually happy to chatter away the first morning after a break, like a weekend or a holiday. But when I find her and Ryan on the floor, she's not dilly-dallying—she's already running laps. It looks like she doesn't want to squander a moment of practice.

"It's 2020," she pants as she cruises past me. "No time to waste."

Ryan turns ever so slightly toward me with his arms crossed over his chest. "Hi," he says simply, like he's testing out the vibe between us.

"Morning," I say, maybe a bit too businesslike.

"How was your day off?" he says evenly, turning his gaze back to Hallie.

I follow suit. It's easier to watch her than to look at him.

"Fine. Yours?" I say, aiming to sound slightly softer this time.

"Fine," he replies.

Hallie jogs past us again, and we fall into uneasy silence.

"Are you cold in here? It's cold in here," he says, sometime after her third lap. "I'm going to go fiddle with the thermostat."

He stays across the gym for longer than it takes to adjust the temperature.

It strikes me that even if I want to pretend the kiss never happened, he may not. Maybe he feels rejected, or embarrassed, or like he misread the situation entirely. Or maybe he came to the same conclusion that I did, that getting involved with each other can irreparably damage the work we're doing. If Hallie overhears our awkwardness, there's no way she wouldn't pick up on the fact that something is off.

I glance at Hallie—she's been doing a variation of this same warm-up routine since she was in preschool. She doesn't need me to hover over her and bark instructions. I leave my regular perch by the stereo and head to the back of the nearly empty gym to find Ryan leaning against the wall and looking at something on his phone.

"Hey, can we talk?" I ask quietly. "Like, for real."

We're far enough that Hallie won't hear us, but still, I'm nervous.

"Hi, what's up?" he says, making a valiant effort to appear casual.

I wring my hands and steel myself for a moment of terrifying honesty. "I had so much fun with you the other night, and I really appreciate that you invited me out," I begin. "It was all amazing, including the kiss, but I . . . I don't think it should happen again. I think we'd be better off as friends."

"Oof," he says coolly. "You're quick to turn me down."

"No! That's not it. I mean, if the circumstances were different, I'd want to give us a real shot."

He raises one eyebrow. "What do you mean?"

I take a deep breath and try to summon the vulnerability I need to pull off this conversation successfully.

"I like you. A lot. I really appreciate that we come from the same world; it makes me feel like you understand me better than most people. I think that if we . . ."

This is mortifying to say out loud, but I have to keep going.

"If we got together for real, it would be incredible," I say. I'm fully emotionally naked in front of him now. "But that scares me, because we could get caught up in whatever's between us, and that could affect our ability to work together."

His face softens. He doesn't look angry—just sad.

"This isn't just about us," I remind him. "It's about Hallie, too. This is a once-in-a-lifetime shot for her."

I see his gaze drift over my shoulder, and I turn to follow it. Hallie is stretching in an oversplit—a split with stacks of mats under each foot and her crotch flush against the floor. She grabs the toes of her front foot and bends over to face her knee. The position requires superhuman flexibility developed over years, which sums up my point exactly. We all have to stay focused on our goal.

He sighs. "You're right. I get it."

"I'd still love to be friends, though, if you're open to it," I add. "Really."

His expression is tough to read at first, but it ultimately crinkles into an attempt at a smile. "Of course."

Me and Ryan, friends. There's something about the idea that's hazy and hard to picture, but maybe that's because *nothing* about my future feels completely solid right now. I've finally saved up enough money to move out of my parents' house, and I'm going to see an apartment this weekend. The idea of moving makes me feel hopeful.

"I'll see you around," I promise Ryan.

He claps his hands authoritatively and calls across the gym, "Hallie, how's that stretching going?"

• • •

For the rest of the morning, Ryan and I stay out of each other's way. I give him space while he works with Hallie on vault. When it's time for me to take over on floor, he tells Hallie he's going to head to the office to answer some emails.

"Tumbling, let's go," I instruct.

She warms up and practices each of the four passes we've chosen for her routine. After a hard landing, she sighs and rolls out her ankle, flexing her foot in different directions.

"Feeling okay?" I call across the floor.

She takes a few experimental steps, head cocked to the side.

"Yeah, yeah. That landing was weird, but I'm good."

"Did you get a chance to see that doctor?" I ask.

"Dr. Kaminsky?" she asks. "Yeah. He checked me out."

"What did he say? How are you feeling?"

She sighs. "Nothing major is wrong, but I can tape it up if it's bothering me."

"Did he order any texts? X-rays? MRIs?"

"It's all fine," she says. "I'm gonna tape up my ankle."

She retrieves gauzy prewrap and athletic tape from the supply closet and sits on one side of the floor with her foot in front of her, methodically winding the materials around her ankle and heel to stabilize the joint.

I sit and join her. She silently fumes when the tape is too tough to rip cleanly. I help her pull off a long strip.

She bites her lip. "I know he's a good doctor, but I don't know . . . I kind of got a weird vibe from him. And my ankle really feels fine, anyway. So it's not like I'd need to go back."

Something about Hallie's quiet, fidgety demeanor and insistence that everything is normal raises a red flag for me. She reminds me of Jasmine, back when we were kids, the way she'd pretend like Dimitri's behavior on bad days didn't bother her. She always cried later, when it was just the two of us. I remember the pressure to stay tightly controlled and focused on training, the way we would push down our feelings until we could barely notice them anymore. I don't want that for Hallie.

"If something's not right, you can tell me, you know," I say slowly, choosing my words carefully. "I'm always here if you want to talk."

She hesitates, glances at the door, and then back at me. Ryan is nowhere in sight. She absentmindedly picks at the edge of the roll of tape.

"Both times I've seen him, he examines my ankle and shows me certain exercises I can do to strengthen it," she says. "But then he also says the reason I have trouble with it has something to do with my hips. So he has me roll down my leggings a little, and he holds my hips and watches me bend over."

She doesn't make eye contact. She keeps picking at the tape.

I don't know enough about medicine to know if she's describing a legitimate professional encounter or something far more sinister. But something feels off to me.

She pulls her knees up to her chest. "He's a doctor," she points out. "My mom was in the room with me both times. She didn't think anything of it."

When Hallie finally looks up at me, her eyes are bright and glassy with tears.

"It's never okay for him to make you feel uncomfortable," I say. "Not even if he's a respected doctor, and not even if your mom is in the room."

"Got it," she says. She digs her chin into her knee.

"I just want to make sure you're okay," I say.

She shrugs.

"It might be helpful to tell your mom," I suggest gently. "That way, she'll be sure not to bring you back to him."

I don't want to pressure Hallie into saying anything she's not ready for, but also, her parents should probably know—and I'm not sure it's my place to tell them. I remember how daunted I felt at her age by the prospect of being vulnerable with my parents. But I wish I had been more open with them.

"Maybe later," she says. "Not right now. And can you please not tell Ryan about this?" she asks.

She looks at me so expectantly, I don't know how to say no.

"Sure," I say, leaning forward to wrap her in a hug.

Hallie leans her forehead against my shoulder and lets me embrace her. I feel this odd wave of maternal instinct, and so I stroke her hair and rub soothing circles on her back. She exhales.

• CHAPTER 11 •

On Craigslist, I found a spare room in an apartment on the edge of Greenwood. The person leasing it, a yoga instructor about my age named Sara McCarthy, was two years below me in Greenwood's public school system, though we didn't know each other as kids. Normally, this would make me wary; I wouldn't want a repeat of my disastrous date with Lucas. But as Sara gave me a tour of the cozy, colorful apartment, she didn't ask any leading questions or pry for uncomfortable answers. She seemed both bubbly and relaxed. The apartment spanned the top floor of a duplex; the living room was painted an electric shade of purple, like Rachel and Monica's apartment in *Friends*; the rent was affordable; the bedroom came furnished. I said yes on the spot.

A week later, I pack my things into the trunk of the Honda and drive across town to move in. Sara helps me carry my suitcases and laundry baskets of clothing out of the car and up the stairs.

"It's fine if you smoke, just open the window first," she says, miming holding a joint. "And I make kombucha every Sunday—you're welcome to have some."

I'm not particularly interested in either offer, but I appreciate her openness.

"Cool, thank you," I say.

She jostles open the door to the apartment and leans one of my suitcases against the couch covered by an enormous hand-crocheted afghan. A pink yoga mat hangs in a nylon carrier on a hook by the coatrack, and a trio of creamy white candles rest on the coffee table.

Despite my protests that there's no need for her help unpacking, Sara seems happy to. She brews us hot, fruity tea and carries it into the bedroom at the end of the hall—the one that's now mine. She lets me have what is clearly the better of the two mugs, printed with a faded graphic of a cat wearing bejeweled cat-eye glasses and only barely chipped. She sits cross-legged at the foot of the bed and folds clothes into neat stacks for me to place inside the old-fashioned armoire by the window, chattering easily as she works.

"So, I'll admit, I know who you are, obviously," she says, pushing her hair behind her ear to reveal a constellation of silver stud earrings.

"Oh," I say nervously.

Maybe I'd misjudged her.

"I mean, like, from years ago," she says. "My little sister went to Summit and practically worshipped you from afar. She'd flip if she knew you were moving in, but I don't know . . . You seem so normal? Is that a weird thing for me to say?"

"Um . . . I don't know? A little?" I say.

I get the sinking feeling that I've just moved all of my possessions into the home of a woman who sees me as Avery, the athlete, not Avery, the regular roommate.

"I'm sure your life has moved on," she says graciously.

I'm grateful she said that—it makes me feel more confident that's true.

"I just recently moved back from six years in LA," I say, as if to prove that I'm not still the girl who grew up in Greenwood.

"I mean, *I'm* not the person I was a few years back, either," she says. "I went to UMass for psych, but then I got pretty into yoga there, and that led to me getting my yoga teacher's training certificate, and here we are. Just couldn't stay away from this ex-*ci*-ting town."

Her tone makes it clear she's kidding.

"I teach at Mind & Body Yoga," she explains, naming the yoga studio not far from Greenwood High. "Since I practiced there so often during summer breaks home from college, I couldn't say no when they offered me a job. I gotta say, I'm jealous that you moved away. I wish I could've done something cool like that."

"I mean, it's kinda like you said, one thing turns into another, right? And then you wind up in a place you never thought you'd be? After my gymnastics career ended, I moved to LA for school, then stayed because of my boyfriend at the time," I say, glossing over the manic years of partying. I'm not sure if she'd approve. "And then when that relationship ended, I didn't have much keeping me there. So I moved back, and luckily, a coaching job opened up at Summit."

"Okay, wait a sec," she says, lowering her voice conspiratorially, even though we are the only people around. "Your boyfriend. You dated that football player, right?"

As soon as she mentions Tyler, it hits me that I haven't dwelled on him in a week. I feel a little proud of myself for beginning to move on.

"Yeah, yeah, I did," I say, trying to downplay it.

I turn toward the closet and hang up my parka so I don't have to face her.

"*That* sounds totally major," she says. "What was that like?"

Her tone sounds hungry for gossip, but I'm not in the mood to give it. I get why some people might be starstruck by the prospect of dating a pro football player, but having actually done it, the sheen is lost on me.

"Uh, lots of muscles, lots of sweat," I say quickly. "But underneath all that, just the same old, same old."

"Huh," she says, chewing that over.

"We just grew apart," I explain slowly, testing out her reaction. "We both changed. We wanted different things."

She dramatically closes her eyes and places her hands together in prayer. "Preach, girl."

I laugh.

"I used to date this guy who . . ." she begins before cutting herself off. She shakes her head. "You know what? No. He's not even worth the breath it would take to explain it."

"Fair enough," I say.

I'm starting to like Sara.

I reach for the scissors on the nightstand to cut open my last box of things. We're both quiet for a minute.

"Actually, I like this new guy," I blurt, surprising myself, even.

"Yeah? Who?" she asks.

I run the odds in my head that Sara would have ever crossed paths with Ryan. Greenwood has just thirty thousand people, but he didn't grow up here, and they seem to run in different social circles. I don't think they know each other. I grab my mug of tea and sink down across from Sara on the bed.

"His name is Ryan. We work together."

"Ooh . . . another coach?"

"Yeah. I actually sort of knew of him when we were younger, and I always thought he was cute. We work pretty closely together now—it's just the two of us training this one incredible gymnast. We think she could have a pretty decent shot at making the next Olympics."

"So has anything happened between you two?" Sara asks.

Right—she is not here to listen to my thoughts on Hallie's athletic career. The question was about Ryan.

"We were work friends up until New Year's Eve, when he invited me out to his friend's party," I say. "We kissed at midnight. And then . . . I don't know, things sort of changed between us? I realized how much I liked being around him. It freaked me out. I don't know."

This is the first time I've ever told this story out loud, the first time I've had a person to tell it to. The events of that night have been playing on a jumbled loop in my brain ever since I left the party in Somerville, but that doesn't make explaining what happened with Ryan any easier.

"Not a good kisser?" she asks, wrinkling her nose.

"No, not that. Not at all," I rush to say.

God, how many times since New Year's Eve have I imagined the electricity of our kiss? Sometimes, I catch myself daydreaming about it at Summit when I know I shouldn't.

"You should go for him," Sara says clearly.

"What?"

"You like him. So tell him that. Go out with him. Do something."

I feel hot, like I'm under a spotlight.

"I can't do that," I protest.

"You can sit here in your discomfort, or you can step outside your comfort zone and try something new," she continues, slipping into what I assume must be a platitude from her yoga classes.

"We work together. It's complicated," I explain. "I told him we probably shouldn't do anything like that again."

"Life is short," she says.

She shrugs and scoots off the bed, then whirls around to face me. "We can be friends, can't we?" she asks.

"Of course we can," I rush to say.

"Good. I was hoping you'd say that," she says, grinning. "I have to get going. The studio does candlelit yoga on Sunday nights. I'm teaching at six thirty and eight o'clock. Wanna join?"

I glance around the bedroom, which doesn't quite feel *homey* yet, though it's shaping into something that feels like mine. This apartment feels like a fresh start. I don't want to leave it just yet.

"Maybe another day?" I suggest.

I don't mean it. It's the way I was raised—unless a workout involves a raised heartbeat and death-defying stunts, I'm not interested. Chanting mantras in downward dog doesn't seem like it'd do it for me.

"Free classes on me anytime," she says, heading around the corner into her own bedroom to get ready.

I sink onto the bed. First Summit, then whatever is going on with Ryan, and now this new place to live. For the first time in a long time, I feel the different elements of my life clicking together. I like this new life.

• • •

After Sara leaves, the apartment is quiet. I drive to the supermarket, pick up an armful of carrots, mushrooms, herbs, and rice, and make risotto for myself. Cooking dinner for one is an endeavor that requires a little too much time, energy, and money for what it's worth, but I need to do something to keep my hands and mind busy. I have to focus on drizzling the pan with precisely the right amount of olive oil and dicing the vegetables the right way so I don't have the bandwidth to think about Ryan. He's been on my mind more than I'd like to admit lately.

I didn't used to be like this—sappy, emotional, with a soft center. I used to pride myself on being able to block out distractions. It's a necessary skill in gymnastics: when you're four feet aboveground, balancing on a four-inch-wide beam, there's no room to notice the trilling of another girl's floor music or the flailing kid cartwheeling past you or the watchful gaze of your coach. There's you and there's the beam. That's it. Tonight, there's me and there's this meal. I wish that could be it. My mind keeps circling back to thoughts I shouldn't be having.

There's nothing worth getting distracted from Olympic glory, least of all a crush—that's what Dimitri drilled into me years ago. But the truth is that however deeply I know Ryan and I can't hook up or date or whatever we were veering toward, I still want to kiss him again. I can't stop thinking about running my fingers through his hair and feeling his powerful hands pressing into the curve of my waist. I *like* him. I liked him back then, too, though I didn't think I could do anything about it. Now, though? I'm not sure. I'm in a new home. It's a fresh start. Anything could be possible.

• CHAPTER 12 •

Monday's practice slips by in a flash. Hallie, clad in a blinding neon orange leotard sprayed with sparkles, whips through warm-ups and conditioning with alarming grit, charges down the vault runway like a sprinter, attacks her tumbling with gusto, and moves with an impressive sense of focus on beam. Nationals—the annual competition that brings together the country's top talent—is one of the most important events of the year, and it's just two months away. The upcoming competition sharpens the pressure. When Hallie's moving in top form, like she is today, practice never drags. It's impossible to look away from her.

She and Ryan have spent the final hour of the day together on bars, drilling her new Tkatchev–Pak Salto combo. It's coming together nicely; right now, she can pull it off just fine, though she has some work to put in before the combination looks effortless. That's the gold standard in gymnastics: making the impossible look not just possible, but *easy*. I've been sitting and stretching on the sidelines, watching Ryan tracking Hallie's movements as she arcs through the air. His arms are outstretched; he's ready to catch her if she falls.

"It's six," he says finally, after what must be her thirtieth attempt at the move.

"What?" she says, spinning around to look at the clock. She gapes. "No! I was just getting into it."

"Time to go," he says. "You know your parents like you out of the gym in time for homework."

"One more?" she pleads.

He laughs. "One more. Then you gotta get out of here."

"Avery, would you film this one?" she asks.

She likes to have video clips to post on Instagram—though, of course, only the most jaw-dropping ones actually get posted.

"Sure," I say, digging my phone out of the pocket of my fleece zip-up and getting ready to record. "Ready when you are."

She takes her position under the high bar. Ryan grabs her by her waist, and she jumps; he helps her reach the bar. She does a move called a kip to swing up so the wooden equipment is flush against her hips, then screws up her face in a look of pure concentration before launching into a handstand, giant, and finally, a Tkatchev followed swiftly by a Pak Salto. Her compact body flings over one bar, then between the two, and it's magnificent. Once the final move is complete, her knees bend, and her shoulders sag into a relaxed swing. She knows she's nailed it. She drops down and jogs over to my spot on the mat to watch the playback.

"I look pretty good, right?" she muses.

"You do," I admit. "I'll text this to you."

"Thanks!" she says. "Okay, now I can head out. I just wanted to nail it once."

She strips off her grips and heads across the gym to pack up for the night. Ryan jumps up to the high bar himself, swings back and forth, and drops back down to the mat.

"You leaving, too?" he asks.

I shrug. "I mean, I guess? My new roommate, Sara, invited me to another yoga class tonight, but I told her practice might run late."

"We never run late," he points out.

"Yoga seems boring. But I can't tell her that," I say.

He laughs. "Gotcha."

Ryan meanders around the bars and leans against one of the silver poles holding up the apparatus.

"So, if you're not doing anything, then, would you want to get dinner?" he asks. He clears his throat and hastily adds, "As friends."

If only he knew how I regret saying that I only wanted friendship.

"Yeah, let's do that," I say. "It'll be cool to catch up outside the gym again."

"Yeah? Awesome. Maybe a bite at Stonehearth Pizza?"

I know the place. Wood-fired pizza with surprisingly healthy toppings, which is a plus, but brightly lit and full of kids—less than ideal.

"I was actually planning to cook tonight. I could make us dinner?"

Too late, I realize that inviting Ryan over might feel too intimate.

"You love to cook, I love to eat," he says, like the decision has been made.

Maybe I'm overthinking it.

"Perfect."

"Cool, I'm just gonna go grab my coat from the office, then," he says.

As we walk together from the bars to the door, I try to pretend that everything is fine and normal, and that I haven't spent the past two weeks wishing for another opportunity to spend time alone with him. When I duck into the changing room to pick up my parka and purse, I spend an extra thirty seconds fixing my ponytail and putting on a coat of mascara from the tube I find in the bottom of my bag. *This is not a date*, I remind myself as I lacquer up my eyelashes.

I find Ryan in the lobby, leaning against the wall and looking at his phone. There's something casually intimate about the way he waits for me; it's something Tyler did when I met him after football practice. But I can't let myself think that way.

"Hey," he says, straightening up when he sees me. "I was thinking I can follow you in my car?"

"Sure thing. Let's go."

He tails me across town, and I try not to look back at his reflection in my rearview mirror too often. I also refrain from turning on the radio, in case he gets an embarrassing glimpse of me bopping my head along to the music. I try to remember exactly how messy the apartment was when I left this morning. I don't think there are any random bras tossed over the arm of the couch, but I could be wrong.

I meet him in my driveway, and we climb the stairs to my apartment together. *This is not a date*, I remind myself, as I unlock my front door and usher a handsome, funny gentleman inside. This is my first time inviting a guest over to my new apartment, and it's a little nerve-wracking. I distract myself by babbling to Ryan about the tortellini soup recipe I was planning to try out tonight.

"So, it's actually a good thing you're here, because it was so much soup to make for just one person," I explain.

"Glad to hear I'm good for something," he says.

I sift through my fridge and cabinets, picking out the right ingredients to make the dinner. Cooking will keep me busy in front of Ryan, which is a relief because it's jarring to see him sit on one of the yellow bar stools in my kitchen, watching me work.

"Hey, do you want some wine?" I ask.

I hope he'll say yes, so I can have some, too. It'll take the edge off.

"Yeah, I could do a glass," he says.

I find a bottle of red wine in the cabinet and give us each a generous pour. The first sip is so flavorful, that alone calms me down a notch.

There's a lull in the conversation as I start to peel and chop an onion. The apartment feels quiet without Sara here.

"Can I help?" he asks. "I'm no chef, but I can follow instructions if you tell me what to do."

I consider the recipe. "Do you think you're up for the challenge of chopping celery?"

He nods. I hand one to him along with a knife and a cutting board, and we get to work side by side at the kitchen table. Our knives *thwack* rhythmically into our respective vegetables, and I realize again that I don't know what to say that will strike the right balance between friendly and polite.

Ryan clears his throat. "Hallie was great today," he says. "Clean, on point."

I'm both relieved and disappointed that he brought up work. It's easy, safe territory—I don't have to worry about accidentally saying anything unprofessional or inappropriately personal. But on the other hand, well, it's *work*. I don't want to be just his coworker.

"Cheers to that," I say, raising my wineglass.

He clinks his to mine. "Cheers. Seriously. Let's just hope she keeps up the good work," he says, sighing.

"I'm sure she will," I say. "You're a great coach."

"I do all right," he says, shrugging. "But you had Dimitri. The best. I'm jealous."

"You're jealous I had *him*?" I ask.

"Yeah," he says, his voice full of awe. "He's a legend. I tried for years to get him to take me on, but he only coaches women's gymnastics. What was he like?"

"Tough," I say honestly, moving on to mince a clove of garlic. "Really brutally tough. I like your style better."

"Really?" He looks skeptical.

"Oh, one hundred percent. Hallie loves you. Dimitri was . . . intense."

"What do you mean?"

"Eh, I don't want to get into it. Let's just put it this way: he had insanely high expectations, and it was impossible to meet them all."

"Huh. I'm sorry to hear you had a hard time with him."

"It's fine," I say.

"I didn't mean to pry," he says.

"It's fine," I say again, using a tone that I hope will shut down the subject. I stand up to start cooking the veggies in a pot on the stove. "I'm fine."

Luckily, Ryan doesn't keep digging.

"Coaching's really the only thing I'm qualified for at this point, so I better make the most of it."

"You went to college, though—what did you study?" I ask.

"I majored in business so I could always have the option of starting my own gym, if I wanted to," he explains. "But I don't think I was the most dedicated student. I went to school on a gymnastics scholarship, and that was mostly what I cared about."

"Would you really open your own gym?" I ask.

"Maybe far in the future. But for now, I've realized I'd be happier coaching than doing anything else, and you don't need a degree to do that—just experience, and obviously, these incredible muscles."

"Modest," I observe dryly.

"It's one of my best qualities," he jokes. "How long were you in college for?"

"Only a year and a half."

He snaps his fingers. "That explains it all, then."

"What?"

"Why you're so terrible at beer pong," he says, eyes sparkling with pure delight at delivering a playful burn. "Most people get a full four years to practice."

"Oh, very funny," I say, pursing my lips and pretending to be annoyed. "As I recall, we won that game. Mostly because of you, but still. We won."

"True, true. So, why'd you leave school?"

My answer tumbles out before I can second-guess myself. "I was completely, totally, and majorly depressed. And also, I partied too much to ever make it to class."

He lets out a low whistle. "That got dark fast."

I wince. "Too dark?"

"Nah, it's good to be honest," he says. "Sorry you went through that."

"Yeah, thanks," I say.

I shrug and turn my attention to the pot on the stove so I don't have to see what I assume is a look of pity. But when I look back at Ryan, he doesn't look like he pities me at all. He nods in a way that makes me think he understands.

"You spend all this time obsessively focused on this one thing, and it becomes your whole identity, and then it's gone," he says quietly. "And then it's like, well, what *now*?"

"Exactly," I say, relishing in the fact that he gets it.

"But you're doing all right now?" he asks.

"Kind of the best I've been in a long time, actually," I say, suddenly realizing just how true that is. "You?"

"Yeah, it's all good," he says.

This time, Ryan raises his glass and clinks it against mine.

"Well, cheers to that," I say.

I want to say something more, to come up with a clever idea to toast to, but I get tongue-tied when he makes eye contact over our drinks. Instead, I finish making the soup and ladle it into two bowls. I'm pleased with how it turned out—savory, hearty, bursting with flavor. It's a simple meal, but Ryan seems impressed.

"This beats Stonehearth, hands down," he says appreciatively, scooping up a tortellini with his spoon.

Over dinner, Ryan regales me with stories from his travels. Years of competing across states and countries sparked his love of seeing new places, and now he saves up for as many trips as he can.

"Next up, obviously, I'm saving to do a trip around Asia after Tokyo—*if* Hallie makes it to Tokyo, of course," he explains. "You ever been?"

"No, I haven't," I admit. "What's been your favorite trip so far?"

He thinks for a moment. "Traveling for gymnastics is always cool, but you don't get tons of time to actually explore or indulge in great food, so . . . hmm. I guess my favorite would be the summer that Goose and I backpacked across Europe together."

I wish I had done something like that.

"And obviously, we saw some of the best beaches in the world," he says.

"Why obviously?" I ask. "I'd think that would be, like, the Caribbean."

He leans in closer and stage-whispers, "Nude beaches."

"You perv!" I squeal. The wine has definitely started to go to my head.

He holds up his hands in protest. "Hey, I'm just a man."

"I don't know if I could ever do that," I muse.

"What, go to a nude beach?" he asks.

"Yeah. I mean, maybe years ago, when I was in shape, but certainly not *now*."

He raises an eyebrow, then looks down in intense concentration at his bowl.

"What?" I ask.

He sips his soup. "You could go," he says, coyly glancing up at me.

"Did you strip down?" I ask.

"When in Rome . . ." he replies.

I feel precariously close to the edge of saying something stupidly flirty, so I shove a tortellini into my mouth to keep myself from speaking. Discussing nude beaches makes me wonder what Ryan looks like naked, which is absolutely the very last thing I should be doing.

We linger after we finish eating. He tells stories about what Hallie was like when he first met her (apparently, "tiny, furiously hardworking, adorably wholesome, and too energetic"—or in other words, exactly like she is today). We go off on tangents about gymnasts we competed alongside a decade ago, musing about the few in the public eye today and the majority who faded into quiet lives. We try to gauge where we fall on the spectrum, and jokingly agree to not let the fame go to our heads.

Ryan runs a finger around the rim of his empty wineglass, and his mouth screws up to the side.

"What?" I ask.

"I was going to suggest another glass, but that's probably not the wisest idea if I have to drive out of here," he says.

"True," I say.

"But this was fun," he says, suddenly serious. "I mean it. I'm glad we did this."

"Me, too," I say.

"Let me pay you for half the groceries and wine," he says, reaching for his wallet.

"Oh, no, no," I protest. "I was going to make all this, anyway."

"Avery, it's fine, I don't mind," he says.

"No, really, I can't let you pay for this," I insist.

"Fine," he says heavily. "But next time, I'll win."

"Oh, next time?" I retort. "We'll see about that."

I like that we can match each other in competitive spirit.

"And in the meantime, let me help you clean this up," he offers.

"Now, that, I can accept."

We spend a few minutes clearing the table and loading the dishwasher. He takes the most annoying task, hand-washing the pots, of his own volition. For a split second, the rhythm of cooking and cleaning together reminds me of living with Tyler, and I forget that Ryan isn't my boyfriend. I feel a dull sense of loneliness, thinking ahead to the rest of the night, once he's gone. It only gets worse once the kitchen is clean and he grabs his coat from the hook by the door.

"I'll walk you to your car?" I offer, lingering by the couch, suddenly feeling shy.

"Oh, you don't have to do that," he says. "It's cold."

"I don't mind," I insist.

It's January in New England, which means that getting ready to head out the door requires serious effort: jackets zipped, scarves wound, gloves tugged on. Outside, it's pitch-black. The driveway is only partly lit by the golden glow of a street lamp. By the time we reach Ryan's car, parked behind mine, I'm not ready for the night to end. There's an easy comfort between us—a type of intimacy that only grows between two people who have lived the same kind of life. Ryan reaches for his car door. I don't overthink what comes next; it just happens.

I lean forward and I kiss him. It feels like the most natural thing in the world. He kisses me back, slipping an arm around my waist, and bracing us both with a hand against the car window. His lips are soft, and his embrace is sturdy and strong. There's a warmth radiating from him, even on this frigid night, and I like the way I fit in his arms. I could stay here happily forever, even if it's freezing, even if we shouldn't be doing this.

And then, suddenly, he pulls back. He pushes off the car and shoves his hands into his pockets. Even his eyes flicker away from mine. Without him hovering over me, I feel cold and exposed.

"Avery," he says softly. "We've talked about this. We know it's not a good idea."

I'm shocked by how much his rejection hurts. It's embarrassing to have to be reminded that my past self made a responsible decision that my present self is too emotional or tipsy or lonely to adhere to.

"I . . . I'm sorry, I just . . ." I stammer.

The easy banter over dinner, the fuss over paying for groceries, the comfort of cleaning up side by side—maybe this wasn't technically supposed to be a date, but it sure felt like one. And what happened next was simply a natural extension of the night. Wasn't it? I sigh, and in the cold, my breath becomes a visible cloud.

"I just thought that maybe you wanted this, too," I say.

He gives me a sad look that makes my entire body feel weighed down with two-ton anchors.

"So you don't want this," I clarify.

It's mortifying to say that out loud, but he has to understand how he made me feel tonight. I want him to recognize that he made me feel like there was possibility blooming between us again.

"I've really thought this through since New Year's Eve, and as much as I wanted this to work between us, you were right—it's just not a smart idea for us to jump into anything," he says.

I hate that he's using my own words against me. I'm afraid if I protest, my voice will come out thin and whiny, like I'm begging for his affection.

"Oh," I manage to squeak out, feeling very small.

He sighs. "I don't want to push you away."

"Right. I know we talked about being just friends," I admit. "I'm sorry if I crossed a line, then."

He looks down at his feet and doesn't say anything. I can feel whatever sliver of a chance of us being together evaporating, and it makes me feel frantic with desperation.

"Do you feel like there's something between us?" I blurt out. "Because I do. I'd be lying if I pretended otherwise."

"I . . ." He trails off and rubs his jaw. I'm overcome by a desire to kiss that spot, but I refrain. "I do. Of course I do, Avery. Come on. You're beautiful, and so unbelievably strong, and I feel so at home talking to you. I like that we're cut from the same cloth: competitive, hardworking, goal-oriented. It's rare to find someone like that who also has room in their life for someone else."

Against my better judgment, a thrill runs through my body. My brain feels like a jumble of confetti and trumpets and parades. And then I notice the way his voice lilts downward at the end, like there's a "but" coming. My heart races and then skids to a stop.

Sure enough, he starts with, "But—"

I have to cut him off. "Here's the thing, Ryan. Whether or not it's convenient, or whether or not it's a good idea, I can't just walk away from the fact that being around you makes me happier than I've felt in a long time."

I sound ten times braver than I feel. It's terrifying to be so honest with him, but I'm in too deep now to turn around. I have to keep going—I owe it to myself to at least try to win Ryan over. I take a deep breath and barrel on.

"And this isn't just about me. You have a great job and a great life, but I know you want more. I bet you've been lonely. That's why you jumped into a relationship right after retiring from gymnastics. That's why you flirt with me, even when you say you know better. I know what it's like to want a real connection and not find it, and it's awful."

Ryan is still just inches away. I take in the soft, dark depths of his eyes, the faint scar over his eyebrow, the smattering of stubble along his jaw, his tensed, broad shoulders. He swallows.

"You're right," he says quietly, not breaking my gaze. "About all of it."

"Okay . . ." I say, feeling hopeful, though not secure enough to relax just yet.

"I'm just not sure that's enough," he says. "Not when there's so much at stake. As long as we're responsible for Hallie, she comes first. There can't be any distractions."

Distractions. The word reverberates uncomfortably and settles into the pit of my stomach. That's what I'd be: a distraction. I can't look at him. I'm not a monster—I don't want my love life to stand in the way of Hallie's shot at Olympic glory. But I don't think it's quite that simple. She would never need to know. I fiddle with the zipper of my jacket.

"Look, I'm not saying no to this. To us," he says, reaching out to tuck a stray piece of hair behind my ear. "I'm just saying we need to think carefully here, because the Olympics are right around the corner. And you, more than anyone, can understand how devastated Hallie would be if she doesn't make it."

I'm sure Ryan didn't mean to do it, but linking my feelings for him now to the depression I felt years ago just crushes me. It's cruel.

"I have to go," I mutter, blinking back tears.

Ryan doesn't protest as I head back inside.

FEBRUARY

2020

• CHAPTER 13 •

"Do you have a boyfriend?" Hallie asks at practice a week later.

I hold her feet as she dangles her upper body off the back of the vault, then muscles her way up into a sitting position. Her abs swell in size by the second.

"What?" I spit out, caught off guard.

I'm very careful to resist the urge to peek across the gym at Ryan. In fact, I've spent the majority of the past week avoiding him, because it's painful enough to replay our awful last conversation in my head every night before I fall asleep. I don't want to have to relive it in his presence, too.

"I asked if you had a boyfriend," she repeats, finishing another rep of crunches.

She rarely, if ever, asks about my life outside the gym. I don't share, either. Did she Google me? If so, there's a handful of tabloid stories about me and Tyler—I hope she didn't uncover those.

I laugh nervously. "No. Why?"

Her face turns beet red, and it's not from the physical exertion. She can do this workout in her sleep.

"I was just wondering because you've seemed kind of sad all week, and I wondered if you got into a fight with your boyfriend," she mumbles, rushing to add, "I just wanted to see if you were okay, *butnevermind*."

"Oh my god," I mutter, more to myself than to her.

The last thing I want to do is to make a scene, because then Ryan will come over and ask what we're laughing about.

"Hallie, no, that's very sweet of you," I say quietly, trying not to attract attention. "I appreciate you checking in on me. I'm fine, just a little tired, that's all."

"Got it, got it, got it," she says. "Uh, sorry for asking."

She dips backward into another crunch. "So, you're single, then? I know my aunt is always trying to set up my older cousin," she says, giggling.

"Hallie, focus!" I say, clamping down harder on her feet. "Ten more reps in this set. Let's go."

We make it through conditioning without any more forays into my personal life. When it's time for her to move on to bars, she skips off to the changing room to grab her grips. I'm relieved she didn't dig any deeper. I remember what it was like when I was her age. I knew that the girls I had grown up with had boyfriends, or at least dates to the winter semiformal. I opted for homeschooling instead of attending an actual high school, but even I heard rumors about my old classmates having sex, saying *I love you*, flirting at beer-soaked parties. I wondered if some people were born hardwired for it, the way I was primed for athletic excellence. I couldn't fathom having the guts to do any of that on my own. (But a death-defying stunt on a sliver of wood? Sure, no problem.) I'm impressed that Hallie was brave enough to ask me about my personal life—and I wonder how much of her curiosity stems from wondering what it's like to have a personal life at all.

My ponytail has loosened over the course of the morning, and it sags toward the nape of my neck. I take down my hair and am in the process of redoing my ponytail when my hair elastic snaps. I don't have another one on me, so I head to the supply closet, tucked in an alcove at the back of the gym. The door is slightly ajar. I push it open farther and nearly bump straight into Ryan, who's running his fingers over the shelves, like he's in search of something.

"Oh! Sorry," I say. "I didn't realize anyone was in here."

"No worries," he says, turning around to glance at me.

He *looks* worried, though, as if he's waiting for me to say or do something inappropriate again.

"Uh, hi," I say.

"Hi," he says, turning back around.

I rack my brain for some witty joke or easy banter to break the tension, but instead, I just freeze up. He tilts his head slightly, like he's waiting for me to say something, anything.

"I just came back here for another hair elastic," I explain, pointing to my awkwardly lumpy hair, still half-stuck in the shape of a ponytail. "Mine broke."

"I see that," he says, pulling the box of hair supplies off one shelf and offering it to me.

I find a fresh elastic, flip my head over, and smooth my hair back into a high, tight pony. I feel more like myself this way.

"Have you seen the blocks of chalk?" Ryan asks. "I know we're running low, but I thought there was at least one more case in here."

I scan the shelves, which are brimming with athletic tape, gauze, Advil, cans of hair spray and butt glue covered in chalky handprints, and water bottles branded with Summit's logo. A colorful pile of latex resistance bands spools in one corner of the closet.

"Uhhh, yeah, here you go."

I crouch down to the bottom shelf, where there's one remaining block of chalk half-hidden in a white plastic bag. Our hands bump when he takes it from me.

"Thanks," he says, turning to lean against the shelves.

Crammed into this narrow closet with him, it hits me that I miss the easy way our conversations used to flow, before I kissed him and messed everything up. Aside from strictly necessary conversations about Hallie's training, we've barely exchanged a single word since then. We've stopped eating lunch together, too.

"How've you been?" I ask.

He exhales with the slightest hint of a laugh and looks down at the chalk in his hands.

"We're really doing this?" he asks, muttering it more to himself than to me.

"Doing what?" I ask, suddenly alarmed that I've crossed a line.

He gestures vaguely at the space between us and makes air quotes. "You know . . . 'How've you been?' Pretending things are all normal, when, in fact, the first time we've spoken about anything but Hallie all week is because we accidentally stumbled into the same closet."

I bite my lip, feeling the sensation of embarrassment flood my entire body. I always thought I had a decent poker face; it's something I picked up from years of competing in front of judges, hiding grimaces when I was in pain or pissed about a low score. It's mortifying that Ryan has seen right through me this whole time.

"Ryan," I say, sighing, doing my best attempt to sound supremely casual. "I am just asking how you are. This isn't some covert sneak attack attempt at rekindling anything. Not that things were, uh, kindled in the first place. Trust me, I got the message."

I cross my arms. I feel like a fool for trying to strike up a conversation with him in the first place.

But instead of looking upset or embarrassed, his expression is apologetic.

"Avery, I'm sorry, no, you're right. I know things have been kind of weird since that dinner, and I'm sorry about that. I'm trying to be a professional here—keep my distance, not make things awkward. This is new territory for me," he explains.

"Same."

He exhales heavily and gives me a hopeful look. "We're not doing too badly, right?"

"What, at keeping this quiet?" I ask.

"Yeah."

"Well . . . Hallie just asked me if I had a boyfriend," I say, not daring to mention that she only wondered because I seemed *sad* about potentially *fighting* with him. That's information Ryan simply never needs to know.

He laughs. "And what did you tell her?"

"The truth, obviously!"

He tilts his head, encouraging me to continue.

"I told her no, I wasn't seeing anybody," I clarify.

"Got it," he muses.

He shifts his weight, and my view of the doorway behind him disappears completely. Nobody can see me in here with him, not even if they tried. I'm close enough to take just one step forward and kiss him, but I know I shouldn't. I inch backward, away from him, but my foot catches on the pile of resistance bands spilling out on the floor and I trip. The shelves are freestanding metal ones; I'm sure everything would topple down onto me if I grabbed them for support. I pitch off-kilter, and Ryan lunges forward to steady me.

I find my balance quickly, but Ryan doesn't let go. Not at first. His fingers are wrapped around my bicep and my waist, and I've braced myself against his chest. He looks down at me. I look up at him. He looks down at his hand wrapped around my torso, like he's just fully registered that it's there, and can't quite believe it. His lips, just inches away from me, curl up in an embarrassed sort of smile. I hate that I like his strong hands holding me up.

Then I hear Hallie's voice calling my name. The sound jolts me out of Ryan's arms. I squeeze past him, through the doorway, and into the main part of the gym so I can find Hallie.

"Avery? Avery?" she calls.

I find her near the bars, clutching her phone, frozen in place.

"Did you see the news?" she asks.

Her voice sounds timid.

"No, what news?" I ask.

She glances at Ryan, coming up behind me, then back to me. She holds her phone to her chest and motions for me to come closer. I get a bad feeling.

"Ryan, could you give us a sec?" I ask.

He looks confused, but ducks away.

Hallie flops belly-down on one of the plush crash mats by the bars. I sit cross-legged next to her. She sighs, hands me her phone, and then buries her face in her arms.

"Just read it," she says, voice muffled and dejected.

My heart sinks when I read the *New York Times* headline on her screen: "Olympian Delia Cruz Accuses Sports Medicine Dr. Ron Kaminsky of Sexual Assault." Of course Hallie isn't the only one he intimidated or abused. I feel so stupid for not realizing she isn't an isolated case. I know Delia, sort of. She's halfway between my age and Hallie's, so we briefly overlapped for a year at competitions, but we were never close. Back when I knew her, she was this bubbly, outgoing kid with a mane of springy, dark curls sprouting from her scrunchie. She used to sneak gummy bears into her gym bag and hand them out covertly in the locker room.

I skim the rest of the story, but after the endless wave of sexual assault allegations against politicians, CEOs, and Hollywood producers over the past few years, the details are sickeningly familiar. Delia says Dr. Kaminsky molested her while allegedly treating her for a hamstring injury. Her mom, like Hallie's mom, was in the room. The *Times* reports that a representative for Dr. Kaminsky vehemently denies the claims.

"I had no idea," Hallie says, voice shaking. "Delia never told me."

I'm at a loss for what to say. I try to imagine what I would want to hear if I were in her shoes, but I come up frustratingly short. It's not like I ever had heart-to-hearts with Dimitri.

"Hallie, this is awful. I'm so sorry you had to find out like this," I manage.

She stares glumly off into space for a long time.

"Maybe if I had said something . . . spoken up . . . this wouldn't have happened to Delia?" she asks.

She looks to me hopefully, as if I have the answers. It's too horrible to comprehend. But this time, I know what to say.

"*No*," I insist. "This isn't your fault. The only person who could've prevented this is him. This is not on you. Please remember that."

I realize that if Dr. Kaminsky did this to Delia, and nearly did it to Hallie, he must have done it to other girls, too. It's too awful to imagine how many others there are, how big this is.

Hallie is still flat on the mat, but now her chin digs into her hands and her lower lip curls inward, like she's trying to prevent it from trembling. I don't know what to do, but I know I have to try *something*. I stroke comforting circles on her upper back, and her eyes start to water.

"Hallie?" I ask tentatively.

"It's just . . . I don't . . ." she begins, hastily rubbing away her tears and sniffling. "This is not supposed to be happening right now."

"I know."

"I have to *focus* right now," she insists.

"Well—" I start, intending to remind her that taking care of herself is far more important than muscling through practice, but she's too incensed to let me speak.

"I hate him, I hate him, he makes me so mad, I hate him so much!" she says, voice curdling with anger.

She's close to shouting now. Other gymnasts and coaches have turned to stare. I want to snap at them. It's like a spotlight follows Hallie around the gym; she's the only one here worth gawking at. But right now, she's not performing. She just needs privacy.

"Why don't we take a break from this and head outside for a bit?" I ask.

I can practically see the first thought that flashes through her head: *No. I need to work.* But then she heaves a sigh, wipes under each eye, and nods silently in agreement. She strides across the floor and the vault runway—the other gymnasts defer to her right of way, letting her cross before they resume tumbling and sprinting—and pushes open the gym's side door. It opens out to the parking lot. There's a set of metal stairs there that we can sit on. It's cold outside, but she's been working hard; I bet the chill feels good on her bare arms and legs.

Hallie perches on the top step, hugging her knees to her chest, and kneads her chin into her kneecaps. She rocks back and forth silently, shaking her head. It looks like there's too much frantic energy to contain in one tiny body. She leaps to her feet and her arms fly out in rage. She lets out an anguished groan into the frigid air and stomps her bare foot against the pavement.

"It's just not fair!" she shouts.

And then she shrinks down into herself. She crosses her arms tight across her body and steers herself into me for a hug. I hold her close and stroke her hair. I guide us to sit down on the steps, and do the one thing I wish someone had done for me, back when I was in pain and enraged and swimming in sadness: I give her a plan. I suggest that if she feels comfortable, she should consider telling her parents the truth about her appointments with Dr. Kaminsky. She agrees to do it, and I offer to be there with her for that conversation, if she wants. And then, as a family, they can all figure out how to move forward—whether that means reporting what happened to her to the police, or simply letting it go. I remind Hallie that there's no pressure to come back to practice today, or tomorrow, or any day.

"The most important thing right now is to take care of yourself," I tell her. "Trust me, even if it doesn't feel like it right now, that matters even more than your training does."

She nods. I hope she believes me.

• • •

The next week is awful. Delia Cruz goes on *Good Morning America*, looking steely and powerful in a sleek white suit, and gives a searing retelling of the most horrific moments of her life. On Twitter, she releases a statement encouraging other survivors of sexual assault to get help. The replies to her tweet are mostly full of love and support, but there's a mountain of replies from hateful trolls, too. I can't even begin to fathom the mental gymnastics they have to employ to convince themselves that she's the one ruining Dr. Kaminsky's life, not the other way around.

Maggie Farber comes forward. So does her teammate Kiki McCloud. And then there's a wave of others who speak up, both household names who competed in the Olympics and athletes who never quite made it into the spotlight: Emily Jenkins, Bridget

Sweeney, Liora Cohen. By the end of the week, there are six names splashed across most of the major TV shows and publications, and a sickening sense that more will come. I feel both shocked and relieved, like I dodged a bullet. It was only by sheer luck that I visited other doctors instead of him.

Tara Michaels, the prominent conservative pundit and self-professed lover of "family values" who wears enough pearly pink lip gloss to single-handedly keep Sephora in business, unleashes a tirade that goes viral. She says it's "disturbing" that America swallows up the stories of these six "unreliable" teenagers without giving a "respected" doctor a chance to tell his side of the story. "Facts are important," she urges, disregarding that most of her own facts happen to be wrong. Half the gymnasts who have come forward are in their twenties by now. Dr. Kaminsky's lawyer already issued a blanket statement denying any wrongdoing. Tara's speech is peppered with racist jabs toward Delia, Kiki, and Emily, whose photos flash on-screen. The producers could have chosen photos of the athletes with medals around their neck; instead, they picked crotch shots—straddle jumps and leaps, taken from below. By the third time I see the video clip circulating online, it has more than ten million views.

The internet churns with impassioned headlines about how America has failed its girls; how gymnastics is just a beauty pageant masquerading as a sport; how this is what happens when parents don't pay enough attention to their own kids. There's a lot of outrage directed at the sport, the parents, the gymnasts themselves—but I don't see enough of it aimed at Dr. Kaminsky. You'd think, given how many powerful men have fallen into scandal over the past few years, that collectively, we'd know how to do this by now.

The gymternet—the blogs, podcasts, and Twitter accounts run by die-hard gymnastics fans with passionately engaged followers—lights up with commentary and analysis of the situation. I tried listening to one podcast episode, but turned it off halfway through. The hosts sounded defeated. There's no pleasure in dissecting this tragedy.

Hallie told her parents about how Dr. Kaminsky had made her feel, and they swiftly connected her to the best children's therapist in the Boston area. She insists on coming to practice each day, though there are dark circles under her eyes and her usual boundless energy sags. She used to keep her phone tucked away in the changing room while she trained, but now she keeps it nearby so she can stay updated in case any more gymnasts come forward. She doesn't seem to want to speak out publicly, and given what the other six gymnasts have gone through, I don't blame her.

What haunts me the most, though, is Ryan's reaction to the situation. Hallie had asked me to tell him the truth about her experience with Dr. Kaminsky.

"I'd feel awkward talking to him about it, you know?" she had explained. "I know he should probably know, but I just can't."

The day the Delia story broke, Hallie decided to leave practice early. She called her mom to come pick her up, and I waited with her in the locker room so people didn't keep staring at her. Once she left, I found Ryan in the gym and told him we needed to talk. We sat in a quiet, empty corner of the gym, and I relayed the entire dismal story. He looked shocked and sad when I summarized what happened to Delia, but downright grief-stricken when I shared how Kaminsky had made Hallie feel. His face crumpled.

"No," he said, shaking his head in disbelief. "Is she okay? How is she holding up?"

"I don't know," I said honestly. "She's angry. Upset. Sad. Who wouldn't be?"

He punched a stack of crash mats, and the solid *thump* of his fist echoed around the gym.

"I told her to go to that scumbag," he spat out. "This is my fault."

"It's not," I said gently.

And because nothing in the world was right, I stepped forward to give him a hug. I held him for a long time.

"I just had no idea," he repeated over and over, looking pained. "Everyone trusted him."

I was at a loss for words again.

"Maybe," I said finally, "that was the problem."

• CHAPTER 14 •

It's been a hell of a week, so on Saturday morning, when Sara invites me to yoga for what must be the fifteenth time, I say yes. Anything is better than sitting around, reading infuriating tweets about the scandal. If yoga can help take my mind off that, I'm willing to try it.

"Yay, this is fab! I'm so excited to have you in class today," Sara says, giving me a quick squeeze of a hug. "You don't have a yoga mat, do you?"

"Nope. You know, I've never actually done yoga before."

"Not a problem. There are extra mats at the studio. You should bring a water bottle and wear something comfortable that you can move in—probably not a leotard, though, just FYI. Like, leggings, tank tops, that kind of thing."

"Trust me, it's not like any of my old leotards even fit anymore," I joke. "I wish."

"Don't do that," Sara says gently.

"What?"

"Make comments like that about your body," she explains. "There's no need to beat yourself up."

"I don't—" I start to protest.

But I do. Constantly. I can't remember a time before I was acutely aware of every inch of my body: every muscle, curve, and soft spot. Dimitri taught us that our bodies were our tools, the same way an artist would use a paintbrush. That's why we had to be so strict and disciplined with the way we ate and worked out, he explained. And at the time, it all made sense: the intense diets, the weekly weigh-ins, the way he punished us with hours of conditioning if we overate or gained weight. Every week, he'd jot down our height, weight, and measurements in a little blue notebook. He wore a withering expression when we failed him, whether we gained a pound or confessed to eating a slice of pizza. That expression still flashes across my mind every time the waistband of my jeans digs into my stomach or I consider indulging in a dessert.

"I'm sorry, you're right," I say. It's awkward to realize that Sara can tell exactly how I feel about my body. "Old habits die hard, you know?"

Sara gives me a kind smile. "Yoga totally transforms the way your mind relates to your physical self. You'll see. I bet you'll like it."

An hour later, she leads me into Mind & Body Yoga. The studio has shiny wooden floors, a row of leafy green plants at the front of the room, and soothing music wafting from the speakers. The other participants in the class—mostly twenty- and thirty-something women, but a few teenagers and a handful of men, too—unroll colorful yoga mats facing the front of the room and begin to stretch. Sara hands me an extra mat, along with two foam blocks.

"In case you need to prop yourself up to get through some of the more challenging poses," she explains quietly.

I try not to scoff, but come on. I'm a former elite gymnast. I think I can survive an hour of yoga.

Sara sets up her own mat horizontally at the front of the room. When the studio is mostly full, she kicks off class by encouraging us to lie down in a comfortable position. I expected everyone to lie flat on their backs, but I'm surprised by the variations: legs splayed out, knees butterflied out to the sides, heads propped up by foam blocks. Sara leads the class through a breathing exercise in a melodic, trance-like voice.

"In through your nose," she intones with a kind but serious expression. "Out through your mouth. And then, when you're ready, another inhale."

After what feels like eons of breathing, Sara slowly leads the class into a sitting position, and encourages us to emit an *om* on the count of three.

"One, two, three, all together, now, *om* . . ." she says.

The class erupts into noise that stretches on for longer than I expected, and I run out of breath before the rest of the class. The second time we try it, I attempt to sustain the sound longer than anyone else—well, second longest, since being the very last person to keep it up would draw more attention than I really want. I'm surprised at the effort it takes.

By the time Sara leads us from a sitting position to a standing one, I'm antsy for the real work to begin. I know that yoga is about relaxation and meditation, but it's exercise, too, isn't it? Eventually, we settle into downward dog. People around me emit little sighs and groans as they sink into the position.

"Beautiful breath sounds," Sara compliments. "It's okay to let go and vocalize your efforts."

From downward dog, we move through a series of poses with names like warrior one, warrior two, half moon, and crescent moon. Sara encourages us to "flow" from one to the next and be "intentional" about our breath, whatever that means. The language of yoga feels funny to me, but I suppose gymnastics has its own language, too. The class moves slowly at first, but soon, we're breezing from one pose to the next in a way that makes me sweat. Sara winds her way through the maze of mats, correcting postures with a touch of her hand and whispering words of encouragement. I can't help but feel competitive about it: I want to perform so flawlessly that she won't have to correct me at all. It would be one thing if I were a couch potato who struggled to get the poses right—but I'm not. I'm a world-class athlete, or at least, *was* one. This should be a piece of cake. I crane my neck to glimpse the way my neighbor, a curvy woman in a pink workout tank that reads HUSTLE FOR THAT MUSCLE, sinks into warrior two, and try to angle my body to match hers.

That's when I feel Sara's hands on my hips. "Like this," she says, tilting my left side forward and my right side back. She trails a finger up the back of my neck, causing me to look ramrod straight ahead instead of at the people around me. And then, as if she's reading my mind, she whispers, "It's not a competition. Just listen to your body and do what you need to do."

"Okay, but is this right?" I whisper back.

She pauses and gives an infuriatingly serene wave of her hand. "There's no such thing as right or wrong, as long as you're focused on your breath and your flow."

"But—" I protest.

It's too late. Sara has already moved on to another student. *This*, I think, *is why I hate yoga.* There's always a right way to do everything.

Once the class has more or less all caught up to downward dog again, Sara takes her place at the front of the yoga studio and demonstrates another sequence of postures. Between the bent knees, angled hips, and outstretched arms, these are a little more complicated. I have to concentrate to get the series right. As I move from one pose to the next, I feel my muscles stretch and quiver; this class is more taxing than I expected. While my thighs quake through chair pose, Hustle for That Muscle Girl's quads look rock solid. I stare down at my legs, willing them to stay locked into place, but the only thing that happens is a fat droplet of sweat drips off my nose and splashes onto my kneecap. I inhale deeply, like Sara taught me to, and I'm surprised to find that maybe—just maybe—it actually does help. Thirteen trembling seconds later (but who's counting?), I breathe a sigh of relief when Sara tells the class to stretch upward into mountain pose, which is just standing up straight.

"You're stronger and softer than your mind knows. But your body knows," she says—whatever that means.

We cycle through the sequence again, and when I end up back in chair pose, I grit my teeth. This time around, I know what I'm up against. I'm determined to make it through the full duration without breaking perfect form.

"If at any point, you're not feeling what the class is doing, take a break," Sara intones in that oddly soothing yoga voice. "Sit in child's pose or *shavasana*. There's real power in tuning in to your body's truest needs."

Real power. *Real power.* Through the burning sensation in my thighs, I want to scream at Sara: *You know what real power looks like? Standing atop an Olympic podium with a gold medal draped around your neck, that's what. Or training hard for thousands of hours until you know you have ultimate control over your body's every movement. Not tapping out when it gets a little bit tough.*

"Chair pose is challenging for a reason," she says, voice floating through the room. "The key is to listen to your body and make adjustments that honor your journey through the pose."

Before I can register what's happening, I'm dropping to the floor and stretching my torso and arms over my knees into child's pose. I'm "honoring my journey." It's embarrassing, but relief washes over me. My thighs relax, my breathing evens out, and the muscles around my shoulders loosen. I'm frustrated with myself for dropping out of the challenge, but when I roll my head to the side and peek out at my classmates from under my arm, it looks like nobody's even noticed me. Hustle for That Muscle Girl resolutely blows out a steady stream of air from pursed lips. The pair of teen girls on my other side don't seem to blink. Sara only comes my way to press her palms into my lower back.

I can't remember ever dropping out of a workout like this before. When I was Hallie's age, if Jasmine or I were tired or in pain, we'd wait until Dimitri got wrapped up in a conversation with another coach or went to the bathroom before we dared take a break. A few moments of rest weren't worth the threat of his backlash. It was impossible to truly relax when you feared he'd deliver a physically taxing punishment or a cruel joke at your expense.

Back then, Dimitri's pressure-cooker coaching style made sense: winners work hard, and we wanted to win. Even if Sara's philosophy is a little new age for me, I hear what she's saying. *Listen to your body; connect to your body; honor your body.* Push yourself when you can, and rest when you need to. It goes against everything I was raised with, but in hindsight, maybe Dimitri should have been softer with us. More forgiving. Less intense. After all, I worked hard all the time, just like he wanted me to, and I still didn't win. I don't regret the way gymnastics shaped my life, but I do wonder if the few fleeting moments in the spotlight were worth the lifetime of pain I know I have ahead of me.

I take a deep breath. Sara's hands have drifted away from me; she's moved on to another student. I concentrate on doing a mental scan of my body. I feel the spongy surface of the yoga mat under my fingertips and the center of my forehead, and I can sense the thin sheen of sweat between my breasts. The soft curve of my belly rests against my thighs, and my hips hinge backward in a comfortable stretch. My feet are tucked under my bottom, and when I wriggle my toes against the mat, I feel the sensation flex all the way up my legs.

More than anything, I feel present, and that makes a sob escape from my throat. It's mortifying to cry here, but somehow, I don't think anyone will mind.

For years, I ignored physical pain and warped my desires into discipline. I controlled my body with the sheer strength of my mind. Maybe now it's time to turn all that around—to let my mind dictate the way my body moves. On my next exhale, I transition into downward dog—my calves feel warm and loose this time around, even as a tear rolls down my cheek and mixes with my sweat. I kneel for a moment to wipe my tears with the hem of my tank top and drink in the cool water that's been waiting for me all practice. I do a sun salutation to catch up to the rest of the group. The simple way my breath and my movements sync up makes me feel airy, light, strong, and yes, powerful.

I make it through the next twenty minutes without taking a break, but I wouldn't mind if I needed to. It's strange—I didn't realize I'd come so far. I mimic Sara's movements as she leads the class from a one-legged balance to core-strengthening exercises to half-pigeon pose, which stretches out your hip flexors like taffy. In the final few minutes of the class, she asks us to lie down on our backs with our eyes closed in *shavasana*. She walks softly around the room with a bottle of lavender essential oil, dropping a dot of it on each of our shoulders.

"I'm going to close out the class with a few words of wisdom from the poet and activist Audre Lorde, and the song of the Tibetan singing bowl," Sara says softly. The little noises around the studio— coughs, sighs, slurps from water bottles—grow still in anticipation. "'Caring for myself is not self-indulgence, it is self-preservation.'"

Then the melodic sound of the Tibetan singing bowl resonates and spirals throughout the room, growing and growing until Sara strikes the bowl and it clangs to a stop.

"You can stay in *shavasana* until you're ready to rise again," she says simply.

I let myself sink into the mat. Energy swirls through my body, but my limbs feel heavy with relaxation. I hadn't wanted to give into Sara's woo-woo, spiritual sort of stretching, but even I have to admit that it felt kind of, well, nice. The combination of exertion and mindfulness makes me drift off into thoughts about the ways in which gymnastics shaped my relationship to my body: my body image, my insistence of pushing through pain, the distant way I regarded my physical self first and foremost as a tool. Over the years, I've tried not to think about it too much. But here, it's impossible to avoid.

Suddenly, Sara is squatting next to me. "How'd you like the class?" she asks.

I crane my neck to look at the clock at the back of the room. Five minutes have passed, and the rest of the class has already rolled up their yoga mats and filed out of the studio.

"It was . . . wow." That's all I can manage.

"You think you'll come back again?" she asks.

Sunlight pours into the studio through the floor-to-ceiling windows, and I get a startlingly clear vision of myself returning to this spot again and again. I could do this, couldn't I? I feel peaceful here, similarly to the way I relax when I cook. The steady movement of the class meant my mind never wandered off to Ryan, Hallie, or even the terrible scandal in the news. Instead, I had no choice but to focus on the flow between poses, my breath, and the sound of Sara's voice. It's not a stretch to see how I could develop a craving for this, unwinding here at the studio after a long day at Summit. And if just one session already feels transformative for me, I can only imagine how it could help Hallie. Maybe this is exactly what she needs to rein in the anxiety she's felt lately.

"Yeah, I'll be back. And next time, there's someone else I'd like to bring, too."

CHAPTER 15

Hallie wrinkles her nose when I tell her about my idea at the end of practice on Monday.

"Yoga? I mean, I already do so much," she says, looking skeptical.

She's cross-legged on the floor of the changing room, stretching the white thigh-high socks she got at her friend's Sweet Sixteen, embroidered with the girl's initials, up her legs. The thick socks strain over her muscular calves, though, and barely graze her knees. She gives a final tug and gives up. I bet the party wasn't as fun as she expected it to be; she probably had to say no to the cake and head home early to stick to her sleep schedule.

"But what if you could have private yoga lessons here at the gym?" I counter. "Barely any extra work on your part, and I think it'll help reduce stress over the next few months."

"I'm not stressed," she snaps.

She looks wild, with a cloud of frizz escaping her ponytail at the temples. But then her expression softens. She must understand, on some level, how that's just not true.

"I'll try it once," she agrees. "*If Ryan thinks it's a good idea, too.*"

"I'll talk to him," I promise.

Hallie shoves her feet into sneakers, stands up, and slings her gym bag over her shoulder.

When she turns to walk away, I catch a glimpse of what's on her screen. I recognize it because I saw it, too, earlier that day—Delia Cruz's Instagram encouraging her followers to donate to RAINN, a nonprofit that supports sexual assault survivors. Hallie's broad shoulders look small and slumped as she disappears around the corner and heads outside to her mom's waiting car.

I know Ryan's still inside, probably cleaning up alone. All the other classes and team practices have wrapped up for the night, and the rest of the coaches have headed home. The lobby is empty by now, too; the usual rows of Lululemon moms playing games on their phones have cleared out of the plastic folding chairs. I head back into the gym to find Ryan and talk to him about setting Hallie up with yoga lessons.

Sure enough, I find him in the back corner of the main part of the gym, cleaning chalk dust and sweat off crash mats with a spray bottle and a roll of paper towels. He's changed the music from its usual Top 40 radio station to what must be his own classic rock playlist.

"Hey, what are you doing back here?" he says, spritzing a mat with soapy water.

"I wanted to get your opinion on something, but while I'm here, can I help?" I ask.

He pauses and looks at the waist-high stack of mats he's yet to clean. They're each eight or twelve inches thick, but still—that's a lot of mats.

"If you really don't mind, sure, take a mat," he says. "What's up?"

I drag the next mat off the stack and pull it parallel to the one he's cleaning. He hands me the spray bottle and I get to work.

"So, I finally went to yoga this weekend, and it was amazing," I explain. "Not just the workout part—though that actually wasn't half-bad—but the mental part of it."

"Nice."

"And it made me think that Hallie could actually really benefit from adding yoga to her routine, especially now and during the next few months."

"Yeah? Why?"

I consider how personal and vulnerable I actually want to get here. I want him to understand how yoga could clear Hallie's head in a way that gymnastics never could. But I don't know if I'm ready to share the rest of my thoughts with him. I don't doubt that Ryan had a hell of a time during his competition days, dieting and pushing through punishing workouts. But I also know that, as tough as it could've been for him, it wasn't the same as what I went through. While puberty signals the end of a girl's gymnastics career, it's the real beginning of a man's: gaining weight and developing muscle only makes him better at the sport.

And Ryan never trained under Dimitri. He probably never worked out on an empty stomach, worrying that his vision would go fuzzy and black around the edges as he sprinted down the vault runway. He probably never tried to convince himself the quaking pain in his stomach was from too many crunches instead of skipping a meal. He wouldn't understand how restorative it was to be in a place in which you simply had to listen and react to your body's needs.

Gymnastics has changed lightning-fast, even in the decade since I was Hallie's age. The top athletes in the sport these days aren't eighty-five-pound waifs like some of the ones I looked up to as a kid—they have real, solid muscle and power, like Hallie does. She's smarter than I ever was, and she knows she can't perform her best if she's starving. But she faces a new set of pressures I never could have imagined: a more difficult scoring system; watching her competitors' skills ratchet up every day on Instagram, just like their follower counts do; the disturbing sexual abuse scandal and its coverage on every news channel in America right now.

"I'm just saying, I think she's going through a tough time right now, and what I loved about the yoga class I went to was the emphasis on self-care," I say.

I cringe at how hokey that sounds, and I try again.

"I don't think it's a bad idea for her to have a place to chill and zone out, where she doesn't have to worry about being the best, or training for some goal," I explain. "She can just stretch, listen to my roommate's cheesy but weirdly effective mantras, and have an hour to herself, away from the news."

"She does seem pretty stressed," he admits, ripping off another square of paper towel.

"I think yoga would be a great way for her to relax," I say.

"Then sure, let's do it," he says. "You're thinking of having your roommate work with her?"

"Sara's awesome, yeah."

"Maybe an hour or two a week?"

"I'll set it up!"

I can't wait to tell Sara.

"Cool, thanks," he says. "You're the best."

He finishes cleaning one mat, drags it back to its regular spot under the bars, and takes off his sweatshirt before starting on another mat. Underneath, he has on a white tank top that reveals the full scope of the Olympic rings tattooed on his bicep. I've seen the bottom edges of it peek out from his T-shirts before, but I've never seen the whole thing. It's not quite as bright as I imagined it would be—instead, the colors are ever so slightly faded, as if it were simply a natural part of his skin.

"What?" he asks, a little self-consciously.

He must have caught me staring.

"Oh, nothing," I say, embarrassed. "I've just never seen your tattoo before, that's all."

I scrub furiously at the mat beneath me until my paper towel begins to shred.

"Oh! Here, look."

Ryan comes over to kneel next to me on the mat. I don't really like most tattoos—you only get one body, and I doubt most things in life are worth permanently etching into your skin. But this one makes my heart beat faster. I know the Olympic Games have their roots in ancient Greece, when men held footraces and threw javelins in a festival to honor the god Zeus. The athletic challenges were revived in Athens in 1896, when the first modern Olympic Games were held. When you remember the history, it's hard not to see Olympic athletes like modern-day Greek gods.

"Can I touch it?" I ask timidly.

He laughs. "Sure."

I run my finger over the outline of the rings. He earned this.

"If you wound up going to the Olympics, would you have gotten one?" he asks.

"Yeah, of course," I say, nodding. "I mean, I'd want a small one, somewhere easy to hide, but yeah."

"Why hide it?" he asks. He flexes his bicep, and the rings jump. "It's an honor to join the club."

"I don't know, tattoos aren't really my thing," I say.

The expression on his face falters just a fraction of an inch.

"But yours, though . . . I like yours a lot," I rush to add. "That's probably the only one I'd ever consider getting for myself."

"If you were to get one, where would you put it?" he asks.

"I used to think about this all the time, you know?" I tell him. "I thought maybe my ankle."

"Huh." He wipes his finger over the bare skin of my ankle, like he's imagining ink there.

"Or the other place I was considering was the side of my ribs."

I brush my fingers along the spot over my tank top. Ryan's gaze follows my hand. He reaches out to gently slide his thumb over the same stretch of my torso. His knuckles accidentally graze the side of my breast, and I pretend like I don't notice, like my skin doesn't buzz with anticipation, like I haven't already imagined what his touch would feel like there.

But then Ryan leans closer, and his hand is on the nape of my neck, and his mouth is on mine. The kiss is slow and sweet, but that's all it is: one kiss. I savor the softness of his lips and the nuzzle of his stubble against my cheek for a long, lingering moment, and then he pulls away. As soon as I register the distance between us, a dull pang erupts in my chest.

"Why did you do that?" I ask in a hushed voice, even though I know there's nobody else around.

"I . . . I've wanted to do that for a long time," he admits.

"But we said we shouldn't," I remind him, hating myself for saying it out loud.

"We said we wouldn't," he says. "But the more I think about it, the more I wonder if we're making a mistake."

I can barely believe what I'm hearing. I go very still, almost too nervous to swallow, as if I could make the wrong move and ruin whatever is about to happen.

"So what are you saying?" I ask.

"I'm saying that I know what's at stake here. We're not wrong to be cautious," he says slowly, as if he's choosing every word with the utmost care. "But, god, Avery, I can't ignore how I feel about you anymore. If I don't tell you this now, I know I'll regret it for a long time. I need you to know that I like you—*really* like you."

There's more urgency in his voice now, and he shifts on the mat to sit up straighter. He takes my hand in his.

"I've had a crush on you from the day we met, you know that?" Ryan says, flushing pink at the memory. "At some competition years and years ago? I recognized you in some arena hallway, and you told me where to find the vending machines."

"I still can't believe you remember that," I say, grinning.

He nods. "Of course. You were hot and insanely talented and so entirely out of my league."

If this were any other moment, I'd brush off the compliment and make a self-deprecating joke, but I'm frozen in awe.

"Trust me, the crush is still there," he continues, squeezing my hand. "But it's more than that now. I want us to give this a shot for real."

Ryan's gaze is brimming with exhilaration and hope, and I know I'll remember the way he looks right now forever. Here's this Greek god of athletic prowess and ambition, made suddenly and startlingly human—full of emotion and desire. He's reached the pinnacle of human achievement, won one of the most coveted honors in the world, traveled the globe, and yet he's here. And he wants me.

"What do you think?" he asks.

There's a slight tremor in his voice—he's nervous. I have a million thoughts swimming through my head right now, and it's surprisingly difficult to pick just one to voice. Finally, I collect myself enough to speak.

"If anything real happens between us, I think we should keep it quiet, just so we don't distract Hallie," I say.

"Absolutely," he says, nodding.

"But if we agree about that, then my answer is yes," I say, scooting closer to kiss him lightly. "I want you. I want this. I want us. We'd be idiots not to give this a try."

"Yeah?" he says, like he can't quite believe I agree.

"Yeah," I say, feeling so happy my heart could burst.

This time, when he kisses me, I can feel him smiling. He cups my cheek with one tender hand, and I get lost in the hypnotic way his lips move against mine. It's like our bodies instinctually know that this is—finally—right. The kiss feels like a celebration.

He guides us down so we're lying on the mat, which is now, thankfully, clean. Somehow, the athletic equipment and fluorescent light overhead fade away, so all that matters is him in front of me. We're lying side by side, facing each other, with the rest of the world and all its distractions blocked out. As deliciously thrilling and tender as our kiss on New Year's Eve was, this is even better. His hands roam from my hair to my hips to the spot on my rib cage he grazed before everything changed. His fingers slip across the hem of my tank top, and I press into him, encouraging him to slide his hand underneath the fabric, against my bare skin.

After keeping a polite distance from him for so long, it's almost unfathomable to me that this is real. I don't care if this is the right place to do this—I don't want to think at all. I kiss the sharp edge of his jaw, then the soft curve of his earlobe, and then a trail down his throat. He groans softly and rolls on top of me, propping himself up on his elbows, with his legs intertwined with mine. I like the solid sensation of his weight on top of me. I let my hands wander across the taut, powerful muscles in his shoulders and down his back; they feel even better than I had dared to let myself imagine.

"Take this off," I say, tugging at his shirt.

Ryan obeys, revealing an exquisite set of abs. I can't help but reach out and touch them, just to make sure I'm not dreaming. They're perfectly solid—this *is* real.

I pull my own top over my head, not bothering to make a disclaimer about my lack of abs. He wouldn't have said all those things if he didn't think I was beautiful, if he didn't want me exactly how I am. And anyway, there's a glint of desire in his appreciative gaze that makes it clear he likes what he sees. It's intoxicating.

He lies back and pulls me on top of him so I'm straddling him. Now I can feel that there's no question of whether he's attracted to me. I lean forward and kiss him deeply; my hair falls like a curtain around us. He unhooks my bra and tosses it to the side. His touch is electrifying. It's been a long time since I've done this with anyone, but that's hardly the reason this feels so good. It's because this is Ryan, and that feels like a victory. I want more of this—I want all of him.

I trail one finger under the waistband of his green track pants, then another. He grinds his hips up into mine, like he wants more, too. I start to tug his pants down, but he stops me.

"Is that too much?" I ask.

He shakes his head and bites his lip. "No, but wait."

He stands up and extends his hand to me, pulling me up, too. He toys with the waistband of my black yoga pants.

"Can I take these off?" he asks softly.

"Yeah," I say.

He slides them off my hips and down my legs. I step out of them and kick them to the side. Before I realize what's happening, he's lifted me up so my legs wrap around his waist. If Ryan were anyone else in the world, I'd probably be self-conscious about my weight in his arms, but there's no reason to worry. I know he's strong enough to handle me. He carries me to a tall block by the metal high bar, usually used for training, though obviously not tonight, and sets me down so I'm sitting at the edge of it. He maneuvers smoothly so my legs are hooked over his shoulders. He looks at me, gauging my reaction, then plants a soft kiss on my inner thigh.

"Is this okay?" he asks.

"Mm-hmm." I nod.

More than okay, I think.

He kisses me again, farther up my thigh, and then again, right at the edge of my underwear. He skims his hands over me, landing with his fingers curled around the lacy fabric at my hips.

"And what about this?" he asks.

I lean back on my elbows and tilt my hips up so he can fully undress me. When his mouth is on me again, I could melt. At first, I want to watch him. But before long, I relax fully, flat on my back on the block. I'm not surprised when, minutes later, Ryan proves that his talents don't solely extend to athletics.

I slide off the block, not 100 percent sure that my legs won't turn to jelly when they hit the floor, and steady myself with a hand against his chest.

"You. Wow," I breathe.

I pull him toward me for a kiss, wrapping my arm around his neck.

"You're pretty 'wow' yourself," he says.

My instinct is to return the favor, but we wind up back on the mat. His pants and black boxer briefs are off now, and he kisses my hair. I reach for him, but then I realize we have a problem.

"Do you have a condom?" I ask.

His face goes slack. "No, I wasn't planning for this at all. There . . . *might?* be one in my backpack, and I'll check, but it's in the office."

He kisses me and gets up to put his underwear and pants back on. He looks like he's about to move toward the office, but thinks better of it. He grabs his shirt and tugs it on over his head.

"Just in case anyone's out there," he says, winking.

"There better not be!" I yelp.

I pull my knees up to my chest and watch him jog across the gym. He disappears around the corner, and once I hear the door swinging shut behind him, I can't help but let out a laugh. It's ridiculous that any of this is happening at all, much less at Summit. But, of course, it would happen here. This is where everything in my life has always taken place.

A minute later, Ryan's back, with a look of triumph on his face. "I found one," he says, shaking the foil packet.

Another minute later, and we're both naked again—sweaty, breathless, and happy. There's a certain stereotype about sex with gymnasts, and I heard enough jokes about it in my early twenties from gross guys at clubs to last a lifetime. The truth is that, yes, while we may be stronger and more flexible than the average person, we're still just regular human beings who like regular sex. Putting your feet behind your head isn't all that exciting when that's just your typical Tuesday morning. That said, there's nothing regular about sex with Ryan. He looks at me with awe, like he wants to memorize this moment. His fingers linger over the tender spots by my waist, the edge of my hip, the nape of my neck.

Later, once we're exhausted, he puts his arm around me and I lay my head on his chest. It's quiet, except for the low hum of the radio and us catching our breath. He kisses my temple and pulls me closer to him, so my thigh rolls over his legs. I kiss his collarbone and drift my fingers over the outline of his tattoo.

"Just in case I didn't make this clear earlier, I, um, like you," I say into his chest.

"I got that, yeah," he says. "I'm really glad this happened."

I grin. An easy silence passes between us. He strokes my hair absentmindedly.

"Sorry to derail cleaning the mats," I say.

He laughs and looks around. "Now we have a *lot* more cleaning to do."

"But we can do it together."

• CHAPTER 16 •

I used to count time in days: thirty days till the start of football season; fourteen days till the rent is due; three days till I run out of clean underwear and have to do laundry. But now it drags out in minutes, ticking by slowly in my head: I know how many minutes it's been since Ryan's last sweet *good morning* text, or the last kiss we stole in the supply closet, or the last time he came home with me after practice and we stayed up until 2 a.m., trading stories over a bottle of red wine. I had forgotten how sweet it is to let yourself fall for someone. I can't help but replay our hookup when I'm washing my hair in the shower, and I snap to attention when I hear his name in the gym. I feel giddy whenever his texts pop up on my phone. On Tuesday night, I was so distracted that I forgot I had brussels sprouts in the oven until the smoke detector jarred me out of my daydreams.

It's nearly six thousand minutes later—four days—when Sara comes to Summit to give Hallie a private yoga lesson. Between Sara's work schedule and Hallie's training plans, Friday is the best day; it also happens to be Valentine's Day, although I don't dare fixate on that. It's too soon into whatever this thing with Ryan is to celebrate the holiday in any real way.

Sara was thrilled when I asked if she would work with Hallie. Without breaking Hallie's trust in me, I told Sara as much as I could—that Hallie is having a tough time in the months leading up to the Olympic Trials, and now more than ever, she needs to reduce her stress and build her confidence. Sara said it would be an honor to help her. And once I told her about what happened with me and Ryan on Monday night, she was doubly excited to come to the gym. I made her promise to play it cool in front of him, especially when Hallie is around.

"Since we're not telling her about us," I explained to Sara. "Because, you know, the whole point is to reduce stress, not add to it."

"Got it," Sara said. "I promise not to gawk."

Of course, the moment she saw Ryan at Summit on Friday afternoon, she gawked.

"He's so cute," she mouthed dramatically the first moment his back was turned.

I take Sara, Hallie, and Ryan upstairs, where there's a dance studio and a party room for children's birthdays. I flick on the lights, illuminating the wooden floors and ballet barres installed against a mirrored wall. Sara sets out the two yoga mats and a pile of foam blocks. Hallie stands with her back to the mirror and one hip jutting out, her arms crossed skeptically over her chest.

"Sara and I are roommates, and she's a great teacher," I tell Hallie, trying to warm her up to the idea.

When I suggested yoga to Hallie, she had balked at the idea. Even after relenting to one private lesson, she still wasn't thrilled to try it.

"Have you ever done yoga before?" Sara asks Hallie.

Her voice has an extra drop of honey in it. It's clear that Sara recognizes this is not exactly Hallie's idea.

"Yeah, once, back in middle school gym class, before I got a tutor," Hallie says flatly.

I can practically read her mind: *This is* exercise?

"I didn't really like it," Hallie adds, as if she can make this lesson disappear just with the sheer force of her surliest teenage attitude.

"Well, this will be totally different," Sara says cheerfully. "Look, I'm not some weirdo old gym teacher who wears basketball shorts with tube socks."

It's a good point: Sara's wearing matching leggings and a cropped tank top in a pink, orange, and purple ombré that reminds me of the sunset. She looks visibly, recognizably strong, and this seems to soften Hallie to her slightly.

"I guess," Hallie says, tilting her head.

"Here, why don't you do the honors of picking today's playlist?" Sara offers, handing Hallie her phone.

"Cool," Hallie says swiftly, nodding.

She starts to scroll through Sara's Spotify.

Sara gives me a bemused glance, as if to say, *Look. We'll be fine*.

"Um, guys? This is a *private* lesson," Sara says to me and Ryan, pointing to the two mats on the floor. "I promise I'll return her in one piece once the hour's up."

"Right, right, we'll be going," Ryan says.

"Yeah, we'll go . . . somewhere," I say, scrambling to temper my voice so I don't sound too thrilled by the prospect of a free hour with Ryan in front of Hallie.

"See you soon . . . and have fun," Sara says.

I follow Ryan down the stairs to the first floor, but when we reach the lobby, neither of us has anywhere to be. He looks blankly toward the gym, then the office.

He steals a glance toward the parking lot. "We could get out of here."

"We can't!"

He shoves his hands into his pockets and gives me an irresistibly flirty grin. "Who'd notice?"

"What if Hallie needs us?" I point out.

The dimple in his cheek winks at me, which I find makes it somehow harder to focus on making good decisions. "I bet you've never broken the rules here in your life," he says.

He's right. The pressure of these four walls somehow makes me feel like a hardworking kid again, terrified to break a rule, lest Dimitri see me.

"Okay, let's get out of here," I agree, pushing open the building's front door, not bothering to even grab my coat.

I bounce down the steps to the parking lot. The gym is on a mostly isolated stretch of road, neighbored by a nondescript office building on one side and thickets of pine trees on all others. Even if we wanted to walk into the town center, it would take longer than the journey would be worth. Ryan catches up to me, jangling his car keys.

"I didn't think you'd actually say yes," he says.

"I can break a rule or two," I insist.

"Reliving your LA wild-child days?" he teases.

Ryan unlocks his car, and I get inside.

"Where to?" he asks, flipping on my seat heater, then turning the radio to his favorite classic rock station.

"Um . . ."

Greenwood is small and boring. Growing up here, if I wasn't at school or in the gym, my only real hobby was trawling CVS for Bonne Bell Lip Smackers and issues of *Seventeen*.

"Come on, you grew up here, you must know somewhere," he prods.

"Let's go to Lolly's," I decide.

"I don't know it," he says.

"You don't know Lolly's? Best chai latte in the world?"

He shakes his head. "In the *world*? I mean, that's a pretty high bar. I don't know if you want to set my expectations there—"

"Oh, shut up."

I give him directions, and ten minutes later, we're inside the tiny café. I haven't been here in a decade, but the peeling floral wallpaper, chintzy armchairs by the brick fireplace, chalkboard menu, and gently piped-in soft rock songs from the easy-listening station are exactly how I remember them. Lolly herself is still behind the counter, though her once-dark hair is now mostly streaked with gray. She's wearing a floral apron and does a double take when she sees me.

"Avery, is that you?" she yelps, coming around the counter to give me a hug.

"Hi!" I greet her, suddenly feeling squeezed by the surprising strength of her embrace.

"I haven't seen you in, gosh, what, a million years? Where's Jasmine?" she asks.

Ryan cocks his head.

"This used to be my spot with Jasmine on cheat days," I explain. "We'd ask for extra whipped cream on the chai lattes and sit here for hours in front of the fireplace."

"The best kids hogged the best seats in the house," Lolly tells Ryan. "Not that I minded, of course."

"I didn't know you were that close with Jasmine," he says to me.

"Those two? My god. Matching orders, matching outfits, all the way down to the matching scrunchies." She turns to me. "How is she these days? I don't see much of her, either."

"Oh, Jasmine?" I ask, stalling for time. Somehow, telling Lolly that I don't see much of her either feels like I'd be letting her down.

I give her a big, plastered-on smile. "She's great. Has a big job. Married. The whole nine yards, all great."

"And you two?" Lolly says, gesturing between me and Ryan.

I try not to look too alarmed. "Oh, no, we're not married!" I say, maybe a hair too loudly. "We, uh, work together."

"I see," Lolly says coyly. "Well, you two look very nice together. What can I get you?"

Ryan follows my lead and orders a chai latte with extra whipped cream. While he pays Lolly for the drinks, I examine the framed newspaper clippings hung by the door. They're slightly yellowed with age, but I remember the thrill I got the day the first one was hung. Lolly saved the *Boston Globe* clippings announcing that two local girls were on their way to the Olympic Trials. Jasmine and I skipped the sugary drinks that day and asked for plain tea; Lolly, who had the round, soft body you'd expect from a woman who made baked goods for a living, had rolled her eyes and told us to live a little. "This *is* us living," I remember telling her, pointing to the newspaper clipping.

The story isn't long, but it features a black-and-white photo of me and Jasmine, frozen at nineteen years old, with our arms slung around each other's shoulders. The date on the framed article feels so far away—a lifetime ago. Next to it, there's a bigger framed article, the paper's front-page story from the day Jasmine returned home from London. There's a larger, color photo of her by herself with a pile of Olympic medals splayed out across her chest. I wonder what the younger version of myself would say if she saw me here now, lying to Lolly about Jasmine, Ryan trailing behind me, out on a furtive break from Summit. I don't think she'd understand how I got into this situation at all.

Ryan sets down the chai lattes on the table between the armchairs, then comes up behind me. He's quiet for a moment, reading the two framed clippings.

"Ah, I see," he says. "You took me here just so I don't forget you're a hometown hero."

"I brought you to a place I loved," I correct him. Sass floods my voice. "And, uh, *was* a hometown hero. Once upon a time. Not so much anymore."

Jasmine's photo floats in my peripheral vision, and I try to block it out.

"Your hometown must be the same way, no?" I ask.

He shakes his head. "Men's gymnastics isn't so much of a big thing. People at home thought it was cool I made the Olympics, but they didn't . . . I don't know, 'crown' me, the way they crowned the women's gymnastics team."

He makes air quotes around the word, and I understand exactly what he means. I wonder if he felt bitter about it, too.

"So it's not just me?" I say, almost embarrassed that I want him to agree and confirm how I feel.

There are times I've wondered if Jasmine's success only looms so large for me because of how tight we were and how close I came to having it, too. I can't see her clearly because of who she is, who we were together. I'm fairly sure she's still a household name. But time makes fame evaporate; maybe her star has cooled long enough that now she's just a regular person again, the kind of former athlete who can make it through her hometown's grocery store without being stopped in aisles four and seven for autographs. But somehow I doubt that.

"Look," Ryan sighs, kissing my forehead. "Forget about Jasmine for now. Let's drink these lattes you love so much."

We sink into the armchairs by the fireplace. There's something different about the steaming beverages in the ceramic mugs, but it takes me a moment to figure it out. A heavy sprinkle of cinnamon forms a pristine heart on top of the whipped cream, and there's a heart-shaped chocolate bonbon on the side of my saucer. I spin around; Lolly is watching us.

"I may have whipped up a little something," she says.

"Happy Valentine's Day?" he says hopefully, like he's waiting for my approval.

I've felt like the most gooey, starry-eyed version of myself all week, but this pushes me even further over the edge. The gesture is just sweet enough without feeling too serious.

"Happy Valentine's Day!" I say, beaming.

He exhales, relieved, and leans across the table to give me a kiss. I feel warm and golden, and I know that has nothing to do with the glow of the fireplace.

"I know this is probably the tiniest Valentine's Day gesture ever, but I didn't want to go too overboard," he explains.

"No, no, anything else would've been too much," I agree. "This is perfect."

"Okay, cool. A lot of the guys I know complain about Valentine's Day, like it's such a hassle to do something nice for the person you're with, or like it's somehow less special to do flowers or dinner on a holiday. But that seems so backward to me."

"What do you mean?" I ask.

"If someone makes you happy, why *not* celebrate that?" he asks, blushing like he's just realized how vulnerable he sounds. He clears his throat and looks away from me. "Anyway, this is just a tiny way for me to say that this week has been amazing. That's all."

I try not to fixate on his words: Happy. Amazing. They make my stomach flutter in the best way.

"Just so you know, I didn't get you anything," I say apologetically. "And now I feel bad."

"Come on, don't feel bad," he says, taking my hand in his. "I came up with this on the spot, and it took two seconds. And anyway, your gift to me is introducing me to this place."

He sips slowly from his latte, considering it. I taste mine carefully, letting the beverage dribble out from under the cloud of whipped cream so as not to disturb the cinnamon heart. It's fragrant and flavorful.

"Yeah, it's official," he says. "You're right. This is delicious."

"I told you! I wouldn't steer you wrong."

"Now I finally trust you."

"What, like months of working together didn't earn that?"

"This sealed the deal."

Chatting in front of the crackling fireplace, nestled into the coziest spot in town, I feel at home in a way I never did in LA. It's not hard to imagine endless winter afternoons curled up in these armchairs with Ryan. It would be so easy, so satisfying, so comfortable. I've learned my lesson already: I know it's not smart to get lost in giddy feelings, daydreaming about a future with a man who might someday break my heart. I don't want to repeat that mistake. But for whatever reason, things with Ryan feel different. I don't worry about losing my spark around him.

Ryan glances at the clock hanging above the cash register. His face falls.

"We probably have to get going," he says.

We drain the last of the lattes, and I savor the sweet, spicy dregs at the bottom of the mug. I hug Lolly goodbye, and she makes us promise to come back before another ten years slip by.

"Because let's face it, honey, I'm not getting any younger," she says, sighing. "And anyway, I like him. Keep him around."

Ryan laughs lightly and reassures Lolly he'll come by for another latte soon.

On the ride back to Summit, I point out landmarks—not Greenwood's most notable spots, necessarily, but the places that marked my childhood here: my elementary school, the sushi spot my family likes to go for birthdays and anniversaries, the house where I attended my first and last boy-girl party growing up. The town looks extra sleepy in the winter. White and gray Colonial homes match the pale sky and dingy snowbanks; the trees are bare and skeletal. Inside the car, though, it feels like summer. Ryan drives one-handed with his fingers laced through mine in my lap as a Bruce Springsteen song blares from the radio.

We slip into the gym with three minutes to spare. Ryan heads into the office, while I sit at the bottom of the stairs, waiting for Sara to finish Hallie's lesson. I hear the Tibetan singing bowl, then silence, and finally, a few murmured words. I can't make out what Hallie and Sara are saying, but when they appear in the staircase a minute later, Hallie has a pleasantly dazed look on her face.

"How'd it go?" I ask.

She passes me on the staircase, and I notice that her typically excellent posture has a new ease to it, like she's gliding.

"That was actually pretty chill," she says.

"Huh, imagine that," I say, resisting the urge to gloat further.

"Thanks for having me in," Sara says, more to me than to Hallie.

"Maybe you'll come back again next week?" Hallie asks.

Sara and I exchange glances.

"I think that's a great idea," I say.

• CHAPTER 17 •

I do dumb things when I'm falling in love. That's what I think for the entirety of the forty-five minutes I spend in the front seat of Ryan's car on Saturday night, nearly nauseous with nerves, as he drives us to Dimitri and Jasmine's house for a cocktail party in honor of my former coach's fiftieth birthday. When Ryan asked me earlier that week if I'd be his date for the night, he told me that if it was too awkward given my strained relationship with Jasmine, I could skip it. But oh, no. I told him it'd be fine. I think I might have even said it'd be *fun*. It was like my brain had entirely evacuated my body: I wanted to spend a night out with Ryan, so I said yes. It was that simple. Even though I haven't seen Jasmine since her twentieth birthday or Dimitri since the 2012 Olympic Trials.

Their house is in a tony suburb, tucked away from the street at the end of a long driveway that winds through looming clusters of pine trees. We park at the end of a row of cars adorned with bumper stickers of gymnasts performing handstands and splits. I smooth down the front of the dress I borrowed from Mom last night when I realized that nothing in my closet could magically make me look three sizes smaller and eight times more confident than I currently am. The dress is rich purple, with an off-the-shoulder neckline and a skirt that skims easily over my hips and thighs. If it were any other night, I'd feel pretty in it.

My heart races as we make our way to the front door. I wonder if Dimitri and Jasmine know that I'm Ryan's date. I wonder if they think about me at all anymore. I mentally review what I'm going to say to them, which boils down to polite but not overly enthusiastic compliments about their home and a few casual comments about how my life is amazing, my job is fantastic, I'm the happiest I've ever been, and everything is actually perfect, thank you very much. My palms are slick and clammy. I pull my hand away from Ryan's to wipe it on my dress.

Ryan heaves the golden knocker—of course it's gold—against the door. Jasmine opens the door and trills an eager "Hello!" She beams at Ryan first. When she registers who I am, her face freezes. For a terrifying moment, she falls silent. But then, just as she was trained to do, she snaps back into action.

"Avery?!" she squeals. "Come here, oh my god. It's been, what, how many years?"

She delivers an enthusiastic air-kiss and half a hug while balancing a precariously full cocktail.

"Hi," I manage. "It's so good to see you again."

She steps back, ushering us into her home. "I can't believe you're here," she says, and it sounds like the truth. "This is amazing."

The house reminds me of my parents' place. It's not decorated in the same style—Jasmine and Dimitri's tastes seem more modern and eclectic—but it's full of the kinds of odds and ends that older people accumulate over a lifetime. There's an expensive-looking credenza in the foyer that holds a single orchid in a hand-thrown pot and an unusual, abstract painting illuminated by a pair of matching silver sconces.

Jasmine shuts the door behind her. Clad in a figure-hugging black sheath, snakeskin stilettos, and the perfect hair and makeup she wears on TV, she looks foreign to me, like my old best friend is acting out a role in a play. She takes our coats and leads us into the kitchen, where a cluster of Dimitri's friends congregate around the marble island set up as a bar. I can hear Jasmine explaining the three custom cocktails they're serving that night, but I can't focus on listening to their ingredients at all, because the crowd of guests shifts, and that's when I see Dimitri.

It's unnerving to see him dressed up in a charcoal-gray sports jacket and tie. He looks older, too, with more pronounced lines settling into his forehead and a cleanly shaven head. His dark, beady eyes and bristling mustache are exactly the same as I remember. He's talking and laughing with a man about his own age while measuring a shot of vodka he pours into a shiny silver martini shaker. His voice booms above the chatter of the party, or maybe my ear is still tuned to listen for it, even all these years later.

"Dimitri," Jasmine calls across the kitchen.

He doesn't hear her.

She rises ever so slightly on her toes and lifts her chin, as if to repeat herself, but thinks better of it and settles back down. It's almost as if she's nervous—like he's still the coach and we're his athletes. She winds her way around the kitchen, stilettos clicking against the hardwood floor, and touches him softly on the arm.

"Look who's here, babe," she says, gesturing at us.

He looks up, and then I see it: a grimace, a glint of disgust. He presses his lips into a tight line, and that's almost scarier. I'm a split second away from grabbing Ryan's hand and whispering that this was all a mistake, that we should just go home, when Ryan waves enthusiastically.

"Hey, happy birthday!" he says, leaving my side to go shake Dimitri's hand. "Thanks for having us. I really appreciate the invitation."

Dimitri sets down the martini shaker, wipes his hands on a dish towel, and smoothly meets Ryan halfway. He shakes his hand slowly.

"This is your date?" he says.

His Russian accent has faded slightly.

Ryan nods and looks pleased, like he's proud to have brought me. "Yes, sir."

"I know her well," Dimitri says. He turns to me and holds out his hand. "Come."

My body's first response is to start moving, and I loathe how very deeply his training has been ingrained in me. I do my best to stand tall and not break eye contact. I don't want to look like a little girl that he can order around anymore. I lift my chin and give Dimitri my firmest handshake.

"Happy birthday. It's great to see you again," I say, straining to offer him a polite smile.

He steps back and lifts my hand, as if he expects me to twirl, and looks me up and down.

"Great to see you," he echoes. "There's so much more of you to see now."

He shoots Ryan a mocking wink, as if he expects Ryan to comment on my weight. I drop Dimitri's hand, but resist the urge to shrink from him. I don't dare glance back at Ryan for support. I can stand up for myself.

"I see you haven't lost your sense of humor," I say.

I pull myself up to my fullest height. In heeled leather boots, I'm an inch taller than he is, and I want him to remember it.

"And you haven't lost your sass," he retorts. He turns to Ryan and adds, "You must have your hands full with her, no?"

"Avery's an amazing coach," Ryan says.

"Wait, you *work* together?" Jasmine interjects, glancing from me to Ryan. "I thought Avery was your date?"

"Uh . . ." Ryan stalls and turns to me for guidance.

"We, um, yes," I fumble. "I'm Ryan's assistant coach at Summit, and I'm also here as his date."

Jasmine wraps her arm around Dimitri's midsection and leans her head on his shoulder. "Aw, another gymnastics power couple, just like me and my babe," she coos.

She looks at him adoringly and presses a kiss to his cheek. I look away; to me, that relationship will always seem wrong.

"Power? How many gold medals between the two of you?" Dimitri asks. He gestures to the living room, and when I turn, I see a wall studded with medals and trophies. "Let's count them up and compare, and then we can talk."

He's not joking. He's keeping score.

The doorbell rings, cutting through the tension in the room.

"I'll get it," Dimitri says quietly. "Jasmine, make sure our guests have drinks."

As he passes us, he ignores me and gives Ryan a respectful nod.

Jasmine takes a deep breath and puts her hands on her hips. "Drinks?" she asks.

"Please," I say.

I glance at the cocktail menu she must have printed up. The names could not be more painstakingly chosen: there's a whiskey-based drink named the Olympia, a wine spritzer garnished with a sprig of jasmine called the Jasmine Fizz, and a twist on the Moscow Mule dubbed the Moscow Man. I choose the Jasmine Fizz by process of elimination—it's the least humiliating option to order. Ryan opts for the Moscow Man, and I wonder if he chose it out of deference to our host. Jasmine steps back to the kitchen island to mix our drinks, leaving us alone.

"That was intense," Ryan mutters to me.

"That's Dimitri for you," I respond.

He raises his eyebrows and nods heavily. "I can't believe I'm actually here at his house."

"*Their* house," I correct, glancing at Jasmine.

I've known about their relationship for six years now, ever since they started dating, but that hasn't made seeing them together any less jarring.

"Are things . . . weird? Between you and Dimitri?" Ryan asks quietly.

I don't respond right away. I look carefully at Ryan, taking in his hopeful expression, his serious, dark eyes, and the tense way his shoulders are set. Despite Dimitri's behavior, I know Ryan idolizes him. I could spoil his impression of him in just a few words, but it seems cruel.

"He was disappointed in me," I say finally. "He wanted me to be an Olympic champion, and when I didn't make it . . ."

The memory comes flooding back. I bite the inside of my cheek and shake my head, as if I can dislodge the reminder of that painful summer.

"He was done with me," I say. "He didn't check in on me. He took Jasmine to the Olympics and never turned back to see if I was okay."

I can't bring myself to tell Ryan about his abusive coaching style, or the way I still hear his taunts about my body every time I look in the mirror, or the fear I felt just now, trying not to flinch in front of this man who used to make me quiver. Not here. Not now.

But Ryan grimaces anyway. The way Dimitri dismissed me is enough to cause him to furrow his brow and sympathetically squeeze my shoulder. He knows how close a gymnast and coach can be; I'm sure he can imagine how awful that rejection felt.

Jasmine sidles up to us with the two drinks.

"Cheers!" she declares, clinking her own Jasmine Fizz to mine.

Ryan joins in the toast, and she peppers him with questions about his work, gushes about how much she misses Summit, and joyfully accepts his invitation to come by sometime. I linger by his side, feeling suddenly like the third wheel. I try to snap out of this tense, dark mood and match her level of enthusiasm, but it seems impossible. Jasmine wears her peppy persona like a second skin. I know she's not really like this. The megawatt smile, the relentlessly upbeat energy—back when we were close, she turned it on for the judges; now, she does it on TV. I'm curious if she lives fully like this now, hiding her sensitive soul, her nervous side, and her darkly funny jokes from Dimitri, smoothing out her quirks until she's a flat reflection of whatever he wants her to be. She always did know how to perform.

"I don't mean to keep you, Ryan," she says, touching him lightly on the arm. "I know you're here to socialize with the other coaches. Why don't you go off and enjoy? Avery and I can catch up."

My stomach drops. Ryan glances at me inquisitively, and I have no choice but to grin back at him.

"Go," I say.

He looks uncertain, but leaves my side to join in on a nearby conversation with three stocky men. Jasmine and I each take a long sip of our drinks. I don't think either one of us knows what to say.

"So," she says.

"So," I respond, searching for the right words.

I have seven years of burning questions for Jasmine, and none of them are appropriate cocktail party fodder. *Do you realize that you got everything I ever wanted? How did you end up married to that monster? Are you even happy?*

"I don't mean to stare, I'm sorry," she says, blinking, embarrassed. "It's just, wow. It's still so surreal that you're here."

"I only moved back a few months ago," I explain.

"From LA, right?" she asks.

"Yeah, LA," I confirm. "I came back for this coaching opportunity. It was just too good to pass up."

She never has to know the truth.

"So, are you two, like, a thing now?" Her eyes dart in his direction.

I wish I had thought to hammer out a joint answer to this question with Ryan before we walked in the door. I don't want to say yes, only to have him find out and think I'm overestimating his feelings for me. It's not like we've had the *What are we?* talk yet. But downplaying my situation with Ryan doesn't feel right, either. I settle for a purposefully coy sip of my drink.

"Oh my god," she says, dropping her voice down to a whispered squeal and clutching my arm. "This is nuts, isn't it? After all these years? We always thought he was so cute."

For a split second, I forget everything, and we're just teenagers again, best friends, teammates. We were so close, we were each other's designated Butt Glue Girl—we'd take turns applying the roll-on adhesive just under the edges of our leotards before competitions so we wouldn't get uncomfortably distracting wedgies in the middle of routines. I've never really understood flashbacks before, but this one comes roaring back with full clarity. And then the moment is over, and I get the ice-cold sensation that Dimitri is watching me, and I duck my head down. I remember to speak quietly and control myself.

"It's very sweet how this has all come full circle," I manage to say. "And you? You and Dimitri? I still can't believe it."

The enthusiasm on her face flickers before she catches herself. "I know. Isn't it funny how life works out?"

"I had no idea you were even into him back then," I admit.

I feel bold saying it, daring her to acknowledge how bizarre her relationship appears to be.

"Oh," she says, blushing. "Well, nothing happened until I was a little bit older, obviously. You had already moved by then. And it just . . ."

Her gaze drifts over my shoulder toward her husband, and she loses focus.

"Made sense," she says finally.

There's another flicker of emotion on her face, but then it disappears without a trace. I think about the way we used to play Fuck, Marry, Kill while stretching at practice, and how Dimitri was too old and weird to be put on the list, even as a joke. We seriously weighed the pros and cons of Kevin Federline, and Tom, the gym's janitor, and even Alexei, a gymnast with a gross rattail we saw at competitions. But Dimitri? Not even once. I cannot fathom one single thing about Dimitri and Jasmine that makes sense.

She looks at me brightly again. "Do you want a tour of the house?"

As she leads me through the home she shares with a man old enough to register for an AARP card, the man who once—when she was twelve years old—poked the side of her bottom left exposed by her leotard, observed it jiggling, and told her to "watch it with the cookies," I feel increasingly disturbed. She shows off the new velvet throw pillows meticulously arranged on the white bed in the master bedroom, and the monogrammed towels hanging in the en suite bathroom. She chirps about the gorgeous natural sunlight in the home office, though I realize neither of them works from home, and tosses a wink when we enter the guest room, or as she calls it, "someday, a baby's room." She does this all while traipsing three or four steps in front of me, far enough away that we never have to face each other. The tour is so tightly packed with minuscule details about where she purchased this rug, or why she deliberated over that paint color, that there is simply no room for me to interject and ask what the fuck is going on.

When the tour concludes on the first floor, Jasmine offers to refresh my drink, which I accept. The minute the glass is full, I find Ryan on the couch in the living room. He lights up when he sees me, scooting to the left and patting the space next to him so that I'll take a seat. He drops away from the conversation with the other two men in the living room.

"You'll never guess what Dimitri said to me while you were with Jasmine," he says, excitement straining through his hushed tone.

I rack my brain and feel a slow sinking feeling in my gut; nothing good could come of this conversation.

"He offered me a job," he says, beaming.

"At Powerhouse?" I ask.

"It would start this fall, after the Olympics. I could bring Hallie— she's young enough that she could train for 2024, and Dimitri and I could train her together," he explains. "I mean, think about it: more resources, better facilities, working with *Dimitri Federov.*"

"Yeah, I got that part," I say.

Ryan's face falls slightly.

"I mean, wow. That's a lot," I continue, rushing to switch to a more congratulatory tone.

"I'm really excited," he says. "I can't believe he wants to work with *me.*"

"What would Hallie's parents think?" I ask, trying to find a hole to poke in this plan.

"I don't know exactly, I'd have to talk to them," he says. The lilt in his voice makes me realize he hasn't thought through this part yet at all. "I can't see why they'd turn down Dimitri. True, Powerhouse is slightly more expensive than Summit, but not by much, and it's literally the best training center in the world. So."

He smiles as if to say, *That's that.*

"If you leave Summit, who else would train her?" I wonder out loud.

He shrugs. "Well, you'd still be at Summit, wouldn't you?"

Training her on floor is already intense—I'm not sure if I'd be confident enough to tack on beam, bars, and vault, too. And anyway, the Conways probably wouldn't trust me to pull that off. So if Ryan leaves and Hallie really does want to train for 2024, the Conways would probably follow him. And that means I'd be left behind.

Ryan sips from his drink and stares off into the distance. It's clear that mentally, he's no longer here at this party—he's in Tokyo, watching Hallie climb the podium; he's at Powerhouse, working as his idol's right-hand man; he's fast-forwarding decades ahead to when *he's* the most respected coach in the entire sport, just like Dimitri is now.

I have to tell him the truth.

"I just . . ." I say, lowering my voice to a notch above a whisper. "I think you should really consider this before you say yes. I don't think working with Dimitri is the right move—not for you, and definitely not for Hallie."

I wish he would understand without making me say it.

"Let's head out?" I suggest.

He kisses my temple and rises to stand. "We've barely been here an hour. Let's stay for a little while longer, cool?"

I hesitate. I don't know what else to say. "Cool."

• • •

We mill around. An older couple asks if I "used to be Dimitri's girl," and I have no choice but to nod—*Yep, that's me. Dimitri's girl.* I get a third drink, just to have something to do instead of watch Ryan laugh at Dimitri's jokes. Finally, he comes to find me in the kitchen.

"You wanna get going?" he asks, touching my arm.

"Yeah," I say, tamping down the instinct to add, *Let's get out of here.*

I rustle up fake warmth to say goodbye to Jasmine and Dimitri. Jasmine insists that we must get together for drinks soon. Dimitri nods silently and stoically at me, then shakes Ryan's hand.

"We'll talk," Dimitri says smoothly.

Ryan looks beatific.

In the car ride back to Greenwood, Ryan invites me to stay over at his place, but I ask him to drop me off at my apartment instead. I turn on the radio, but he turns it off a few seconds later. It's quiet, with just the hum of the engine to keep us company.

"You don't seem all that happy about Dimitri's job offer," he observes.

"It's flattering that he asked you," I say evenly.

"But you don't think I should take it," he counters.

"I . . ." I stare out the window as houses and trees whiz by us in the darkness. "I am incredibly grateful for Dimitri. He changed my life. He could've made me an Olympic champion, if things had gone differently. But he's not a nice person, or a good person, or a person who would treat Hallie fairly."

"He's tough and old-school," Ryan says, shrugging. "That's what makes him legendary. Coaches aren't made like that anymore."

"He's tough, yeah, but he's . . ."

I trail off and bite my lip. I want to say *abusive*, but that's not a word you throw around lightly.

"Did you hear what he said about me? Basically calling me fat?" I ask, changing tactics.

"What?" he asks, sounding disgusted. "I didn't notice."

"Yeah. 'There's so much more of you to see now,'" I recite.

Ryan sighs heavily. "That's not cool."

"Exactly, it's not. Imagine hearing that, but worse, all day, every day, when you're thirteen years old," I say.

Ryan flicks on his blinker and makes a turn, so it takes a while for him to respond. I get the sense that he's grateful for the extra time to formulate a response.

"I'm sure he's not a saint, but this is the opportunity of a lifetime," he says finally. "I get one shot at a job like this, and there's no better coach in the entire sport. Every boss has their shortcomings—there's no 'perfect' job."

I hate that he makes air quotes around the word. It makes me feel as if he thinks I'm overreacting. I study his profile in the moonlight. I wonder what would happen if I described to him in unflinching detail what it was really like to spend the most impressionable years of my childhood with Dimitri. I can't muster up the energy to explain what he's really like if Ryan will only defend him.

I sigh and slump back in my seat.

"It's late," I say. "We don't have to talk about this now. If you're happy, I'm happy for you."

He reaches across the gearshift to hold my hand. His warm fingers weave through mine and rest in my lap.

"Thanks for coming with me tonight," he says, squeezing my hand.

I don't squeeze his back.

MARCH

2020

• CHAPTER 18 •

Nationals are a week away, and Hallie is still struggling. She can't control her power on her forward tumbling pass—the front hand-spring, front full-twisting layout, front double-twisting layout—so I suggested she add a stag jump on the end. That way, any energy that comes bounding off the tumbling goes directly into a real, choreographed *move*. She'll get points for a jump, rather than a deduction for not sticking the landing. A stag jump should be pretty: one knee bent at a ninety-degree angle in front of your body, with your other leg trailing out long and straight behind you, and your arms thrown triumphantly in the air. But Hallie's is tense and tight, and it throws off her timing going into the next segment of her routine. Once she loses her cool, it's hard to recover. The rest of the routine gets rushed.

"Okay, let's move to the tramp," I suggest. "We can work on your form there."

We've been finessing this one second of her routine for fifteen minutes now, and I can tell that Hallie is running low on both energy and patience. It's true that the trampoline is a less physically taxing place to jump repeatedly than the floor is—the elastic power mesh bounces you right back up, obviously—but also, no matter how old or sophisticated a gymnast gets, there's still nothing quite as joy-inducing as playing around on a trampoline. And more than perfect form, more than excellent technique, what Hallie *really* needs right now is to feel good. Going into a competition, an athlete's mental headspace is just as important as her physical well-being, if not more so.

She trudges over to the trampoline, and after a few lazy bounces, she gets serious.

"Stag jumps?" she asks, confirming her task.

"On every bounce," I say. "Focus on getting that back leg nice and straight."

She swings her arms to get some momentum, then bounces into shape. With each jump, she thrusts her right leg a little harder behind her.

"That leg needs to come up faster," I observe. "That'll keep the jump short and sweet, which is what we want."

She nods like a little soldier and jumps again.

"Faster," I insist. "The leg comes up quick and high, then snaps back."

"Snaps back," she repeats, continuing to bounce.

At the height of each jump, her chin tilts up and her fingers flick out with style. She looks like a star up there. It's gratifying to see her improve after months of working together.

And after seeing Dimitri last week, that's what I need: I have to know that I'm helping Hallie, not hurting her. If I pass down what he did, I would never forgive myself. Hallie screws up her mouth in concentration as she tracks the distance between her and the trampoline. Her full body weight plunges down on the black mesh and she rebounds brightly into the air once more. Her limbs soar jubilantly into shape; at the peak of her jump, she beams. She knows she nailed it.

• • •

I haven't seen Ryan outside of practice since Dimitri and Jasmine's cocktail party. I've gone to yoga after work twice, and on the nights I've been free, he's had plans with friends. All week, I've felt starved for attention; I had forgotten what it's like to crave somebody like this. I could physically feel the way I yearned for quality time with him—sometimes, low in my gut; other times, like an actual pang in my chest. When he texted me yesterday evening to ask if I'd be free for a date night tonight, I replied *yes* practically while my phone still buzzed with the incoming message.

He texted confusing instructions: *I have a secret plan for us. Wear something warm, and make sure you have socks.*

Socks? *What's the plan?* I wrote back.

He replied, *Like I said—it's a secret ;)*

I knew I wasn't going to weasel the truth out of him, so instead, I tried to puzzle out what we could possibly be doing—hiking? skiing?—and took great care to find a matching pair of socks without any holes. Tonight, after drilling stag jumps with Hallie on the trampoline, Ryan and I waited until Hallie had left the gym's premises in her dad's car before we both climbed into his car. We decided earlier that I'd stay over at his place and he'd drive me back to the gym the next morning. The plan made me feel as if we were serious and committed, or at least on the way toward it.

"So, now you can tell me where we're going," I say once he's pulled out of the parking lot.

"Nope," he says.

"Not even a hint?" I ask.

He's resolute. "You'll just have to wait and see."

He talks about how much fun he had dreaming this up, and how it'll be the perfect way to chill out in the midst of Nationals prep, but I just can't focus. My mind ping-pongs from sleuthing out where he's taking me to our last in-person conversation about Dimitri's job offer. We haven't had a chance to discuss it. There's so much I could say to him—and as much as I want to ask how he's feeling about what Dimitri said, I don't want to ruin the romantic mood.

He drives through the town center and pulls into Osaka Sushi. The familiar wooden sign gives me a burst of nostalgia, but it takes me a moment to piece together why he's so excited.

"I told you about this place, didn't I?" I say, suddenly recalling. "When we were driving through Greenwood after Lolly's."

"Your family likes to come here for special occasions," he says.

"Ryan! You remembered." I take off my seat belt so I can properly lean across the car to give him a hug and a kiss. "But wait, the socks? Warm clothes? Was that just to throw me off?"

I'm overheating in a thick turtleneck and knit scarf. There are gloves stashed away in the pockets of my parka.

"That's for after dinner," he says, winking as he gets out of the car.

• • •

Ninety minutes later, when we're happily filled up on a sashimi plat-ter and a sake flight, I still don't know where we're going next. But Ryan did insist on heading out of the restaurant as soon as the bill was paid, rather than lingering at the table. I get the sense we're on a deadline. In the car once again, I feel warmed by the sake from the inside out, touched by the romantic gesture of bringing me back to Osaka Sushi, and high on the anticipation of discovering where this adventure all leads. Whatever desire I had earlier tonight to ask Ryan about Dimitri has faded away. It's not that I don't care—it's that moments like this don't come around often. It's not every day that a gorgeous man throws together a surprise date packed with personal touches at a series of secret locations. I slide my hand into Ryan's and squeeze a silent thanks.

Finally, the jig is up: he pulls off a main road down a narrow street that winds into the town forest. He drives slowly through the heavy thicket of pine trees until we reach a clearing. There's a cul-de-sac full of cars streaked with winter grime parked near an outdoor ice-skating rink. Although it's a dark night, the rink itself is bright, thanks to white floodlights and golden Christmas lights wrapped around aluminum poles. I've been to this rink a few times for my elementary school classmates' birthday parties, but it's only now, as an adult, that I see how charming this spot really is.

"This is so *sweet!*" I exclaim, getting out of the car.

"Do you skate?" he asks.

He looks hopeful but hesitant, the way people do when they hand you presents with the tags still attached in case you want to return them.

"I haven't skated in years, but I always liked it as a kid," I say.

"Me, too," he says.

A rink attendant in a red clapboard shed asks for our shoe sizes and hands us clunky skates. We lace them up and totter to the edge of the rink. He steps over the threshold first, then extends his hand so I can steady myself as I step onto the ice. I take a few tentative glides with my hand hovering over the railing in case I lose my balance.

We make a slow first lap side by side, getting used to being on the ice. There aren't many other people here—three couples in casual clothes and a single skater in athletic gear who makes sharp turns and elegant spins—so it's calm enough to go at our own pace.

"So far, so good, but I bet I'll fall flat on my ass at least once tonight," I say.

"I'll catch you," he says.

"Don't you dare. I'll probably pull you down with me," I warn.

"You're not gonna fall," he predicts. "I remember you on beam back in the day—your balance is absurd."

"Don't jinx it," I say.

He's right, though; by our second lap, I feel sturdier, and by our third, I've regained my confidence. I slip my hand into his and trust my balance enough to plant a kiss on his cheek as we glide. I can't help but see flashes of the future—maybe we'll hike this spring, canoe this summer, train for a half marathon together this fall. We're both used to solitary sports, but there's something appealing about tackling new adventures as a pair.

As we continue to skate circles around the rink, we whisper theories about the other couples—which ones seem happily in love, which seem more like old roommates who couldn't give a damn about each other—and resolve to never fall into the latter category. We trade stories about ice-skating experiences as kids, and the Olympic skaters we've met over the years. On some laps, we don't talk at all, content to enjoy the twinkling lights nestled into the forest and the blur of our hazy reflections gleaming on the slick ice. With Ryan, silence doesn't feel like pressure.

But there's one question I can't get out of my head.

"What's all this for?" I ask finally.

"A guy can't take a girl out?" he replies.

"Of course, of course. But, I mean, this is spectacular."

His cheeks go pink, and I don't think it's just from the thirty-five-degree weather.

"Don't get me wrong, I love seeing you in the gym," he says slowly. "And at your place, and at mine. But I've never really treated you to a real date night, and you deserve that."

"Oh!" I say, touched.

"In case you haven't noticed, I'm not, uh, the fanciest guy," he says sheepishly.

"*You?*" I joke back. "Huh, never would've guessed."

He smirks. "And I thought about a gourmet dinner somewhere, but I know you love to cook. I know you'd rather cook than be waited on."

"True," I admit.

"So I thought your old favorite sushi place would be a treat, and this would cap the night off perfectly. I hope you like it?" he finishes.

"I love it," I say. "Thank you for planning such a fabulous date."

I don't mean to, but I flash back to a "date night" with Tyler. Or, rather, it was supposed to be a date night. Instead, we watched *Fast & Furious 6* in silence while we ate Easy Mac. He had told me not to bother with cooking a special meal for date night. He didn't get that cooking for him felt like another way to show my love. He fell asleep before the movie was over. But this feels entirely different—it's thoughtful and personal. He put care into choosing something I'd like.

"So you'll keep me?" he says.

I can hear a note of restrained laughter in his voice.

"Eh," I joke, pretending like I'm attempting to make up my mind. "I'll keep you."

I skate to a stop and pull him gently toward the railing. I steady myself against it and kiss him deeply, slipping my fingers under his scarf to hold him close. It's true that there's a certain thrill about kissing someone for the first time, when you can only guess what it'll feel like, how your bodies will respond to each other's, and if there will be sparks. But this is thrilling in a different way: comfortable, familiar, easy. I can anticipate the way his lips will move against mine. I *know* there will be sparks. I can't believe how lucky I am.

The rink is quieter now; we're among the last people left. It's a picturesque moment, but I know there's a bigger reason tonight makes me so happy. Being here in his arms feels exactly right.

"What an incredible night," I say.

I have to stop myself from uttering the three little words that almost roll off my tongue next.

"*You* are incredible," I say, swallowing the too-soon words and choosing the safer ones instead.

He nuzzles closer and kisses me again. When he pulls back, he hesitates, like he's trying to determine exactly what to say next. I wonder if the same words are running through his head, too.

"I . . ." he says.

My stomach does a backflip.

He gazes at me for a moment that feels like an eternity.

"I'm really glad you're here with me," he says, pulling me closer for a kiss.

Everything about it—the steady pressure of his hand on the curve of my hip; the scent of pine; the slippery surface of the ice beneath our feet—I commit to memory. I want to remember every detail, because this is the night I know for sure that I am falling in love with Ryan Nicholson, and there's nothing I can do about it.

• CHAPTER 19 •

A chill runs up my spine when I enter the National Championships arena in Miami. The nervous energy hanging in the air feels just as real as the mingled scent of chalk dust and sweat. I follow Hallie and Ryan around the perimeter to find a spot to settle down, and I can't help but drink it all in: the crunch of errant bobby pins underfoot; the spare cans of hair spray and bottles of butt glue rolling out from unzipped gym bags; the ritual gestures of gymnasts warming up; the satisfying *scrchhh* of grips being Velcroed on and off wrists; the anxious parents snapping gum in the bleachers. I savor every bit of it. I feel as if I've come home again. The moment I walked through the door, I straightened up, lifted my chin one notch higher, and tightened my ponytail. This time around, though, nobody's watching me. This isn't about me.

We're here for Hallie. It's her day. She finds a bench on the far side of the arena, closest to the beam, that has yet to be claimed by anyone else and drops her duffel on it.

We're all clad in matching navy tracksuits embroidered with Summit's logo over our hearts. Hallie removes her jacket, revealing a gleaming, emerald-green, long-sleeved leotard. It's spangled with Swarovski crystals across her collarbone and down the center of her chest, like a glittering necklace or a piece of armor. If she goes to the Olympics, her competition leotards will be chosen by the American Gymnastics Federation, and she'll probably be clad in red, white, blue, or all three. But for now, she can wear whatever she likes. I know this leotard is one of her favorites because it brings out the green flecks in her hazel eyes.

There are armies of gymnast-coach teams just like us scattered across the venue. I spot Delia Cruz rolling her wrists in supple circles to warm up for bars. Maggie Farber and Kiki McCloud sit with hands over their faces while their coach tames down their ponytails with hair spray. Across the arena, Dimitri reclines on a bench while his group of Powerhouse gymnasts stretch silently. I recognize their faces and names, though I don't know them personally. His star student is Emma Perry, a fiercely talented competitor who's probably the front-runner of the entire sport. He has Skylar Hayashi and Brit Almeda, too—the former is a vault specialist who began performing flawless Amanars at fourteen years old and has only gotten more intimidating since then; the latter is a decent if less memorable athlete who brings in reliably fine scores but doesn't quite have that X factor. I don't think Ryan has broached the subject of Dimitri or Powerhouse with Hallie or her parents yet. In the frenzied lead-up to Nationals, there hasn't been time.

Each gymnast's competition roster is assigned randomly. When the schedule flashes on the big screen that looms above the arena, Hallie's face hardens. She's up first on bars, which means she'll spend the rest of the day rotating through vault, beam, and then floor. She doesn't complain, though; she knows NBC's cameras have likely already begun swirling, and she's smart enough to understand that her reaction to the news shouldn't be a dismal one.

"I just want to get floor over with," she whispers to me.

"I know. I'm sorry. Let's stretch," I suggest, stepping forward to place myself protectively between her and any cameramen who might be approaching with a long lens.

She dutifully nods, slips off her track pants, and stands to begin her warm-up. She runs through the same basic set of moves she's completed daily since childhood—bending over her knees in a pike, rolling out her wrists, straddling her legs wide—but this time, every movement is packed with intention: pointed toes, straight spine, sucked-in core. She waves at a pair of little girls in the bleachers holding up a sign with her name printed on it in colorful marker.

An announcement cuts through the noise of the stadium: fifteen minutes until the competition begins, which means it's time for Hallie to warm up on bars. She's on the same rotation as Delia and Brit, and the three gymnasts take turns chalking up and practicing elements of their routines. There's an unintentional hierarchy: Brit defers to Hallie because she's the stronger athlete, and both girls defer to Delia, because she's become something of a legend, a mother hen, a spokesperson for the horrors of the sport ever since the accusations broke. Today, Delia's leotard is teal. I heard Jasmine discussing it during her TV segment; teal is the color of sexual assault awareness.

At the one-minute mark, Hallie signals to us that she's all set.

"Last-minute pep talk," Ryan says. "Huddle up."

Ryan wraps a protective arm around Hallie's shoulders and slides a nonchalant arm around my waist. Hallie's breath is shallow. This isn't her first rodeo; it's clear that she knows as nervous as she is, she has to fake it till she makes it. Otherwise, she'll psych herself out.

"I just want to tell you one more time how proud I am of you," Ryan says, locking eyes with Hallie. "You're strong, you're tough, and you have trained so hard for this for so long."

She blushes. "Thanks."

"And don't let the prospect of floor rattle you all day," he says. "You have nothing to worry about."

"I don't?" she asks, surprised.

"The new choreography? Fantastic. The updated tumbling passes? Genius. I've known you a long time, and I've never seen you as poised or as elegant as you've been performing lately."

Hallie exhales. Her shoulders visibly relax.

"Oh," she says, almost laughing to herself. "Right."

"Avery?" Ryan prompts.

I didn't prepare anything to say. When I was competing, it's not like Dimitri ever gave any sort of warm, touchy-feely pep talk like this one. A gruff request to stop whining and keep my chin up, maybe, but nothing like this. I swallow.

"You have no idea how good you have it," I say. "How easy this will be. How prepared you are. You are a natural superstar, and you have Ryan, who's amazing, and you have an incredibly supportive family cheering you on."

The words come easily because they're the truth.

"Every single day, I am so proud to work with you, because you never give up and you never lose what makes you *you*," I continue, ignoring the lump forming in my throat. "I'm lucky to be on your team. And I can't wait to see you rock this competition."

I squeeze my hand around her shoulder. I didn't expect to be so emotional, but seeing Hallie here, just inches away from a competition that could make her a front-runner at Olympic Trials, I'm overwhelmed. I break the huddle to give her a tight hug.

"Thank you, guys," Hallie says, her words muffled into my hair. "Seriously. Thank you."

An event coordinator taps Hallie on the shoulder. "It's time," she says.

Hallie glances at each of us. "Bye."

"You got this!" I call out.

Ryan goes with her. He's there to hover by the high bar through-out the duration of her routine, ready to lunge forward during her riskiest release moves when she's most likely to fall, in case he needs to catch her. I don't want to be a distraction, so I'll watch from the sidelines.

Hallie reaches into the chalk bowl to add one more layer of dust to her grips, and nods to Ryan that she's ready. Moments later, an announcer's voice booms over the loud speaker. A hush falls over the crowd in the bleachers.

"First up on bars is Hallie Conway," the voice booms.

The audience roars a cheer. "Let's go, Hallie, let's go!" I call out, clapping.

Hallie strides to the center of the low bar, totally transformed. She stands tall, suddenly looking five years older and twice as se-rene as she really is. She raises both arms to the table of judges and beams, performing the customary salute of respect that every gymnast does at the beginning and end of each routine. I see a judge flick to a new sheet in her notebook and peer over the tops of her thick-rimmed glasses.

Hallie takes a deep breath, then jumps on the low bar and swings up into a perfect handstand with such easy grace that I forget to be nervous for her. She transitions smoothly to the high bar, then pirouettes in a handstand, and executes a clean Tkatchev–Pak Salto combo, flinging herself backward and soaring smoothly down to the low bar. Everything is tight, as it should be: vertical handstands, straight knees, pointed toes, rock-hard core. The routine concludes with a mesmerizing series of giants—swinging, 360-degree circles around the high bar—and then she's slicing through the air into a double-twisting double back tuck. The moment she hits the mat, she's sturdy and sure of herself—she sticks the landing. The audience erupts into a cheer as she arches backward.

Hallie waves to the crowd, turning to face each corner of the arena to blow grateful kisses.

Giddy, she crashes sideways into Ryan for a one-armed hug.

"Amazing job," I say, high-fiving her in a burst of chalk dust when she makes it back to the bench. "You nailed it."

"That felt great," she says.

"Because it *was* great," Ryan says.

Thirty seconds later, the judges confirm what everyone knows: It was a beautiful performance. They award her a 15.025—and anything in the fourteen range or above is incredible. By the end of the first rotation, she's in fourth place—Emma, Delia, and Kiki have just barely edged her out for the top spots. Hallie's face falls slightly.

"Don't worry, you have three more rotations to go," Ryan points out. "The rankings will change."

"Yeah, but I just finished bars," she protests.

Nobody has to say out loud what she really means: her best event is now over, so it could all go downhill from here.

"Vault's next," I say brightly. "Just focus on nice, solid landings, and you'll be just fine."

Per the rules of the competition, she competes twice on vault. Judges score both efforts, then take the average as her final score. Her first run, an Amanar, is impressive. But any success there is canceled out by the deductions she receives for the two extra steps she takes upon landing her second vault, a Mustafina.

I know the rules of the sport well enough to know better, but it still seems incredibly unfair that Hallie gets points docked for her dynamite energy. She's like a high jumper in a ballerina's body—if she were a track-and-field star instead of a gymnast, her explosive power would make her an Olympic champion. But not here. My nerves feel frayed as I watch the judges grimly turn over the final score: 13.250. Hallie slips to fifth place. The mood on the bench is tense.

Her third rotation is beam, and if there's one event that demands confidence and precision above all else, it's this one. When I was a gymnast, beam was always intimidating, but at least I felt in control of the experience. If I shook or bobbled or fell, it was my own fault. But now, as Hallie competes, that sense of control crumbles. My muscles spasm as I watch her move. When she pirouettes, I crane my neck, as if I can manipulate the speed of her spin. As she wobbles on the landing of a front aerial, my stomach and glutes and thighs clench hard, as if I can keep her centered on the beam through sheer force of will. Her tumbling pass—a back handspring, whip back, back layout that's usually just pure fun to watch—tilts slightly off center. One foot curls desperately around the beam, while the other leg ricochets sideways in a last-ditch attempt to regain balance. She stays on, but just barely. After her dismount, she salutes limply to the panel of judges and trudges into Ryan's arms.

Hallie makes it back to the bench just as the stony-faced judges reveal her score: a flat 12.850. That means she's officially slipped down to ninth place. I feel sick. As long as she doesn't completely bomb floor, she should qualify to compete at Olympic Trials. (The top fourteen competitors will go to Trials.) But there's no guarantee of that—anything could happen at a competition, especially with her confidence at an all-time low right now—and ninth place is a brutal, embarrassing spot to be in, even out of seventeen total spots. Ideally, she'd be in the top five or six, if not fully in the top three for medal contention. I hate to imagine Jasmine's commentary right now. It can't be good.

Ryan spots Hallie's empty water bottle and goes to refill it.

"I'll be back in a minute," he promises.

Hallie scowls and slumps down further in her seat. There's a beat of silence between us.

"I'm completely failing," she says morosely. "I'm messing up over and over again on live TV, looking like a total idiot."

"Hey, scoot," I say, moving to sit next to her. "You're not an idiot. At all. I promise."

She slides over a few inches but doesn't look at me. She's staring at the big screen, transfixed as Emma sticks a powerful double-double on floor and makes it look easy.

"I'm in ninth place," she spits out. "*Ninth* place. That's for idiots."

"You have to stop calling yourself an idiot," I say.

She gives me a look full of skeptical contempt that reminds me she is still a surly teenager. She might have traded in the typical trappings of a teen girl's life for the discipline, demands, and pressures of a fully grown adult athlete's, but this is one thing she can't change. She's a sixteen-year-old girl, behaving the way any sixteen-year-old would.

She scrunches up her face. "I didn't work this hard to be all the way down the scoreboard."

"I know," I say carefully. I try to figure out what to say to lift her spirits. "But maybe there's more to it than that. What if you can just appreciate the fact that you've worked so hard to be here? I know you get so much joy out of performing. Just go out there and have fun showing off what you can do, you know?"

She tilts her head and stares at me.

"You're nuts," she says. "You've lost it."

"I'm just trying to show you the silver lining," I insist. "Because there is one."

"If you kind of squint," she adds.

"Squint really carefully, yeah," I say. "You're here. You deserve to be here."

She takes a long sip of her water and shakes her head slowly.

"You sound extremely yoga right now," she says.

"I'm just jealous that you get to go out there and deliver the hell out of your next routine," I say. "You're living my dream."

She sighs dramatically.

"I'll go slay on floor if you promise to stop talking like a corny Oprah knockoff," she says.

"Deal," I say, extending my hand.

She shakes it. "Deal."

An event coordinator waves Hallie over to start warming up for floor. I shout ridiculously supportive comments as she walks away. But once she's gone, the pit in my stomach returns.

• • •

Floor warm-ups fly by. Brit delivers a surprisingly lovely performance to a delicate piece of classical music, and Hallie whispers to me that she must have gotten new choreography. Up next, Delia strides calmly onto the floor to perform a knockout routine that inspires the audience to give her a standing ovation. On the big screen, you can see tears glittering in her eyes as she waves to her fans and hugs her coach. The moment is powerful and heartbreaking. When the judges award her the breathtakingly high mark of 15.275, it's clear she's earned every bit of it.

Meanwhile, Hallie is trembling. She rises from the bench and shakes out each leg so her knees don't buckle beneath her. More than any other moment in her life, the pressure is on.

"Let's go, Hallie!" I call out.

"Come on, Hal, you got this," Ryan says loudly.

"We had a good talk while you were gone," I say. "I think she'll be okay."

"If she's not, I think her parents will skin us alive," Ryan mutters.

Hallie's name rings out over the loudspeaker, and the judges flick to new sheets of paper in their notebooks. She salutes at the edge of the blue mat, then struts into position. There's a high, clear *beep* to signal that she should prepare herself, and then the opening notes of her new floor music. This is her first time performing the routine I crafted in competition, and I'm anxious to see how it's received.

Hallie throws herself into the first few fierce steps of her choreography, just like we practiced, and I am so proud. She's a swirl of limbs and piercing gazes as she pivots, backs up into the corner, and lunges into her first tumbling pass. She whips across the floor with enough energy to power a fleet of Maseratis, rocketing skyward at the end into the stag jump we drilled on the trampoline. Her leg levers up elegantly behind her, and she lands on beat.

She beams and surges onward through a frenzied attempt at her leap series. She'll get a small deduction for failing to hit the full 180-degree split, but it's a marked improvement from the first time she tried that combination. When she slides down to set up her wolf turn, I cringe and grab Ryan's hand. His palm glistens with sweat. Hallie's brows knit together as she steels herself to spin. I can't breathe as I watch her rotate cleanly. It's the best wolf turn I've ever seen her do.

On her second tumbling pass, she flies high above the floor and sticks the landing. As she prances through her choreography, I whisper a prayer. *Please keep this up. Please let this be okay.* Hallie attacks her third and fourth tumbling passes with pure grit. She spirals through the air and digs in her heels when she lands. As the music hits its final note, she throws her head back into the dramatic pose we practiced so many times in the Summit mirror. Her chest heaves as she tries to catch her breath. There's a second of silence, and then Hallie climbs to her feet, saluting the judges with all the energy she has left. The crowd claps as the judges continue to scribble down notes.

Ryan and I intercept her along the side of the floor for high fives and hugs, and we walk back to our spot together. Her breathing is ragged.

"Hallie, that was unbelievable," I tell her excitedly. "The best I've ever seen you perform."

"You were awesome," Ryan confirms.

She pants and gives a half-hearted thumbs-up. "Don't congratulate me until the score is ready," she warns.

"Don't worry about the score; that was phenomenal," I insist.

I hope, of course, that the judges reward her for one of the best floor routines she's probably ever done in her entire life. But I'm also nervous—they don't award medals for personal improvement. Her score will be compared to the other gymnasts'.

The judges deliver their score: 13.475. It moves Hallie up to seventh place.

Hallie lets out a low moan. "That's not good enough," she wails.

"That's a full point higher than you got at Worlds!" Ryan crows. "That's a real improvement, Hal. You should be very proud of yourself."

A full point! Selfishly, I glow with excitement.

"If this were Olympic Trials, seventh place wouldn't be enough to make the Olympic Team," Hallie says, sounding panicked.

Ryan kneels down in front of her and takes her hands. "But this isn't Trials," he points out. "You have months to go. So much can change between now and then."

Hallie looks suspiciously around the arena. "Yeah, but everyone else will be training to improve, too."

I want to say something reassuring or encouraging, but everything I come up with sounds hollow or worthless. Seventh place is a complicated place to be: she's not knocked out of Olympic contention by any means, but she's not a shoo-in, either. It would be exciting to land here if this were Hallie's first elite competition, but it's not. She didn't come this far to only make seventh place. It's an uncomfortable middle ground, achingly mediocre when gymnasts are used to flashy wins or spectacular failures. Hallie could go either way from here . . . or she could float into obscurity, never quite making a name for herself in this sport.

"I know today wasn't what we hoped for, but I'm still proud of you," I say finally.

Hallie zips up her tracksuit and pulls the hoodie down low.

"Bars was beautiful," Ryan adds. "Vault was pretty solid, too. Next time, we'll work on—"

"I can't think about that now, all right?" Hallie snaps.

She shoves her feet into her Uggs and slings her gym bag over her shoulder.

"I can't stay here anymore. Bye."

She makes a beeline for the nearest exit.

"Wait!" Ryan calls out to her.

"I'll catch up with you later, okay?" he tells me, darting after Hallie.

My first instinct is to follow them, but I know Hallie doesn't want a full audience right now. If she wanted me with her, she would've told me. Instead, she wants to grieve today's results alone. I don't blame her. So I sink down onto the bench and watch glumly as other gymnasts gleefully celebrate their wins. My heart hurts.

• CHAPTER 20 •

I'm still alone an hour later. I don't want to be. Ryan and Hallie never returned to the arena, and my text to him went unanswered. I head back to the hotel. I had originally assumed that Ryan and I would share a room—we spend two or three nights a week at each other's places, anyway, and I was even looking forward to our first trip together as a couple. But Ryan had pointed out that it'd look suspicious for us to share, especially since Summit had already paid for us to sleep separately. Our rooms are at opposite ends of the seventh floor; Hallie and her parents have a larger suite on the eighth.

When the elevator doors slide open on the seventh floor, I step out in the cool, blandly carpeted lobby. There's an array of kitschy beach-inspired decor hanging on the wall—shiny pink seashells, dried-out coral and starfish—alongside black-and-white photos of the Miami skyline. I should turn left and head down the hall to my room, but instead, I turn toward Ryan's. I knock, but he doesn't come to the door.

I walk the long stretch of hallway back to my own hotel room. The maid has been here: the bed is freshly made and my jumble of clothes and extra shoes and phone charger are stacked neatly on top of my luggage. I kick off my shoes, flop diagonally across the bed, and try to resist the urge to check my phone. Instead, I stare at the white stucco ceiling for a few moments, ruminating on Hallie's disastrous performance today and wondering if she simply had an off day or if I had failed to properly prepare her. Too depressing.

I miss Ryan. I feel silly admitting it to myself, because I just spent the entire day with him, but I do. When we're working, it doesn't really feel like we're spending time together—I can't fully relax around him when I know other people are watching us. If I had to guess, he's probably still with her, comforting her, and that makes me feel even worse: heartbroken for Hallie, ashamed over how I failed as a coach, depressed by what this means for my career, and self-indulgent for wishing Ryan could be here with me instead. I don't want him to come over and analyze what went wrong today. I just want him here as my boyfriend.

I get up to shower off the day, if only because there's nothing else I really want to do (and everyone could benefit from bathing after spending time in an arena that smells like feet). The hotel room's bathroom is outfitted in cream-colored tile with vanity lights over the mirror that feel like the height of glamour compared to my apartment in Greenwood. I linger longer than I need to in the shower. When I get out, wrapped in a fluffy white hotel bathrobe that feels wonderfully thick and heavy over my shoulders, I'm relieved to see a text from Ryan—until I read it.

Hey, sorry, I'm actually not free to hang out right now, he wrote. *Let's talk later?*

His words make me feel lonelier. I spent countless hours in LA waiting for Tyler to text me back, to come home, to want to see me. Eagerly waiting for scraps of attention is the most pathetic feeling in the world.

Sure, I type.

I consider delaying my response by several minutes to give him a taste of his own medicine, but that's too juvenile to feel rewarding. I should know better than to behave like a child. I press send.

I'm too restless to sit around this room, so I get dressed and head downstairs to the hotel's restaurant. Vending machine snacks aside, I've barely eaten all day, and it'd be good for me to get some real food. I didn't realize it until now, but I'm hungry. The restaurant's vibe mimics the beachy decor from upstairs: the upholstery on the chairs looks speckled like sand, and nautical bits and bobs like buoys and fishing net hang from the driftwood bar.

"Just one?" the hostess asks.

"Just me," I say, pretending to be cheery and fine about that.

She scans the crowded room.

"So, it'll be about fifteen or twenty minutes for a table for one, but I could seat you now at the bar, if you'd like," she offers.

"The bar's fine," I say.

There aren't many free bar stools, either, though I see one crammed between two larger men, and another . . . Oh. Next to Jasmine. I move toward the seat between the two men, but she sees me before I can sit down. For a split second, neither of us says anything.

"Hey!" she says, waving me over.

"Will that seat work?" the hostess asks.

Jasmine is watching expectantly.

"It's fine, thank you," I tell the hostess.

I wedge myself into the seat on Jasmine's right. She's dressed for TV: gleaming lipstick, sleek blowout, lemon-yellow shift dress. There's a glass of white wine and a leafy green salad in front of her.

"I wondered if I'd bump into you," she says, giving me an air-kiss by my cheek.

"Good to see you," I say, even though the prospect of a conversation with her makes me anxious.

The bartender slides a menu my way, and I order a glass of wine as quickly as I can.

"Plus, uh, whatever salad she's having," I add.

"It's delicious," Jasmine gushes.

She *would* grow up to be the kind of woman who raves about lettuce.

"It was so interesting to watch Hallie compete today," she says. "You know, knowing you coach her now."

"'Interesting'?" I echo.

That sounds like a euphemism for *bad*.

"I loved her new floor routine," Jasmine insists. "I made a note of it on-air, even—I was talking about how you choreographed it yourself, and how excited I was to see Hallie compete it for the first time today."

"Oh," I say, surprised. "That's actually very nice of you. Thank you."

"I'm sure she would've liked to do a little bit better in the rankings today," Jasmine says. "But, hey, you know I always love to root for the underdog."

She winks, as if there's a camera waiting somewhere to catch her reaction. There's not.

"She's a good, hard worker. I think she'll bounce back just fine," I say.

"She's not tough to discipline?" Jasmine asks.

The question catches me off guard. "We don't really need to discipline her."

"Sure," she says skeptically.

"No, really. It's actually been really interesting, figuring out a coaching style that's different from the one we grew up with," I continue. "You remember, Dimitri always said he was hard on us because that would be best for us. But with Hallie, I don't know, she just works hard."

Jasmine doesn't respond right away. Instead, she sips quietly from her wineglass. I regret speaking so candidly about Dimitri in front of her.

"I'm sorry, I don't mean to imply anything about the way he coached. I know, obviously, things are different now that he's your . . . husband."

The word still leaves a bad taste in my mouth.

"No, it's all right, you don't need to apologize," she says, twisting her diamond engagement ring and staring down at her salad, like she's trying to find the right words. "I know he . . . I mean, he was . . ." She trails off and sighs heavily.

"Is he still like that? I mean, when it's just you two?" I ask tentatively.

I know I'm prying, but it occurs to me that Jasmine might not have anyone else she can talk to like this. We used to confide in each other all the time—more often than not about the man who's now her husband—but I wouldn't be surprised if she stays tight-lipped about what he's really like among her new set of friends.

My salad arrives. Jasmine pauses, politely watching the busboy set it down in front of me. She looks grateful for the opportunity to collect her thoughts before she speaks.

"He's a good man," she finally says in an even voice. "He provides a beautiful life for us, and he is so respected in the community, and he makes me happy."

I know what Jasmine looks like when she's not being totally honest. I've seen it before, back when we were kids. It was easy to lie about doing two sets of reps of crunches instead of three, or to pretend we didn't eat the extra whipped cream on our chai lattes at

Lolly's. I'm not married, so I can't judge firsthand what's normal and what's not in her relationship. But she doesn't sound like a woman in love. She sounds like a defense attorney.

"Right," I say.

Discomfort clings to me like an itchy, too-small sweater. There's more I want to know.

"But what's it . . . *like*? Being married to him? I mean, I can't imagine," I say.

It sounds like I'm openly gawking, and I guess I am. I've spent years wondering what their relationship could possibly be like, and after getting a glimpse of it at their party, my curiosity has only intensified.

She gestures to the bartender for another glass of wine.

"I mean, you know him," she says, shrugging. "Sometimes, he has his . . . moods," she admits. "You remember those."

"Yeah, I do."

"And he . . . he's particular, you know? He likes things to be a certain way. Sometimes, he gets upset when things aren't right."

"He used to take it out on us," I say bitterly.

Maybe that's a step too far, but Jasmine doesn't disagree with me.

"He meant well, but it wasn't right," she says.

"It took me a long time to clearly see how that affected me, because at the time, it all felt so normal," I say. The words come more easily now, since I know Jasmine will agree with me on this point. "Or, at least, if not normal, like everything was in service of a greater goal."

"Glory," we intone at the same time, like we've heard thousands of times before.

In the back of my head, I hear the word in a guttural Russian accent, and I bet she does, too. For a moment, the past seven years collapse, and I feel like we're just kids again—giggling friends who finish each other's sentences. It makes me miss how we used to be. Nobody has ever replaced her.

"But I think that's changing, no?" she says. "Dimitri's old-school, but he's pretty much the only one left."

"I mean, Ryan and I do our best," I concede. "Hallie's mostly pretty easy, but even so, we don't push her any harder than she'd push herself. I mean, god, the world is not a good place for gymnasts right now. You know what I mean."

"I do," she says heavily.

We don't even need to say it out loud.

"But as horrible as that is, this isn't the first time there's been a scandal like that—awful things like that have happened before," I point out.

"In dark, shady fucking corners, yeah," she says grimly.

"The rest of the sport, though? I think it's getting a little better," I say.

"I think I see that, too," she says. "At competitions, it's like . . . *whoa*. The girls all have muscles and thighs and don't hide the fact that they eat."

We both look limply down at the remaining salad on our plates.

"I don't know about the girls Dimitri works with, but Hallie has personality. Sass. Or, as he might call it, attitude," I say.

"Nothing we were allowed to have," Jasmine adds, shaking her head.

"Ha. No. But Hallie's good. Happy."

"She's okay with food?" Jasmine asks.

"She eats, she does yoga, she's confident . . ." I say.

Jasmine lets out a low whistle, understanding the implication: Hallie's not like we were. "Good for her."

"She has a tutor, but she has a whole plan: Olympics first, then college. She talks about going to law school someday. For her, there's a whole world out there," I explain.

I don't have to spell it out for Jasmine. For us, there was no other world. We're here, after all, aren't we? I stab a piece of lettuce with my fork.

"I wanted to be a fashion designer," Jasmine says suddenly. Her eyes are spacey, vacant, like she's dreaming about some far-off memory. She turns sharply toward me. "Did you know that?"

"Maybe?"

I vaguely recall her sketching evening gowns and spindly high heels on a long car ride to a competition. We must have been twelve. She erased and redrew and erased and redrew each line on a model's body until it matched the vision she held in her mind.

"But then, you know, everything just happened. London and then the post-Olympics tour and then all these motivational speeches at gyms and then Dimitri and NBC, and here we are," she says, shrugging like she blinked and it all just fell into place, like one domino after another. She gives a short laugh. "What was I supposed to do, duck out and learn to sew?"

My question comes tumbling out before I have time to realize that it's a rude one. "Are you happy?" I blurt.

The words hang in the air. Jasmine uncrosses and crosses her legs, catching one stiletto along the rung of the bar stool and taking a long sip of wine.

"Of course I'm *happy*," she says finally. "I just wonder, sometimes, what else could've happened—would've happened—if we'd grown up differently."

"Without Dimitri, you mean," I clarify.

"With a different coach, more options, another life," she says, gesturing vaguely around the restaurant.

The wine is getting to her now; there's a looseness to her energy, so unlike the sensitive, tightly wound girl I used to know.

"Which is why," she continues, "you can't let Ryan take the job."

"What job?" I ask.

"The one they're talking about right now," she says, pointing above us, like it's obvious. "Upstairs. In our suite. No matter who they'll coach together for 2024—Hallie or someone else—that girl deserves better."

"Ryan's with Dimitri?" I ask blankly.

I have the sickening sensation of being the last person to know what's going on, and I hate it. I don't want to have to play catch-up with my own boyfriend's whereabouts and career.

"Where'd you think they were?" she asks, alarmed, as if she suddenly realizes that I've been in the dark. "Oh, honey."

I groan.

"You can't let Ryan take the job," Jasmine says, her tone growing urgent now. She clutches my arm. "I shouldn't say this, and if you tell anyone I did, I'll deny it, but keep Hallie away from Dimitri. Let her be good and safe and healthy. Let her have a future outside of this world."

"What's your room number?" I ask.

"Room two twenty," she says, rolling her eyes. "Like 2020—for good luck."

"Of course he would request that."

"I'll cover your meal if you cover for me," she says, holding a finger to her lips. "Go."

I race to the elevators.

• CHAPTER 21 •

The moment before I knock on Dimitri's door, my stomach tightens and my mind spirals into tight focus. It's the same sensation I used to get right before I saluted the judges and strode forward to perform a routine. I knock.

Dimitri opens the door. Surprise flits across his face.

"Hi," I say.

He doesn't greet me.

"Your girlfriend's here," he calls over his shoulder.

He cocks his head and clicks his tongue, signaling for me to enter. Somehow, that's more humiliating than him shutting the door in my face. There was a time I spent more of my day with him than with my own parents. Now he won't even use my name.

The suite is far larger and nicer than the room I'm staying in. The bedroom is identical to mine, but there's also a lounge with a pair of upholstered armchairs and a love seat arranged around a coffee table. There's a crystal decanter of whiskey with two matching, half-filled glasses. Ryan rises from one of the armchairs, confused.

"Avery? What are you doing here?" he asks.

"I'd like to talk to you," I say, hoping my voice comes out steady and strong.

"I'm in the middle of something," he says helplessly. "I texted you earlier, remember? I said we'd catch up later?"

"I know," I say.

"Is everything okay?" he asks.

There's real concern in his voice.

"Well, yeah, I'm fine, but . . ." I wish I had prepared something more convincing to say ahead of time. "I just . . . I really would like to speak with you. Now."

"Where are your manners, girl?" Dimitri says, looking amused. "We're working out business here."

The way he calls me *girl*, it's like he's hurled me more than a decade into the past. He has a knack for making me feel so small. It makes me burn with rage, especially because I know he's right—I barged in here without an invitation—but I can't apologize. I can't bow down in front of him and pretend to be sorry. I'm not.

Ryan looks from me to Dimitri and back again.

"Go," Dimitri says, waving his hand to dismiss us both. "Ryan, we'll talk again tomorrow."

"No, Dimitri, it's fine . . ." Ryan starts to protest.

But Dimitri's already halfway to the bedroom. We've been dismissed.

"All right, bye, thank you for everything," Ryan rushes to say.

I hate how furious and flustered and thrown off course I feel, just from spending one single minute in Dimitri's presence. But maybe it's for the best—maybe this is exactly the raw, hateful energy I need to fully convince Ryan he can never work with that man.

Ryan follows me out of the suite. I turn to face him the minute the door closes behind us, but he shakes his head, pressing a finger to his lips, and ushers us farther down the narrow hall, toward the elevator. I jab the up button.

"What was that?" he says finally. "Are you really okay? Is Hallie okay?"

"I'm fine, she's fine," I insist.

We enter the empty elevator, and the tight quarters make it feel impossible to keep my thoughts to myself. We're so close, he can probably hear what I'm thinking.

"What were you talking about?" I demand.

The edge of my voice sounds hard. Angry. Ugly.

"I've made up my mind. I want to work with Dimitri at Power-house," he admits.

For a moment, I feel too bitter to speak.

"But you know he's not a good guy," I say.

The elevator doors *ding* open on the seventh floor, and I follow him to his room.

"I know *you've* said that," he says carefully.

I grab his arm and stop walking. "That's not fair."

He sighs and pulls his arm away. "Okay. It's not, you're right. I'm sorry."

Now, in his hotel room, I stare at him expectantly, waiting for him to produce any explanation that makes sense. He sits on the edge of the bed, and I join him reluctantly. My heart pounds. I just want this conversation to be over with.

"I think this is a mistake," I tell him plainly. "Dimitri would crush Hallie. You see how rudely he treats me, don't you? He'll be ten times worse to her, day in, day out. He'll yell at her if she doesn't perform up to his insanely high standards of perfection, and then he'll scream at her if she dares to cry or fight back. He'll call her cruel names. He'll make her keep a diary of everything she eats and he'll review it once a week while she stands on a scale in a leotard. He'll punish her for gaining half a pound. He'll isolate her from her friends. Ryan, I know you think he's a legend, but he's a nightmare."

Ryan bites his lip and shakes his head. I can't tell if it's in disbelief or disagreement.

"I'm sorry that you grew up like that," he says in a strained voice. "I really, really am. Please don't get me wrong. He must have changed—he's not like that anymore."

"I don't believe that," I say firmly. "And anyway, it's not worth the risk. Girls who train with him don't grow up to have healthy, normal lives."

"Well, look at you," Ryan says, shrugging. "You turned out fine."

"Exactly! Look at me," I say. "It's been a long road to feeling remotely okay."

It's increasingly impossible not to shout. It feels like a match just caught fire in my chest. I ignite with anger. I've seethed silently about this in the past, but I've never let it all out before.

"Since I moved back to Greenwood, I've finally, slowly, just barely started to cobble together a real, adult life that I'm proud of," I explain. "A lot of that has to do with working with you. But I am twenty-seven years old. *Twenty-seven!* It took me the better part of a decade to get here. I was reeling. I had no education, no ambition, no goals, no full-time job. That's not me. That's not who I was supposed to be. For years, my life just . . . stalled. And I couldn't get back on track."

"You can't blame that all on Dimitri," Ryan says softly.

"He's certainly not innocent. He pushes people down so they can't get up," I fire back. "And look at Jasmine. He broke her down so hard, she never left. He's despicable."

"Kaminsky's despicable. Dimitri's just tough," Ryan says.

"I'm telling you, what you're doing is just plain wrong," I argue. "No decent person would do this."

"I'm not feeding Hallie to the wolves, Avery," Ryan says. "I'll be there with her. I'll protect her."

"Does Hallie know you're doing this? Do her *parents*?" I ask.

He sighs. His face contorts, but I can't tell if it's with guilt or exasperation.

"We've been talking about it for weeks," he admits. "I didn't include you in the discussions because I knew you would never work with Dimitri."

My anger blooms into rage, then betrayal.

"And when did you think you'd tell me?" I ask. My voice breaks. "I'm not just your coworker. This isn't about you ditching your job. I'm your *girlfriend*, Ryan. You're supposed to tell me things, not go behind my back."

He sighs. "I'm sorry for not telling you about my plans sooner."

I shake my head. I'm too overwhelmed to speak. What is there to say? I don't recognize the person I'm arguing with.

"I feel so stupid," I say finally.

"Why?" he asks.

I shudder and the words slip out before I can register what I'm saying.

"Because this whole time that I've been falling in love with you, you've been keeping secrets from me."

Ryan bites his lip. His eyes search mine for a long time.

"I . . . I didn't know," he says. "That you felt that way," he clarifies.

I look away, cheeks burning hot. There's a painful, stretched-out silence. I wait for him to say those words back to me. If he loves me back, he won't take the job. He'll make things right. But he doesn't say a word. I feel tears threatening to well up and a painful lump building in my throat, but I know I won't cry. It's a skill I learned long ago, honed so Dimitri would never see me more vulnerable than I could handle. The irony of it all feels bitter. I clear my throat.

"Please don't take the job," I say. "That's all I can say. That's the only thing left to say."

I rise from the bed. I can't stand being close to him right now.

"Avery, I'm sorry," he says. "I wouldn't do this if I didn't really believe Dimitri's changed. He's a legend. He's going to make Hallie a star."

"Do you want her to be star? Or do you want him to make *you* a star coach? You'll leave me and Summit behind in the dust."

"I'd take you with me, if you wanted to come," he offers.

"Right, sure, because that's ideal: working alongside an emotionally abusive asshole and the guy who doesn't love me," I snap. "Sounds great."

He leaps up from the bed. "I didn't say I didn't love you," he says.

I take a deep breath. "Do you?" I ask. "Do you love me?"

He wavers for a moment, like he's going to say something. But he doesn't.

"We're done," I say, walking quickly to the door so he can't see the tears springing to my eyes for real this time. "We're over."

I turn the door handle hard and storm out, hurrying toward my room at the opposite end. I wait for the sound of him chasing after me, begging me to change my mind. But there's nothing except the cool hiss of Ryan's door as it eases shut behind me.

• CHAPTER 22 •

The day after I get home from the National Championships, needing a distraction, I text Sara and entice her to be home at seven for one of the most exquisite meals I have under my belt: seared scallops on a bed of fresh corn and roasted hazelnuts, swirled in a creamy, paprika-infused brown butter sauce. Scallops cost a breathtaking twenty-four dollars per pound at the grocery store, and their soft, delicate white bellies make them tricky to cook without charring the skin and leaving the insides raw. In other words, don't bother attempting to make them unless you know what you're doing and have a reason to splurge. I'm making a pound and a half of them tonight because I want to feel talented and productive and like myself again as I recount the story of my breakup to Sara. I lost sight of who I am over the course of my relationship with Tyler; I need to prove to myself that I haven't forgotten that again while dating Ryan.

I've unloaded the groceries and preheated the oven when Sara walks in and drops her yoga mat by the door. She taught a class tonight, so wisps of blond hair frizz up from her topknot, and her

cheeks glow pink. It's true that teaching yoga isn't as physically taxing as doing it, or so she tells me, but she's still one of those girls who
never sweats. As a person who spent a good chunk of her teenage
years sweating on national television, I'm jealous.

"You're officially my favorite person, do you know that?" she says,
taking in the paper-wrapped scallops and the ears of corn. "This
looks amazing."

"Thanks, but save your compliments for when you taste it," I say.
"Hey, do me a favor? Will you shuck the corn?"

"Sure thing. Looks fancy. What's the occasion?" she asks.

I look up carefully from the paprika I'm measuring. "Ryan and I
broke up," I say.

Sara gasps and gives me a sympathetic look. "I'm so sorry," she
says, hugging me.

"Well, technically, I broke up with him," I add. "We had a fight,
and . . ."

I press my lips together into a tight smile so they don't tremble.
I can't let myself cry again—not now, not after I've spent the better
part of the last two nights crying myself to sleep. It feels important to
add the technicality that I was the one to break off the relationship.
I can't stomach being the girl who gets dumped twice in six months.

Sara sinks into the kitchen chair next to mine, and while I slide
the chopped hazelnuts into the oven and pat each scallop dry with
a paper towel, I recount what happened. I don't have to litigate
Dimitri's wrongdoings for her; I say he was emotionally and verbally
abusive, and she understands.

"The most embarrassing part is that when we were arguing, I
accidentally told Ryan I was falling in love with him," I say.

As mortifying as that was in the moment, I discover the humiliation feels just as fresh recounting it the next day. Sara visibly cringes.

"Did he say it back?" she asks.

"Nope," I reply. "If he had, maybe things would've gone pretty differently."

"Do you really love him?" she asks.

I sigh. The question sounds deceptively simple—yes or no. But there are too many other emotions swirling through my head right now to make sense of the situation: sadness, anger, embarrassment, shame, regret.

"I guess I'm just confused," I say, puzzling through the thoughts out loud. "I thought I loved him. But the way he's acting? Going behind my back, taking that job, not listening to what I'm saying about it? That makes me question who he really is."

The realization stings.

"I'm really sorry he let you down," Sara says softly. "He should've believed you."

"That's what's so weird about it, though! He was devastated over what Hallie went through. He believes all the other gymnasts who have come forward about Kaminsky—it's not that he's one of those men's rights activists who's all about guys being innocent until proven guilty. He's always cared. Just not now."

"Maybe because now, this issue is personal for him? It's about his career, which means he's not thinking as clearly as he should?" Sara guesses.

I groan at how infuriating the situation is and drizzle olive oil into a hot skillet. I gently place the scallops one by one, listening to the sizzle as they bathe in oil. Cooking scallops looks intimidating, but it really all comes down to precise timing and skill—just like gymnastics. Not that I ever really want to think about gymnastics ever again, especially not right now.

"And then, ugh, the next day, we had to fly back from Miami together," I say. "Me, Ryan, and Hallie, all in one row."

"That really blows."

"Yeah, sitting between my secret ex and a kid who's mourning the potential end of her athletic career for three hours was a real treat."

"How's Hallie doing?" Sara asks.

I shrug and flip the scallops. "Not great," I say. "Her confidence is shot, she's stressed beyond belief, she's frantic that she'll fail at Trials."

"Yikes," Sara says.

I finish the recipe, mixing bright yellow kernels of corn with the rich, slippery sauce, and plating it carefully all together so it looks like a real gourmet treat. I turn around and I'm just about to set Sara's plate in front of her, when she makes a sour face.

"What?" I ask.

She bites her lip and slides her phone across the table toward me.

"I hate to show you this, but this just popped up on my feed, and I think you should see it," she says, wincing.

The screen is filled with Ryan's most recent Instagram, a photo of him I must have missed. His arms are slung around Dimitri and Jasmine's shoulders, and his satisfied smile gives me goose bumps. Dimitri looks the same as always—gruff, like he's only posing to humor them. I search Jasmine's face for clues, but she's wearing that blankly beautiful newscaster look again. It's impossible to tell what thoughts are running through her head. The background of the photo looks familiar, but I can't quite place it until I spot the glint of medals against the wall behind them—it's Dimitri and Jasmine's house. They're cozy enough to do dinner at home together now, I guess.

"I can't believe I have to work with him for months," I say, groaning.

It's late March; Trials are at the tail end of June, with the Olympics stretching from late July through early August.

"You gotta focus on Hallie? Forget about him?" Sara says. I think she means it like a statement, but the absurdity of working on a three-person team with your ex for months is too much, even for her. "Channel your energy into the right places, block out the distractions, all that kind of stuff."

I try not to grimace, but right now, I need something a little stronger than yoga. There's half a bottle of red wine left corked on the counter, although it feels like a bad omen to pour a glass from it: Ryan and I opened it together last week. But the only other drink with a buzz to it is Sara's home-brewed kombucha, so wine it is. Fittingly, the flavor has turned bitter. I drink it anyway.

"It's just not fair," I say, pushing away my plate of scallops.

Tears prick at my eyes. I inhale deeply to calm myself down, but it doesn't really work.

"I want to be strong about this," I say. "I don't want to let this drama with Ryan get to me. I h-h-hate that I'm the kind of person who gets so thrown off course by stupid, dumb *feelings*."

My shoulders start to shake with gentle sobs, and I wish I could disappear into a black hole. I don't want Sara to see me like this. It's embarrassing to lose your shit over a guy you've only dated for a handful of months, especially when Sara met me shortly after a breakup with a *different* guy. If it walks like a duck and talks like a duck, it's a duck, right? And if I look like a boy-crazy mess, well . . .

"Avery, you've got to give yourself a break," Sara says, interrupting my spiraling thoughts. "It's okay to feel sad. Breakups are sad! That doesn't make you weak."

"Ryan's not sad. He's 'networking,'" I say, making vicious air quotes.

"He posted one picture," Sara says gently. "That doesn't tell you what he's really feeling on the inside."

I nudge a scallop with my fork. I wish I could know what he was thinking: if he believes what I said about Dimitri; if he regrets not chasing after me; if he's wondering how I'm doing right now, the same way I'm wondering about him. I miss him, even though I know I shouldn't. He crossed a line, and he was wrong—I feel this on a cellular level—but the only comfort I crave is a hug in his sturdy arms. It strikes me as heartbreakingly unfair that the one person who would lift my spirits best is also the person who crushed them.

I want Ryan to stroke my hair and whisper apologies into my ear and promise me he'll take my word more seriously next time. I need him to tell me he cares as deeply for Hallie as I do, and that he wants to protect her and girls like her, no matter what the cost, even if it means his career doesn't zoom up the ladder as quickly as he'd hope. I took it for granted that I could trust him. Now I realize I shouldn't have.

"Sweetie, it's going to be okay," Sara promises.

She tries to catch my gaze, and because I don't want to ruin her night, too, I let her.

I muster up enough energy to pretend like her advice is helpful. "Right," I say.

"Let's eat," she suggests. "Dinner looks incredible."

But I've lost my appetite.

APRIL

2020

• CHAPTER 23 •

I'm in a terrible mood. I'm fifteen minutes late to practice because
I couldn't overcome the overwhelming dread of getting out of bed.
The sight of Ryan's spare blue toothbrush in my bathroom made me
crumple. I don't want to face him, but calling in sick would be worse.

I stride across the lobby, past the life-sized cutout of Hallie, beyond the poster with my face hanging dustily from a forgotten spot
on the rafters, onto the floor. Ryan is chatting with another coach.
His shoulders are hunched, and he leans his chin onto his fist as
he talks; from the awkwardly self-conscious way he speaks, I'd bet
anything that he's discussing Nationals, even though I'm out of ear-
shot. Once he notices me approaching, he shifts ever so subtly. He
straightens up and clears his throat. He gives a small nod of recognition in my direction but doesn't pause to say hello. The way he
brushes me off looks so subtle to an outsider, but it stings because
it's light-years away from his attitude toward me even just a few days
ago. I can't believe I said that I was falling in love with him and was
met with silence.

Hallie's not here yet. I cruise to the water fountain just to have something to do. I lean against a low practice bar and look at my phone to kill time, but I can't fully relax. The energy in the gym is all wrong. I can feel Ryan not even halfway across the room. Most of the kid gymnasts are too young or too casual about the sport to have understood the full ramifications of Hallie's performance at Nationals—if they're even aware a competition took place, they probably think it's cool that she went at all—but the older, elite-track girls understand. So do their parents. *Especially* their parents, the ones who watch Hallie as if she's a weather vane that can evaluate the gym's worthiness and predict their own daughters' success.

Hallie slinks into the gym ten minutes later with her tracksuit hood shielding half her face and quietly settles down in an empty corner of the floor to warm up. I head over to greet her, but she barely looks at me. Ryan joins us, squatting down to Hallie's level on the floor and giving me a respectable amount of space. Luckily, Hallie is so caught up in her own morose world that I doubt she'll even notice the tension between me and him.

"Actually, I'm just gonna warm up by myself, if you don't mind," Hallie says, slipping her AirPods into her ears and shutting us out.

This isn't like her. She hasn't been her typically energetic, goofy, fun-loving self since before Nationals. This isn't good.

"Okay," I say uncertainly.

"Just let me know when you're ready for conditioning, okay?" Ryan asks.

She gives a curt nod, slides into a wide straddle, and slumps forward so her cheek rests against the floor. Sometimes, coaches will sit behind a gymnast in a straddle and press her down flatter into the floor for a better stretch; all *I* want to do is give her a hug. I hate seeing her so sad like this.

Normally, if Hallie were working on her own, Ryan and I would hang out. But I have nothing to say to him—not anything appropriate that I could say here, anyway. From the way he avoids me, I don't get the sense he's interested in speaking to me, either. So, instead, I do a little ab work until I panic that it makes me look like I'm peacocking for him. I get up and straighten up the supply closet, even though nothing is really out of place. I bounce lazily on the trampoline, turning back tuck after back tuck just because they're simple and fun. I go to the bathroom and run my hands under the faucet for three times as long as I need to, just because I feel lonely and out of place in the one spot that's always felt like home. I loathe everything about today. Nothing about this entire disastrous situation feels right—nothing.

Eventually, I wander back into the gym and perch on one of the beams to watch Hallie condition with Ryan from a safe distance. After her shaky performance at Worlds last fall, Hallie returned to the gym with a powerful vengeance. She threw herself into her practice with dynamite energy, ready to shape herself into a better athlete. But this time, returning from Nationals, her spirit couldn't be any different. Across the gym, she's supposed to be drilling sets of reps on bars: chin-ups, pull-ups, and leg lifts. She dangles loosely from the high bar and works with sloppy form. If she cared about the outcome, she'd work better. Work harder. She's throwing today's practice away.

I don't know the specifics of the ups and downs of Hallie's athletic career as well as, say, Ryan would, but I know enough: she was a supernaturally talented kid, and when her coaches said she had a real shot at an elite gymnastics career if she took training seriously, her parents made sure she had every advantage: a private coach at Summit, summers at training camps, a tutor so school would be more flexible. She always performed well enough in competitions to nab medals and level up. For Hallie, the Olympics probably never felt like a long shot. And now, to come so close and still worry you're not quite good enough? That can't be easy.

I feel for her. I wish circumstances were different—it's only human to need some time to rebound, recharge, and return with a better attitude. But time isn't on her side, and if she wastes the next few weeks or months by sulking, she's letting a lifetime of hard work and sacrifice wither and die. It sounds dramatic and unfair, but so is this sport.

Hallie trudges my way, clutching her side and breathing hard from the workout Ryan just gave her.

"Ryan says we should start with floor today," she says.

So, apparently, he won't even speak to me unless it's through her.

"Sure, let's go," I say brightly, trying to lift her mood.

"You want me to warm up tumbling first?" she asks.

That's our usual routine, but today, I want to try something different.

"Actually, let's hold off on that for now," I say. "I want to go over the video of your Nationals routine together."

She groans. "Do we have to?"

"Yes, we do, because that's how we'll know what to target over the next few weeks," I insist, using my most authoritative voice.

It's often all too easy to feel transported back in time at Summit, and to lose sight of the fact that I'm actually a decade older than Hallie, but it serves me well to remember I'm in charge sometimes.

"Let's go, I have it on my phone," I say.

"I hate this," she mutters. "You're the worst."

"You'll thank me when you win a medal on floor at the Olympics, okay?" I say.

She rolls her eyes. "Yeah, right."

We sit with our backs to the cool concrete wall and watch the routine on my phone screen. If it's cringeworthy for me to watch her stumbles and mistakes again, this time with Jasmine and Barry's sharp commentary playing in the background, I can only imagine how she feels.

"Ignore the commentary," I say, turning my phone on silent.

To a casual viewer, Hallie's routine gleams. She looks like a superstar dream. But to me, the mistakes are obvious: her leap series doesn't hit the requisite 180-degree splits; there's just a hair too much power on one tumbling pass; her poise drops as she loses energy toward the end of her routine. The second the video is over, Hallie pushes away the screen.

"I get it," she says darkly. "I suck."

"You don't suck," I retort.

She pulls her knees up to her chest and rests her chin on top, looking very, very small.

"I'm not going to sugarcoat this for you," I warn her. "You gave an amazing performance at Nationals, but you need to deliver an even stronger performance at Trials if you want your athletic career to continue. If you don't use this moment to learn from your mistakes and grow, you might as well just quit now."

That catches her attention. She stares at me, dumbstruck and horrified.

"Quit now?" Hallie repeats.

"I get that you're sad, I get that you're jealous of girls like Delia and Emma, I get that none of this went the way you hoped. But you're still here, in fighting shape, and you have the opportunity of a lifetime coming up in just a few short weeks," I remind her.

She sighs and doesn't look at me for a long time. "I'm just afraid that it won't matter what I do to prep," she admits. "Like, what if I'm not good enough? What if that's just it? Some people have what it takes, and some people don't."

"You can't think like that," I say.

"But what if it's true?" she asks. "I mean, how many millions of little kids take gymnastics classes? And then, what, only four people actually make the Olympic team every four years? Come on."

She's right, but I don't want her to think that way. A failed Olympic hopeful probably isn't the most convincing person to deliver a pep talk right now, but I'm the person she's got. I fumble for the right words; I think back to the girl I was moments before competing on floor at Olympic Trials in 2012, and what I've so desperately wished I could have said to her. What I wished I had known.

"There are no guarantees at all," I say finally. "Not in gymnastics. Not in life. But you have to give this the best goddamn shot you have, I swear to you, because it's the one chance you have."

Her lower lip trembles, and she buries her face in her knees.

"Now get up," I command.

I stand, hands on my hips. For a moment, I worry that I've gone too far. She doesn't move. But then she pushes herself off the ground to stand up. Her cheeks glisten with tears, and her chest rises and falls with emotion, but she's here. Standing. Ready to work.

MAY

2020

• CHAPTER 24 •

The calendar slips into May before I know it. Each day at Summit is tightly packed: Hallie's schedule is dominated by heavy-duty practice and punctuated by appointments with a revolving door of professionals: yoga and meditation sessions led by Sara, acupuncture and massage by a team of sports medicine doctors I found at Children's Hospital in Boston, visits from a nutritionist to map out her pre-Olympic meals. I give so many pep talks, I spend my lunch breaks Googling inspirational quotes. My nights are busy, too: I hang out at home with Sara, go out for drinks with Jasmine more regularly now, and visit Mom and Dad for dinner when they complain it's been too long since they've seen me.

I'm glad I'm mostly busy, because even with the little free time I have, it's too easy to dwell on what happened with Ryan. The sadness creeps in during idle moments when I least expect it: I'll be washing my hair in the shower when I realize how badly I miss kissing him. Or I'll be waiting by the stove for water to boil when I get the urge to text him—and I can't anymore. When I'm lying in *shavasana* at the end of yoga class, I should be relaxed. But instead, I rake over every memory I have of Ryan from February and March, trying to spot the moment I missed him betraying me. The last thing I want to do is let the weight of the breakup crush me. I have to keep moving in order to eventually move on.

When practice wraps up on Monday night, I'm heading out of the lobby when I see a missed call and a text from Jasmine. I pause in the doorway of the building to read the message.

Do you happen to be free tonight? Would love to talk to you. It's important.

I'm about to text her back when I hear a noise behind me—someone clearing his throat.

"Oh, sorry," I say, stepping outside into the warm spring night. It's finally nice enough that you can get away without a jacket, and blips of music float by as cars drive past with their windows down. "Didn't mean to block the door."

I turn and flinch. There's Ryan, awkwardly ruffling a hand through his hair.

"I didn't mean to scare you," he says.

We've worked alongside each other just fine, but that's the key word: "alongside." Not *with* each other. Outside of communicating the essential logistics of Hallie's training schedule, we've barely spoken two words to each other since returning from Nationals. I'm afraid that if I start, I won't be able to stop, and I'll blurt something embarrassing and emotional.

"It's okay," I say.

That much, at least, I can manage.

He moves past me toward the parking lot, then stops and turns.

"Everything all right?" he asks.

"Yeah, I just got a weird text, that's all," I say.

I don't tell him it's from Jasmine. From what she's told me, he and Dimitri are spending more and more time together. I don't want whatever I say to Ryan to get back to Dimitri.

"I hope she's okay," he says.

He looks concerned, but he doesn't move from his spot on the pavement. If our relationship had unfolded differently, I'd be able to tell him everything. He'd reassure me things would be okay. But now, ten feet sits between us, and it feels like ten miles. I know that neither one of us will close the distance.

"Yeah, it'll all be fine," I say.

I cross my arms and lean back against the door frame. He seems to get the message—I have nothing more to say to him. He waves good night and gets into his car. I wait until he drives away to text Jasmine back.

I'll come over now, I tell her.

• • •

I'm nervous pulling into Jasmine's driveway. We've seen each other plenty of times since Nationals, but always in public—never at home. Together, we've split oysters and sauvignon blanc at a French bistro, shared a big veggie pizza at Stonehearth in the town center, and even met up on a Saturday afternoon to get manicures together (I rarely indulge in them, but she promised it would be fun, and I have to admit, it was pretty nice). There's an unspoken agreement: we don't hang out around Dimitri. I don't know if he'll be home tonight.

I heave the gold knocker against the door and hear the pitter-patter of bare feet inside. Jasmine opens the door looking unlike I've seen her in years. Her face is free of makeup, so completely so that I can see the dark circles beneath her eyes and a blemish forming on her cheek. Her hair is unceremoniously pulled back into a low ponytail, and she's wearing saggy gray sweatpants and an oversized T-shirt. She looks both embarrassed and relieved to see me.

"I'm so glad you came," she says, pulling me into a hug. "Thank you so much."

I step cautiously inside. The house is quiet. "Of course."

"He's not home," she says, as if she can read my thoughts. "It's poker night. He'll be out for hours."

"Oh, okay."

I mean *Oh, good*, but I didn't want to sound too enthusiastic.

She leads us through the kitchen, where she pours me a glass of rosé to match the one she's already drinking, and then into the living room, where we settle onto the ivory-colored sectional beneath the wall of medals. She pulls her feet up under her. On the glass coffee table beside us, a fragrant candle burns brightly.

"I know we don't really do this," she says, gesturing at the couch between us. "Or at least, not for a long time."

A decade ago, there was nothing unusual about us spending hours in each other's bedrooms, sneaking snacks and talking about the movie stars we thought were cute. But that was before London, before she got married, before we grew apart and grew up.

"We can do this," I say. "We're friends."

She gives a small smile at the word "friends" and sips her wine. "Yeah."

"So . . ." I say, trying to prompt her.

I don't want to push her, but I know she didn't call me over here just to chitchat.

"I have news," she announces.

"Okay," I say gently.

I can't help but race through the options: she's not pregnant—she's drinking wine—but maybe it's something about Dimitri and Ryan, or her career, or worse, a health scare of some kind, or something terrible with her family.

She gives me a nervous look and takes a deep breath, as if she's psyching herself up to say whatever it is out loud.

"I'm going to leave Dimitri," she says.

Her voice is low and quiet, as if she can't quite trust that we're really alone.

"Oh my god, Jasmine," I breathe. "Wow."

She nods. "I know. I haven't told him yet. I need to get my life in order first. But . . . I've decided."

"How long have you been thinking about this?" I ask.

"Part of me has known for a long time that marrying him was the wrong decision," she explains. "It felt right at the time, but I was swept up by him, and I was so young, and I wasn't thinking straight. He had a way of intimidating me—more so back then—and when he said we should get married, I wasn't brave enough to say no. But . . ." She hesitates, then admits, "Part of the decision came from talking to you."

"Me?"

I clap a hand to my mouth. I never hid my contempt for him, but I never outright told her to leave him, either. Meddling in a marriage, encouraging a wife to leave her husband—it all feels too adult for me. I'm way in over my head.

"It started at Nationals," she recalls. "At the bar, remember? Nobody has ever dared to tell me to my face that Dimitri is . . ." She stops short and scowls. "An emotionally abusive asshole. But you did. You know what he's like, better than anybody."

"Not as a husband, though," I say.

"Even still," she says. "Once you said it, I couldn't ignore it. It gnawed at me for days afterward. Everything he had said and done over the years, I brushed it aside. But you didn't, and it made me think that I shouldn't, either."

"Of course," I say.

"Our relationship wasn't balanced, you know?" she continues.

"There was never a time when it felt like I had the upper hand, ever. It was always him. We were gymnast and coach and then husband and wife, but the dynamic between us never shifted. We were never equal partners, the way you're supposed to be."

"I wondered about that," I admit. "When I first heard you were together, I just . . . I couldn't make any sense of it."

"I didn't know how strange the relationship was," she says. "I didn't see how unhealthy it was."

"You deserve so much better than him," I say. "I mean, nobody deserves him at all, but especially not you."

I'm relieved for her, but I'm afraid for what I've set into motion. I know that, on average, it takes women seven attempts to finally leave their abusive husbands for good. I wonder where Jasmine will go; I'd let her stay with me and Sara, if she wanted to, even though the prospect of Dimitri banging on our door late at night makes me feel sick with nerves.

"I think I know that?" she says tentatively, like she isn't ready to fully commit to the idea just yet. "I mean, I look at my life, and the only common thread throughout all the different parts—gymnastics, TV, marriage—is that Dimitri has always been right there behind me, making me feel small. Everyone else cheers me on. But with him, it's always . . ."

Jasmine falters, and her expression crumples.

"Nothing is ever good enough for him. *I'm* not good enough for him," she says. Her voice gets high and tight. "He says I'm too anxious, too sensitive, too mediocre."

"Maybe you'd be less anxious if he didn't *make* you so anxious," I point out.

I don't know if she even hears me—now that she's started to spill how she really feels, she barrels on, spitting out the insults Dimitri has hurled her way over the years.

"The dinner is late," she recites. "And my cellulite is bad. I supposedly interfere with his schedule. I really don't think all that is true, but no matter what I do, the comments keep coming . . . I thought marriage was about being on each other's team, you know? But not mine."

She gingerly places her wineglass on a coaster on the coffee table and sinks back into the cushions with a hand pressed over her mouth to muffle her sobs. For a moment, her shoulders shake, and I reach across the couch to hug her. She leans into the embrace, and we stay like that for a long time. I rub her back and wonder, with a sickening feeling in my gut, what it must be like for her to prepare to leave the man she has been with for most of her childhood and the entirety of her adult life. I can't fathom it. She is so incredibly brave—she always has been. I hold her until she steadies herself, returning to the normal rise and fall of her breathing.

"I'm sorry for getting emotional," she says quietly, wiping away her tears.

"Please, there's nothing to apologize for," I insist.

She shrugs.

"You know, I'm here if you need anything—any help at all," I tell her.

"There's a lot I need to figure out," she says, sighing. "All my money is in a joint account, and I'll need a place to live, and I need to find a good divorce lawyer. That stuff, I can do on my own. But maybe, when it's time, you'll help me pack up and move out?"

"Of course," I promise.

She suddenly looks shy. "Or even if you just continue to be my friend, that's more than enough, you know. I can't tell you how grateful I am that we came back into each other's lives. Really and truly just blown-away grateful."

She gives me the most tender smile, and I feel so touched that she sees me as a person who will have her back again. It's heart-breaking to watch her reckon with the broken pieces of her relation-ship, but I'm proud that she trusts me to help her heal and move on. Before Nationals, I never would have guessed in a million years that Jasmine and I would be friends again—could be *best* friends again, the kind of presence in your life where it doesn't matter if you cry in your sweatpants or your voice cracks when you reveal the gnarled insecurities and fears that keep you up at night, because that person loves you for you and loves you for good, forever. I didn't think a friendship of that magnitude could abruptly drop dead and be revived nearly a decade later. But this time, I'm glad to be proven wrong.

• CHAPTER 25 •

A few days later, as I'm jamming my feet into sneakers and getting ready to head out of my apartment for practice, Jasmine sends me a text.

Another one, she writes, copying a link to a news story.

The text shows a preview of the NBC story, with the headline "A Seventh Gymnast Accuses Dr. Ron Kaminsky of Sexual Abuse" and a photo of Skylar Hayashi taken at a competition. I feel disgusted as I click on the story and wait for it to load. I don't know much about Skylar other than that she's one of Dimitri's gymnasts, she only competes on vault, and as far as I've seen, she can stick perfect landings in her sleep.

I sink down on the couch to read more. NBC reports that Skylar came forward on Twitter early this morning, writing, "I have some difficult news to share. Like many of my fellow athletes, I survived sexual abuse by Dr. Ron Kaminsky. For those of you who may be suffering in silence, I encourage you to seek the help you deserve. #MeToo." NBC notes that Skylar accused Kaminsky of abuse following similar allegations from Delia Cruz, Maggie Farber, Kiki McCloud, Emily Jenkins,

Bridget Sweeney, and Liora Cohen, and that Kaminsky's criminal trial is set for this winter. The American Gymnastics Federation, the sport's governing body, issued a statement this morning in support of its gymnasts' bravery, but that doesn't feel like enough to me. They must have known what was going on. Didn't they?

Reluctantly, I head outside and drive to Summit. I know Hallie is going to be shaken up today, and I wish I had a way to shield her from all of this pain. What Skylar and Hallie and all the other girls are doing is already painful enough. They've already sacrificed enough of their childhood, their freedom, their health, and their families' peace of mind in order to be where they are. It's unbelievably unfair that grown men, monsters, can step in and make everything even worse.

When I spot Hallie glumly sprawled across a crash mat, I don't have to ask if she's seen the news. I can tell.

"Skylar," she says heavily. "You saw?"

"I did," I say.

"Out of everyone, I didn't think it would be Skylar," she says, shaking her head. "I mean, out of all of us, she's, like, the normal one."

"What do you mean?" I ask.

Hallie sighs. "She has school friends. She has a boyfriend. She's really pretty and goes to Aruba with her family every winter, and she went to a Post Malone concert last month."

"This can happen to anyone," I say gently.

"Yeah, but you'd just think . . . ugh, god . . ." Hallie says, trailing off. "You'd hope that not everybody's life would be ruined, you know?"

I nod, because what else is there to say?

Ryan approaches us gingerly, squatting down so he's on Hallie's eye level. He glances at me and gives a nervous half smile as a greeting.

"Hi. How are you doing?" he asks Hallie.

She shrugs at him and looks at me. "Bummed, I guess."

"Because of Skylar's news?" he asks.

She nods. "Yeah."

"I don't want to push you too hard today," he says. "I'm sorry you're having a tough morning."

I'm surprised by how gentle he is with her. Trials are six weeks away—there isn't time to take it easy, especially not when Hallie's less of a shoo-in for the Olympic team than we all had hoped.

"Thanks," she says. "I mean, I'm okay. It's just . . . unfair."

"It is. It really is," he says. "Is there anything I can do to make things easier for you right now?"

She gives him a skeptical look.

"I'm here if you want to chat," he says warmly, sounding like a coach and a protective big brother all rolled into one. "Or if you want to smash things, I can bring in my old printer and a hammer. Or we can skip practice today and pick up tomorrow."

She laughs. "No, I'll be good. I appreciate all that, really, but no smashing necessary."

"Okay. Just let me know," he says.

"Will do."

He starts to rise, but appears to think better of it. "If it's any comfort, I have a tiny piece of news that might cheer you up," he says.

"Trials are canceled, and I can go straight to the Olympics?" Hallie guesses.

I think I know where Ryan is going with this, and I don't like it.

"Don't get your hopes up," I mutter.

"Well, I've been talking with Dimitri, and he seems really excited about training you for 2024, if you still want that," he says, offering a small smile.

There's no way Dimitri would have ever used the word "excited." Ryan's exaggerating.

Hallie beams. "Well, that's nice!"

"Just passing along a compliment," Ryan says.

"I mean, I guess a lot depends on what happens this summer, but . . . without making promises, I think I do still want to keep 2024 open as an option."

"Cool," Ryan says, high-fiving her.

"Dimitri's intense, isn't he?" Hallie says, turning to me. "I mean, he's the best, but he's intense. Right, Avery?"

"Yeah, he's intense," I say darkly.

"Avery," Ryan says quietly, as if he's warning me.

He shoots me a meaningful glare, and I hesitate.

"I'm sure whatever happens, you'll be amazing," I tell her diplomatically.

It's the truth. Not the whole truth, but there's only so much I can say without crossing an inappropriate professional line.

She squeals and drums her hands against the mat. "Eep, thanks."

Ryan smirks. "Glad I could cheer you up. Let's get to work."

• CHAPTER 26 •

I shouldn't have been surprised that Jasmine got her shit together to leave Dimitri pretty quickly. Within two weeks of her telling me she wanted to divorce him, she had already contacted a good divorce lawyer, funneled away enough money into a separate bank account in order to put down a deposit and the first month of rent on an apartment in Cambridge, and officially broke the news to Dimitri. She told me she was going to do it on a Friday night; I spent all evening holding my breath, waiting for the frantic phone call that she needed help. I stayed in and watched a movie on Netflix with my phone resting in my hand, just in case. But the call never came—just a text at nearly midnight, asking me to come by the next morning to help her pack up her things. I was relieved.

So, on Saturday morning, for the final time, I drive to see Jasmine at her house. It's a gorgeous seventy-five degrees outside, but I get a chill waiting on the front step for her to open the door. It's hard to imagine that after nearly a lifetime with Dimitri, she'll be leaving him behind for good. She opens the door in white jeans and a pink tank top and throws her arms around me into a hug.

"Thank you for coming!" she says.

She seems relieved to see me, which is, I guess, better than the alternative—miserable.

"I'm happy to," I say. "Is Dimitri home?"

She wrinkles her nose. "No. He was at least nice enough to leave me alone while I packed today."

"So, then, last night went okay?" I ask.

She heaves a sigh and starts to trudge up the stairs to her bedroom. "Yes and no. At first, he was furious. He screamed at me. He wanted to know if I was cheating, and he accused me of sabotaging Tokyo by throwing this distraction his way at a 'crucial time,'" she says, rolling her eyes and making air quotes with her fingers. "He was mad at me, but ultimately, he didn't argue with me. I mean, he can't pretend like our marriage is happy. I think we'd *both* be happier with a divorce."

"Wow."

It's a tiny, meager thing to say, but words just aren't forming for me. I can't imagine standing up to Dimitri like that. I'm impressed by her bravery.

We enter her bedroom, and I try not to think about the would-be baby's room down the hall. The crisp white bed is covered with folded piles of clothes, and there's a stack of cardboard boxes piled in one corner of the room. On the nightstand, there's a roll of packing tape and a black Sharpie alongside Jasmine's engagement ring and wedding ring, and a silver photo frame turned facedown.

"He told me that he would ruin me, that I'd never work in the sport again, that I was an 'ungrateful bitch' who was giving up the best life with the 'greatest man' I'd ever know," she recalls, spitting out each brutal word. "But, I mean, fine. Nothing worse than anything he's said before. And, most important, he let me go."

"He let you go," I repeat dumbly, trying to absorb how casually Jasmine tosses off his cruel remarks.

I remember how horrible he was to us years ago, but it's different to hear of him hurling insults like that at his wife. It's depressing.

"He said he was angry with me, but he wouldn't stop me," she says. "His exact words, I think, were that I'm now 'an adult woman who can make her own choices.'"

"As if you weren't when you got married," I say, filling in the implication.

"Barely," she admits. "I was twenty-one. I had been on a few dates with guys my own age, but he was the first person I dated. He was the only man I'd ever really known."

Someday, when a little more time has passed, Jasmine will eventually dip one toe in the dating pool, and she's going to discover an entire world out there: electrifying first dates; butterfly-inducing texts; real, equal love. Maybe heartbreak, too. But at least this time around, she'll be standing on her own two feet, away from Dimitri's shadow.

"So. Help me put everything into boxes?" she asks.

"Of course."

We work side by side, stacking her jewel-toned shift dresses, workout clothes, and thick winter sweaters into cardboard boxes, securing them shut with strips of tape, and labeling each box with thick, definitive black lines of Sharpie. I don't want to dwell on the reason she's moving out, but there's still so much I'm dying to understand. Once she leaves here, that will all be in her past—today feels like the last chance I have.

"Do you ever think you would've had a real relationship with Dimitri if he weren't our coach first?" I ask.

She looks up from the box she's taping shut with a sour, stunned expression. "No. We wouldn't have known each other."

"How did it happen? We weren't really . . . talking then," I say awkwardly.

Even after all these years, I still can't picture it.

She returns to taping the box, maybe so she doesn't have to look at me as she explains this part.

"I did a TV segment at a news station in Boston after the Olympics," she recalls. "He came with me—he was on-air, too. Instead of driving me straight back home afterward, he said he was in the mood for a drink, and so we went out to this Irish pub."

He probably didn't invite her out; he probably just told her they were going, and that was that.

"He ordered beer after beer after beer," she says. "I didn't order anything; I was just twenty, not old enough to drink legally yet, and I was too afraid of being recognized to even try. He gave me sips of his beer when he thought the bartender wouldn't notice. And then, right there at the bar, he kissed me. I didn't know what to do—it's not like I was going to say no to him."

"Were you okay with that?" I ask.

"Not at first! I was terrified," she says.

"But as time went on, it wasn't so bad?" I ask.

"You have to remember, Avery, I didn't have anything to compare it to," she says sadly. "No other boyfriends. My mom had been single practically my entire life. It's not like I had other friends my age with regular relationships, either. So . . . in time, it felt normal. That's all I knew. Plus, he was established, respected, he had money . . . When he wanted to get married, it didn't even cross my mind to say no. I thought this is just what people did."

She pushes the box to the side and starts on another one.

"We were so sheltered," I say.

"Mm-hmm," Jasmine agrees. "It's nice that Hallie has you, someone she can talk to, someone she can trust. We didn't have anyone like that at the gym growing up."

She absentmindedly fidgets with her necklace, surveying the spread of clothes still laid out on the bed.

"I guess," I say. I still find it hard to take a compliment.

An idea comes to me, half-formed and fuzzy.

"We could do something," I say, trying to pin down the exact thought. "I mean, we could help these girls. We've been through enough to know what they need."

"You mean like a support group?" Jasmine asks.

"Yeah," I say. "I mean, gymnasts know to take care of their bodies . . . but I don't know if most of them take care of their minds, too. I didn't. What if we help connect girls to mental health resources? That way, they can get the support they need, no matter what they're dealing with."

"That would be so cool!" Jasmine says.

"If anyone could do it, it would be us," I point out. "I mean, mostly you—you still have a real name in gymnastics. You could get people to care."

Jasmine leans onto the bed, too, and tilts her head.

"We could do that, couldn't we?" she says, awestruck. "We could really help."

"This could change girls' lives," I say.

Jasmine gives me a knowing look. I don't have to spell it out for her. The fact is if you train and compete as an elite gymnast, you get hit one way or another, if not multiple ways: maybe you get molested by a doctor or maybe you fail out of college because you're too depressed and disoriented to give a shit anymore. Your body breaks down: your spine aches if you stand for too long, or your ankle is held together with metal screws, or you never fully shake off the habits you picked up to starve yourself.

"I like this a lot. And god only knows I'll need something to keep my mind off . . ." She waves her hand vaguely around the bedroom. "All of this."

We finish packing up Jasmine's bedroom and bathroom quickly. The entire time, we work through ideas: what the group needs to do, how to make it happen, and even a name. We settle on the Elite Gymnastics Foundation, which would provide mental health services and support to top gymnasts.

I feel the same flood of adrenaline and desperate sense of longing I felt when I first fought for the coaching job at Summit. It's not a new feeling, either; I remember the tangled rush of emotions from my own gymnastics career. Wanting things—wanting things so badly, my heart races and the hair on my arms stands on end—makes me feel alive and full of energy. Right now, I feel like I could stick a double-twisting layout flyaway off the high bar.

I'm not naïve—I don't expect two former athletes to change the sport overnight. But if gymnastics taught me anything, it's that if you work long and hard at something, astronomical, unfathomable success can be yours.

When Jasmine tapes up the final box, we carry everything downstairs to the foyer so the movers can pick them up later this afternoon. (All those years of conditioning really did come in handy.) We sit on the cool tile floor in the front hallway, leaning against the cardboard boxes with our feet splayed out in front of us.

"Girl, thank you," Jasmine says, exhausted.

"This? This was nothing," I say truthfully.

I'm happy to help her with whatever she needs. She should know that by now.

"I don't mean just the boxes," she says. "That was clutch, but I mean everything—the boxes, your friendship, this idea. It's a *big* idea."

"It is," I admit. "And there's nobody better in the world to do it with. It has to be you and me."

Suddenly, her eyes sparkle, and she bolts upright.

"Huddle up?" she asks mischievously.

The old memories of our competition ritual, our good-luck charm, come flooding back.

"Let's huddle up," I say, beaming.

We loop our arms around each other's shoulders. I'm not sure what to say.

"We can do this," she declares.

I squeeze her tighter and join in.

"We can do this, we can do this, we can do this," we chant.

It feels like coming home.

• CHAPTER 27 •

It's tough to focus at practice on Monday. When I'm working one-on-one with Hallie—warming up, drilling tumbling, fine-tuning her techniques on floor—I feel present. But otherwise, my head is adrift. I clean crash mats and wonder about Jasmine's move out of Dimitri's house; I organize the supply closet and daydream about the Elite Gymnastics Foundation. The idea felt fresh and exciting when I first came up with it, but here, at Summit, it feels even crisper. I watch Hallie sprint down the vault runway and catapult herself through the air, and my heart surges with the desire to protect her. Brainstorming with Jasmine felt more abstract, but here, it's impossible to ignore the very real person at risk right in front of me.

That's why I have to talk to Ryan. I can't sit by and watch as he takes Hallie into a dangerous situation. Arguing with him didn't work the first time, but maybe then, I didn't give it all the effort I had—maybe I held back out of fear of damaging our relationship. That's not a concern I have anymore, obviously. If he ignores one last-ditch effort to deter him from joining Dimitri, then at least I can say I've truly tried my best. But I have to try now, before it's too late.

After Hallie has left for the night, I wait for Ryan. I sit on the stairs in the lobby that lead up to the second floor, which positions me with the best view: from here, I can see half the lobby, the door to the gym, the door to the office, the door to the bathrooms, and the exit. No matter where Ryan is, I'll be able to catch him. Sure enough, two minutes later, he rounds the corner from the office.

"Wait!" I call, springing up from my seat on the stairs.

"Hey," he says. "What's up?"

"I need to talk to you," I say.

He looks surprised. "Oh! Believe it or not, I was actually coming to find you."

"Why?" I ask.

He tilts his head. "There's something I'm hoping to get your opinion on. If you're open to talking to me about it."

This is practically the most communication we've had all day.

"What's going on?" I ask.

He's piqued my curiosity.

"You first," he says. "Let's sit in the office?"

We sit down. I gear up to tell him what's on my mind, but my thoughts get tangled—I don't know where to start. So much has changed since our breakup: my renewed friendship with Jasmine, her separation from Dimitri, what I can only imagine is Ryan drawing further into Dimitri's inner circle.

"So, you might know that Jasmine and I are close again?" I start.

"I've heard," he says, nodding.

"We've been talking a lot about how the culture of gymnastics at this level is just totally messed up, particularly for girls," I explain. "I mean, even injuries aside, there are the issues with food and body image, mental health, sexual assault . . . and we want to do something about it."

"That's great," he says.

"We're launching a support network," I continue. "We're calling it the Elite Gymnastics Foundation. We'll connect gymnasts to mental health professionals."

"Impressive," he says. "You're the perfect people to make that happen."

His compliment warms me, but I can't let it soften me toward him.

"Well, you might want to wait before you start saying nice things to me," I warn. This is my last-ditch attempt to get him to listen to me: "I need you to turn down the Powerhouse job."

He looks surprised.

"So, that's actually what I wanted to talk to you about. I went to Powerhouse on my lunch break today. It was . . . intense."

I purse my lips. "I'm sure it was."

"I've heard your stories about what it was like to have him as your coach, but seeing it firsthand felt different," he explains. "I didn't like the way he treated his gymnasts. He made fun of them for getting winded during conditioning; he called them 'sloppy,' 'lazy,' 'useless.' He came up with these absurd punishments, like running laps for falling off beam during just a regular practice."

"I don't want to say *I told you so*, but . . . Ryan, come on, what did you expect?" I ask.

"It made me have serious doubts about taking the job," he admits.

I'm shocked but hopeful.

"Well, obviously, you know what I think," I say.

"I guess I just wanted to confirm with you—do you think what I saw today was a one-off, bad day? Or is that who he really is?" he asks, squinting like he already knows the answer.

"That's just him," I say.

Ryan leans his elbows onto the desk and presses his fingers to his temples. He exhales a ragged sigh.

"Okay, then," he says, more to himself than to me, with a small shake of his head. He looks up at me with a resigned expression. "Then that's that."

There's too much at stake for me to jump to conclusions.

"That's . . . what?" I clarify.

"I can't take the job," he says.

I'm reeling at how quickly he changed his mind. I can't wait to tell Jasmine. I almost can't quite believe that I'm hearing him correctly. Despite how much I hoped Ryan would come around, deep down, I don't know if I ever really believed he would.

"It's not the dream job I thought it was—not if he's like this," he explains.

My heart races as I tell him emphatically, "It's not. You're right."

"I'll talk to the Conways and tell Dimitri I won't be working for him," he says.

That's the next step that will make all of this feel real.

"I can't promise the Conways will accept my decision, though," he warns. "If they got excited about Powerhouse, they might choose to transfer there, anyway."

That makes my stomach flip—not only would Hallie still work with Dimitri, but if she leaves, Summit may not have much use for me anymore.

"If they still want Dimitri, they can go see his gym for themselves," I suggest.

"Right," he says. He pauses and bites his lip, then continues in a soft, serious tone. "I'm sorry it took me so long to listen to you. I should have trusted your opinion of him from the start. This isn't an excuse at all, but I had a hard time wrapping my head around exactly how abusive he really was. I knew he wasn't an easy coach, but everything you've told me is so different from the way I was trained—I just didn't get it at first. And maybe I was starstruck by him. But

I understand now, and I apologize for taking so long to get here. I understand if this isn't possible, but I hope you can forgive me."

He looks somber but heartfelt. When he offers up a hopeful smile, his dimple flashes beneath his tender, dark eyes.

"Thank you for saying that," I manage. "It means a lot—it really does. Apology accepted."

He ruffles a hand through his hair in relief and shoots me a grateful look. "I'm really glad to hear that."

If Ryan and I broke up because he wouldn't listen to the truth about Dimitri's abuse, and now he's come around and apologized, where does that leave us? I can't help but wonder if the same question is on his mind. But even if we are on the same page, I'm not ready for us to move forward together again. All those months of hurt and distrust can't dissolve in an instant. A single apology doesn't reverse the pain I felt because of him.

And yet . . . I can't lie to myself: my feelings for Ryan never went away. I shoved them down so I could stomach working with him day in and day out, and I tried to distract myself with Jasmine, with Sara, with cooking elaborate meals. Even still, I crave the easy way we used to joke around; I miss his secretly romantic side; I can't forget how everything else melted away when he touched me. When we were together, he made me feel seen and understood—and I've spent enough time in the wrong relationship to grasp how special and rare that is.

I stand up to give him a hug. He holds me close to his chest. We fit together like we always did, with his chin resting on top of my head and my cheek nuzzled against his shoulder. It strikes me as unfair that love isn't like a switch you can flip on and off at will; despite the storm of conflicted emotions I have over Ryan right now, he's the one person in the world whose hug will make me feel better.

I pull back just enough to look up at him. He meets my gaze, and there's a heaviness to his expression that I can't quite read. Is it regret? Or longing? Either way, it makes my heart ache. For a split second, I feel his body tense beneath my arms, like he's about to steel himself to kiss me. But then, just as quickly as it arrived, the moment disappears.

Ryan backs away, digging in his pockets for his car keys, furtively looking over my shoulder to the door.

"I should get going," he says stiffly. "I'm glad we had this conversation."

I nod. "Same—me, too."

We exit through the lobby. He holds the door open for me.

In the parking lot, we walk in opposite directions to our cars, but I hear him call my name before I get inside.

"Yeah?" I say.

"Thank you. I mean it."

He drives away, and I watch his headlights vanish around the corner. I shouldn't miss him already, but I do.

• CHAPTER 28 •

Ryan invites me and the Conways in for a meeting before practice the next morning. Kim, Todd, and Hallie look anxious when they arrive. I'm secretly glad Ryan included me in negotiations about Hallie's career this time around.

"Thanks for coming in on such short notice," he says as we take seats in Summit's office.

"It sounded important," Todd says.

Kim frowns. "And vague."

"Is everything okay?" Hallie asks.

Her parents dart confused glances from me to Ryan. I bet they're surprised to see me here.

"Things are fine, but there's something I wanted to discuss with you," Ryan says.

He comes around the desk to lean against it, hesitating like he's trying to find the right words to explain his mistake. This can't be easy for him, even if he understands now how crucial it is to turn down Dimitri's job offer. Thick tension fills the room.

"Avery and I have been debating the pros and cons of moving to Powerhouse for months," he begins. "She knows Dimitri better than any of us. And from what she's told me about her experiences with him and having seen him interact with his gymnasts, I can't recommend that Hallie trains at his gym."

Kim and Todd look surprised; Hallie looks deflated.

"What does that mean?" Kim asks.

"You told us he was the best," Todd says, narrowing his eyes. "I mean, his track record speaks for itself."

"It does," Ryan hedges.

He looks at me for backup. I appreciate that he doesn't take the liberty of revealing uncomfortably personal details to the Conways without my permission.

"He's emotionally abusive," I confirm. "Bullying, name-calling, fits of rage . . . He lashes out when girls get sick or don't perform up to his standards. He might be responsible for a lot of gold medals, but he's not a good coach. He's toxic."

Hallie's jaw drops. "Whoa."

"You're sure about this?" Todd asks.

"Believe me, I trained with him for five years," I say. "I know what he's really like. And I didn't even get the worst of it."

"Oh my god," Kim says, appalled.

"Well, Hallie's not going there," Todd says flatly.

"Yeah, no, he sounds horrible," Hallie says. She gives me a sympathetic look.

"I'm glad you understand," I say. "Thank you for listening."

For so many months now, I've felt powerless to stop Hallie from getting hurt. To see how quickly and effectively I could change her fate is mind-blowing. I'm so grateful that the Conway family came around to my side immediately.

"It was my mistake to recommend a move to Powerhouse earlier,"

Ryan says. "I really do apologize for that, and I hope you can trust my judgment going forward."

Hallie nods in approval, but Kim and Todd exchange worried glances.

"You have to understand—we've put Hallie's career, our family's lives, in your hands," Kim says. "We've always trusted that you know what's in her best interests."

"I . . . I understand that," Ryan says, faltering.

Todd piles on. "I don't mean to be rude, but I have to ask: can we trust you?"

"*Dad*," Hallie says, slinking down in her seat and covering her face with her hands. "Don't be so dramatic."

"This is important, Hallie," Kim says.

Ryan straightens up. "You can trust me. You can trust both of us," he says, nodding at me. "I couldn't do this without Avery."

I watch Kim and Todd chew that over for a few moments. She sighs heavily.

"All right," she says. "All right."

Todd gives me a small smile. "Thanks for everything you do," he says.

"Of course, you're welcome," I say.

"So I'm going to tell Dimitri we're both staying put—you and me," Ryan says to Hallie, who appears to be recovering from the humiliation of her parents having an opinion about her well-being. "That is, if you still want to keep training."

"Yeah," she says. "The more I think about it, the more I really do want to train for 2024. No matter what happens this summer, I've worked too hard to retire at sixteen, you know?"

Ryan grins. "That's what I like to hear."

JUNE

2020

• CHAPTER 29 •

Then, bam, it's June. While the rest of the country starts to slow down for summer vacation, time speeds up for us. The Olympic Trials take place on Saturday, June 27, and the Olympics begin less than a month after that, on Friday, July 24—soon enough that I have a running countdown in my head that tracks how many days we have left. I don't need to check a calendar; the days tick down automatically for me. It's twenty-five, then twenty-two, and now we're in the teens. This is what I've been preparing for since last October, and what Hallie has been looking forward to for quite literally her entire life.

The Olympics are just close enough now that regular people are getting excited. On one lunch break, Hallie squeezes in a phone interview with Kiss 108, the local Top 40 radio station; on another, she takes a call from a *People* reporter. A whole crew from the *Boston Globe* arrived during practice one afternoon to take pictures and interview her for a front-page story. Ryan shooed the journalist and photographer away after forty-five minutes, insisting that Hallie's energy was best spent on training at the moment. As the reporters packed up their camera equipment, her face fell just a little bit. I don't blame her.

Competitive gymnastics isn't like football or baseball in the sense that the general public will tune in for a big game or even be aware when the sport is in season—it gets one blip of fandom every four years. So, even though throwing a new responsibility on top of preparing Hallie for the Olympics seems like pure lunacy right now, Jasmine insists that we have to capitalize on this moment in order to gain media attention. She wants to launch the Elite Gymnastics Foundation publicly *now*, before the Olympics kick off, while elite gymnastics is having its moment in the sun. If we wait until after Tokyo, the public's interest in whatever we have to say may be lost. People will only see Hallie and her Olympic cohort as buff Miss America stand-ins—shiny, patriotic trophies—not flesh-and-blood young women battling real systemic issues. And then, well before the first crisp day of fall, gymnastics will have fallen off most people's radars.

So, while Hallie has been slipping out of the gym for interviews and heading home early to rest up as much as possible, I've been working alongside Jasmine to transform the foundation from a hazy idea into a solid reality. I text and email as much as I can during the day, and on nights and weekends we hole up in my living room to get work done. Maybe it's because we trained alongside each other for years, but we're a strong team now, too. Within a week, we've contacted a slew of former gymnasts to get them on board with publicly supporting this initiative and to collect donations. We've used that money to hire a web designer to create a site. And most important, we've started to assemble a team of mental health professionals, including therapists who have worked with athletes and sexual assault support group leaders. They'll provide services either in person or remotely, depending on where the gymnasts live. We've gotten them to agree to working pro bono up front, and our goal is to fund-raise to pay for their services so there will never be any question if a gymnast can afford to access help.

Jasmine hooked us up with a five-minute spot on NBC's morning news show for Monday, June 8, so we'll be the first story breaking after the weekend. The goal is to announce the launch of the Elite Gymnastics Foundation, spread awareness for the sport's desperate need for reform, and, of course, raise money. NBC is the obvious choice, given Jasmine's connections; she's a familiar face, so their viewers will be primed to hear what she has to say.

My alarm blares at five thirty on Monday morning. As I shower, I try not to dwell on how nervous I am. It's been eight years since I've spoken to a reporter or been on TV. Doing press used to feel exciting—I liked when my competitions were broadcast live for viewers at home, and any questions thrown my way were easy to answer: How hard had I been training lately? Was I happy about my big win? Were the London Olympics on my radar? This is entirely different. I'm publicly calling out the failures of the sport that gave me everything.

Jasmine dictated specific instructions on everything from what to wear to how to speak. She says I need to wear a simple, professional, solid-colored top or dress—no prints, because they look distracting on camera, and no green, because the green screen will turn me into a floating head. I own nothing remotely right, so I've borrowed a coral-red shift dress from her closet that I can just barely squeeze into. Jasmine promises the camera will only film me from the waist up. I've never mastered the ability to blow-dry my hair, but I do my best attempt at' it while running through the sound bites I've practiced. Jasmine will do most of the talking on-air, but I can't be entirely mute. It's funny, I was never afraid to hurtle myself into the air and perform impossible-looking stunts, but saying a few lines to a camera crew strikes me as terribly intimidating.

I step into my most professional-looking pumps to give myself a confidence boost, pour coffee into a thermos, and drive to NBC's studio. Jasmine meets me in the lobby. She's in a bright blue wrap

dress with fluttery cap sleeves that show off her toned arms, re-
minding viewers of her athletic past. She chose these outfits on
purpose: red and blue to remind everyone that even if we criticize
the American Gymnastics Federation, we're still wholly in support
of Team USA.

"You ready?" she asks as the security guard at the front desk
scans my driver's license and double-checks my name against his
computer.

"I barely slept last night," I admit.

She looks closely at me and scrunches her nose. "The makeup
artist can cover up your dark circles—no worries."

Jasmine leads us to the fourth floor, where the receptionist
greets her by name, and then through a maze of hallways until we're
in the greenroom.

"Every guest on the show waits here to go on," she explains.

The room isn't actually green—it's white with gray carpeting,
brown furniture, and multiple TVs tuned in to the show. A handful
of people sit around in suits and dresses like ours; they have faces
that seem vaguely familiar, or maybe it's just that everyone on TV
looks more or less the same: conventionally attractive but airbrushed
in an eerily bland way.

A twenty-something producer in a headset comes flying toward us.

"Hiiii, you're in hair first," she says to Jasmine, then glances
down at her clipboard. "And you, Avery? You're in makeup."

"Oh, I actually did both at home," I say.

Jasmine shakes her head. "Everyone gets touch-ups," she insists.

The producer drops me off in a room just big enough to contain
a single chair in front of a mirror decked out in lights and a table
full of beauty products. A makeup artist dabs concealer under my
eyes, as Jasmine promised, and slicks on hot pink lip gloss before I

can protest that I don't really feel like myself in so much makeup. Next, the producer brings me to the room next door, where a hairstylist finishes the transformation with a curling iron and an intense blast of hair spray. When she's done, I look like . . . well, I look just as polished and professional as Jasmine always does. With a pang, I realize that if my life had turned out differently, none of this would faze me. I wouldn't be bare-skinned in a ponytail at Summit; I would be contoured and curled at NBC. This would be my reality.

I find Jasmine back in the greenroom. On TV, the meteorologist talks about the seventy-five-degree days coming this week. Jasmine stares vacantly in the direction of the TV, but she's not focused on the screen. Her knee bounces up and down. I understand why she's nervous—my heart is pounding, too—but I'm surprised the pressure is getting to her, of all people.

"You okay?" I ask gently.

She turns toward me, and her jittery knee slows to a stop. "Yeah," she says. "Yeah, I will be."

"You sure?" I ask.

"I'll be fine once I'm out there, trust me," she says. "It's just . . . this is bigger than anything I've ever done before."

"You've been on this same channel, what, a hundred times? A thousand times," I remind her.

"Commenting on *other* people," she says. "This time, the spotlight's on us."

I grab her hand, and she gives mine a squeeze.

Soon, the producer breezes back into the greenroom. "Come with me," she says to us, jerking her head. "Commercial break just hit."

We follow her down a hallway and around a corner into a dark studio space jumbled with lighting equipment, rubber cables, and, further back, a glossy, L-shaped desk with two open seats for us diagonal from Cynthia King, the news anchor. Another producer clips tiny microphones to the necklines of our dresses. If I hadn't watched Jasmine do it first, I would have been bewildered: Jasmine expertly threads the thin cable over her shoulder, hiding it under her hair, and turns to let the producer clip the mic's battery pack to her bra underneath her dress. I follow her lead, flinching at the feel of his hands. He zips my dress up again and gives the first producer a thumbs-up. We're ready.

"Thirty seconds," she barks. "Go."

I follow Jasmine onstage, letting her take the seat closest to Cynthia, who greets her warmly. In contrast to the dimly lit backstage, the lighting here is bright and white and blinding. Cynthia, clad in a pearly pink dress with a neat bob and gravity-defying eyelashes, looks like a *Real Housewives* star in the sense that she could just as easily be thirty-five or fifty. She says hello and asks how I am, but I'm too nervous to squeak out anything more than a hello. She and Jasmine make pleasant small talk, which seems frankly insane to me with just seconds to go before we're on live television, but Jasmine looks unfussed. I'm relieved that she's settling into her element.

"The producer says it's Jasmine Floyd, not Floyd-Federov now, right?" Cynthia confirms.

"Floyd's perfect, thanks," Jasmine says.

Cynthia cocks her head like she's connecting the dots. "You're leaving your husband the coach, and speaking out about abuse in the sport?" she asks slowly.

Jasmine freezes next to me. "Well, um . . ."

"Five, four," the cameraman calls out.

Cynthia raises an eyebrow, shuffles her papers, and clears her throat.

The cameraman falls silent, flashing three fingers, then two fingers, then pointing straight at us.

"Welcome back. The Olympics are just around the corner, but before you get too excited about watching the gymnastics, you might want to hear what two former athletes are saying about the sport," Cynthia begins. Her voice is strong and smooth like honey. "Olympic gymnast Jasmine Floyd and her former teammate Avery Abrams claim that the culture of competitive gymnastics puts young athletes at risk, and they're launching a new organization called the Elite Gymnastics Foundation to offer these gymnasts what they believe is much-needed support. Ladies, tell us more."

"Thanks for having us, Cynthia. It's always great to be here," Jasmine says weakly.

We've practiced that Jasmine will deliver the announcement of the foundation, but now she seems shaken. I glance at her, unsure if I should take over her lines. On live television, every second feels like it stretches out for ten minutes. But finally, thankfully, she collects herself and launches into the speech we wrote together.

"As many people unfortunately saw with the recent sexual abuse claims against Dr. Ron Kaminsky, gymnasts aren't always safe. And as two former elite gymnasts ourselves, we know there are other issues out there that threaten the athletes' well-being. Not every gymnast out there is struggling, but there are real challenges in this sport. I'm talking about eating disorders, depression, anxiety, emotionally abusive coaches, and yes, sexual abuse. There's a serious lack of regulation from the sport's governing body—the American Gymnastics Federation—and given our personal experiences, we know how challenging it can be to advocate for yourself to get the help and resources you need in order to thrive. That's why we're launching the Elite Gymnastics Foundation, an organization that offers mental health support for elite gymnasts."

"That's very admirable," Cynthia says. "We've heard a lot about the allegations against Dr. Kaminsky—who, by the way, is set to face trial early next year."

A chill runs through me. Delia, Skylar, and the other girls should have justice.

"While I'm saddened to hear of the mental health issues that plague top gymnasts, I'm also not exactly surprised," Cynthia continues. "It seems like a particularly high-pressure sport—and who is looking out for these girls?"

"The sport's toxic culture is a real problem," I agree. "That's why our first step was to create what we're calling a wellness network for elite gymnasts. We've assembled an excellent team of professionals, including therapists and sexual assault educators, to provide top-notch care for these athletes. Gymnastics is a mind-body sport—gymnasts, mostly adolescents, train hours a day to keep their bodies strong, but it's equally important for them to take care of their mental health, too."

I pivot to the sales pitch. "This is important work, but it's not easy, so we are raising money on EliteGymnasticsFoundation.com to fund these initiatives."

I'm surprised at the steady way my words flow. It feels as if the lights and cameras and unnatural stage makeup fade away, and all I need to do is explain why I'm here.

"Avery, for you, this is personal, isn't it?" Cynthia asks.

I knew this question was coming. It was part of our pitch to the network—a good sob story will catch people's attention more than anything else we could say. Neither of us is ready to talk publicly about Dimitri yet, but there's still plenty I can say.

"It is," I confirm. "I suffered a knee injury during the Olympic Trials in 2012. Physically, I was able to bounce back after a few months, but I was depressed. I didn't seek out help, but I should have. This organization would ensure that nobody feels alone. Gymnastics is a solo sport, but that doesn't mean you're on your own."

Jasmine and I wrote five different versions of that line before we hit on the right one, and maybe the familiarity of it stirs something in her.

"Nobody has to be alone," she adds. Under the desk, she grips my hand. "I'm grateful to be partnering with my friend Avery here."

"That's a great message. Now, Avery, you're hopefully heading to the Olympics in Tokyo later this summer, isn't that right?" Cynthia asks.

"I'm coaching a young gymnast named Hallie Conway, and I have to tell you, she is such a superstar," I say. "I can't wait for you to see her compete at the Olympic Trials."

"I wouldn't miss it," Cynthia says. She turns away from us to face a different camera, and wraps up the segment. "This has been Jasmine Floyd and Avery Abrams, cofounders of the Elite Gymnastics Foundation. Back to you, Michael."

The network cuts to a commercial break, and the producer shuffles us quickly offstage, unclipping our mics and sending us back to the greenroom.

"I'm shaking," Jasmine whispers.

"You were great," I reassure her.

"I lost it," she says. "Her comment before we went on threw me off. *You* were amazing."

"I don't think we sounded so bad," I admit.

"Next time, I'll be better," she insists.

"Next time?" I ask.

She beams. "Girl, this is just the beginning."

In the greenroom, I dig my phone out of my purse. I'm caught off guard by a text from Ryan. After the breakup, our endless stream of texts came to a sudden halt; now we rarely text, and only about work.

I caught you on TV, he wrote. *Very impressive. Just wanted to say congrats—what you and Jasmine are doing is so cool.*

I had mentioned the segment to him, but I didn't think he'd bother watching it. It's one thing for him to pay lip service to our cause, but this shows he actually cares. I'm happy to hear from him. I slip my phone back into my purse without mentioning it to Jasmine.

• • •

I drive directly from NBC to the gym, where I change out of Jasmine's dress into an old pair of Soffe shorts and a faded T-shirt with Summit's logo splashed across the chest. I pull my hair back into a ponytail but don't bother scrubbing the gloss off my lips.

"*Whoa,*" Hallie says when she sees me on the floor. "Why do you look so fancy?"

I hesitate to explain where I was earlier that morning. I haven't told her anything at all about the Elite Gymnastics Foundation because it felt too embarrassingly personal. But now that she's asking, I don't have a choice.

"You probably haven't heard about what I'm up to," I confirm.

I doubt she watches cable news—and anyway, she's been in the gym all day. But I also wouldn't be surprised if this was lighting up her Twitter feed.

"Jasmine—Jasmine Floyd—and I went on NBC this morning to announce the launch of our new organization that helps out top gymnasts," I explain. "You know how I connected you to Sara and got you into yoga? Think of that, plus connecting people to therapists and other experts who can help gymnasts stay healthy."

She squeals a little. "Avery!"

"What?" I laugh nervously.

"I'm so proud of you," she says.

It's a funny thing for her to say—if anything, *I'm* proud of *her.* That's how this relationship dynamic is supposed to go. But, hey, Jasmine and I created the foundation for the sole purpose of making life healthier and happier for girls like Hallie. If she's on board with the idea, I'm elated.

Hallie sashays across the gym and finds Ryan filling up his water bottle.

"Ryan, Ryan, Ryan!" she calls.

He turns to look over his shoulder.

"Hallie, Hallie, Hallie, what's up?" he mimics.

She leaps—and I mean literally executes a perfect, 180-degree split leap—in front of him. I wish I was her age and had that much energy on a Monday morning, or ever at all.

"Did you hear what Avery's up to? It's super cool! And very fancy. See how fancy she looks?" she says.

He laughs. "I heard. Pretty amazing, huh?"

"Guys, stop it," I say bashfully. "Don't we have work to do today? There are just—"

"Eighteen days left," Hallie groans. "I know, I know."

• • •

Maybe it's because the Olympics are drawing closer, or maybe it's because of Jasmine's near celebrity status, but either way, the response to the NBC segment is thrilling. The story gets picked up by other outlets, including ESPN, *Sports Illustrated*, the *Boston Globe*, *Cosmo*, and BuzzFeed. Jasmine and I are invited on GymCastic, the gymternet's most revered gymnastics-themed podcast, and a wave of current and former elite gymnasts urge their Instagram followers to donate to the foundation. Within three days, we raise nearly ten thousand dollars. It's far more money than I could have hoped for.

We were disappointed that AGF never reached out to us directly, though when prodded by *Cosmo*, the organization apparently "declined to comment." Predictably, the worst reaction came from Dimitri. He called Jasmine five times, and when she refused to pick up, he left a voicemail threatening that we better not say a word about him. She saved the voicemail—just in case we ever need it.

It's nerve-wracking but exciting to have the foundation getting this much attention so early on. It feels like yet another good omen: now that I've encouraged Ryan to turn down Dimitri's offer and work alongside Jasmine to make a real difference in this sport, I feel more capable and confident than I have in a long time. People say good things come in threes. And this summer, there's only one goal left to tackle. It's a big one. But I'm ready.

• CHAPTER 30 •

By Friday, of course, the countdown has dropped to just fifteen days. In two weeks' time, Hallie will be about to compete at Trials; in six weeks, she could potentially be marching with the rest of the United States Olympic fleet at the opening ceremony in Tokyo. This afternoon, though, the only place Hallie is going is back and forth across the length of the beam. Ryan and I watch patiently as she drills her tumbling pass—a back handspring, whip back, back layout step-out—over and over. The goal is for her to smoothly connect each move into the next and finish the series with a satisfying *thwack* of a clean landing, no wobbles whatsoever.

As a rap song blares from the speaker, Hallie stands with her toes a millimeter from the edge of the beam and stretches her arms out in front of her, centering herself. Her chest rises and falls as she takes a deep breath. Then, in one sleek, catlike motion, she swings her arms behind her and lunges backward into the tumbling pass. The back handspring is solid, but she's probably been doing that since she was nine years old. What's trickier is the whip back, a fast-moving, arched flip in which her hands float a foot above the beam, and safely transitioning from that to a soaring back layout, which requires rotating high in the air with her body and legs extended to their fullest length. She lands with one heel just inches from the opposite end of the beam, and teeters ever so slightly to catch her balance. It's not good enough, and she knows it.

"Again," Ryan calls.

She looks a little frustrated with herself, but she nods and scurries back to the other end of the beam to start over.

Ryan turns to me.

"So, uh, I've been thinking about ways to support the foundation you and Jasmine are launching," Ryan says, looking down at his feet.

"What?" I ask, surprised.

"Yeah. It's an amazing cause and I want to do my part," he says, shrugging.

"Oh, uh, wow. Thank you," I say.

"I hope this isn't overstepping anything, but I called a few places around town to see who might be willing to host a fund-raiser," he says.

"You did *what*?" I blurt.

He speeds up nervously. "Jade Castle agreed that if we wanted to partner with them for a fund-raiser, one hundred percent of the proceeds for drinks ordered there would go directly to the Elite Gymnastics Foundation, as long as we tip the bartenders."

He looks directly at me now, and I'm almost too stunned to speak.

"Ryan, oh my god," I say.

He winces. "Or if you hate the idea, I don't have to do anything at all. I haven't agreed to anything with Jade Castle yet—I just called to ask."

"No, are you kidding me? That's so ridiculously nice of you, really," I say.

I can't believe he really did this. It's not out of character, exactly—I know he's a thoughtful person, and I'm sure his friends would have no problem drinking enough to raise a sizable chunk of money—but I'm blown away that he would do all this for me.

Hallie flips across the beam and sticks the landing. She leans dramatically into a bow.

"Good one," Ryan calls. "Again."

He drops his voice and turns to me. "I wanted to find a way to show you how sorry I am for almost taking the Powerhouse job. I made a huge mistake by not listening to you from the moment you told me what Dimitri's really like, and I hate that I upset you by taking so long to come around. I know this isn't enough, but I hope it's a step toward showing you that I really do care about keeping Hallie and the other girls safe and happy."

His apology that night at Summit was one thing, but this is on another level entirely. This shows me that he's listening and learning, and isn't that all anyone can ask for? He made a mistake and isn't just owning it—he's fixing it. I wish we were somewhere else so I could give him a hug.

"Thank you," I say, squeezing his arm. "I really appreciate that. This fund-raiser sounds really helpful."

He exhales, relieved. "Jade Castle had a big birthday party reservation cancel, so they actually have space for us at seven o'clock tomorrow night," he offers. "Unless that's too soon, in which case, we can figure something else out."

My stomach drops, and it's not just because Jade Castle was the scene of my disastrous first Tinder date after moving back to Greenwood.

"Oh! I would, but I actually have dinner plans tomorrow," I lie.

I'm not ready to spend time with Ryan outside of work. If I'm honest with myself, I know I'm not fully over him yet. That's why we've barely spoken about anything except for Hallie since our breakup, and that's why I can't bring myself to open Tinder again, even though the app sends plenty of reminders that people nearby have swiped right on me.

"Oh, no worries, we can schedule this for another time," he says, scratching his ear and blushing.

"Uh, no, go for it. I don't have to be there—what matters is that people are raising money," I say awkwardly. "And maybe I could swing by later."

"Are you sure?" Ryan asks.

I hesitate. "Have an amazing time."

Hallie finishes beam and heads to vault next. I'm not her coach for either event, so even though I watch from the sidelines and offer encouragement, there's unfortunately enough space for my mind to wander.

I'm touched that Ryan would organize a fund-raiser. I'd worried that I'd trusted him too easily, and felt duped that I'd fallen for a guy who would shove the worst moments of my life under the rug so that he could climb the career ladder. In the aftermath of the breakup, it was easy to boil everything down to simple black and white: he was wrong, he was a bad guy, and so we were over.

But life isn't so black and white. People are complicated, and they can grow. I certainly have. I can't deny that between Ryan turning down Dimitri's job offer and him organizing this fund-raiser, I'm starting to see him in a better light. He wants to learn and make amends. He's open to changing his mind, even when it comes at a personal cost. Despite the frost between us ever since Nationals, it wouldn't be fair to ignore that he's taken significant strides to earn my approval again. The next step might be forgiveness.

I sit on the edge of the blue floor and pick at a piece of fuzz coming loose from the fabric. Sixty feet away, Ryan leans over the vault table, explaining something I can't quite hear to Hallie. He talks with his hands, and she nods along. Hallie's attention is tightly fixated on what he's saying; I can tell from the serious way she stands with her hands on her hips, biting her lip. She trusts him, doesn't she? Maybe I should trust him, too.

• • •

SOS, what are you doing tomorrow night? I text Sara on my lunch break.

I'm eating last night's leftover tilapia and zucchini straight from the Tupperware in my car. Ryan's invitation, however casual, made me too jittery to eat within the same building as him.

I have a friend's housewarming party at 8, wanna come? she texts back.

Ryan invited me to drink with his friends tomorrow night at Jade Castle, I write. *It's a fund-raiser for EGF.*

Her response pops up before I can continue typing: *???*

I lied and said I had plans with you. I don't wanna go alone. But I do think I might want to go. Please come with me? I text.

It sounds so pitiful laid out like that, but I know Sara won't judge me.

How's this: I'll come with you for a bit, then head out to the party once you find your footing? she asks. *Slash you have two drinks and feel fine.*

That second one sounds about right, I write. *Thank you. Love you.*

I finish the fish and text Jasmine to join us. She knows, of course, that Ryan turned down Dimitri's job offer, but I think she's still skeptical of him—or anyone who would willingly associate with her ex, to be honest. I can't blame her. I care about her opinion, and I'd feel less guilty over my storm of conflicting emotions toward

Ryan if I had her approval of him. I want her take on this situation. I'm strangely relieved when she texts back that Ryan's fund-raiser sounds amazing. She says she wants to go.

• • •

On Saturday night, I arrive at Jade Castle a little after eight with Sara and Jasmine by my side. The restaurant's lounge is dimly lit and crowded, filled with vaguely familiar faces I've seen around town. I spot Ryan standing with a cluster of people by the window, holding a beer and in the midst of conversation with some guys. He's in a pair of dark jeans and a light blue button-down shirt with the sleeves rolled up. I don't recognize most of the people he's with, but I spot his friend Goose with his girlfriend, Melissa.

I catch Ryan's eye.

"Hey! You made it!" he says, choking down beer, looking surprised to see me here.

He winds his way through the crowd and tentatively gives me a one-armed hug.

"We finished dinner and figured why not come by?" I say.

It's close enough to the truth. Jasmine brought over a bottle of wine for the three of us to share while Sara and I dabbed on makeup and put on sundresses. I felt more comfortable coming here tonight with a little liquid courage in my system.

"Oh, wow, nice," he says. "Can I get you a drink?"

"We can get our own," Jasmine says, cutting in.

"All for a good cause anyway, right?" Sara says.

Ryan gestures to the bar. "Of course."

Sara orders a vodka soda, and I ask for the same. Jasmine squints at the array of spirits lining the back shelf of the bar and sighs at the row of draft beers.

"I'll have a prosecco," she says.

The bartender gives her a weary look.

"We don't have that here," he says, without bothering to check.

"Jasmine, this isn't the fanciest place," I say quietly, nudging her.

She grimaces. "Another vodka soda, sure." Under her breath, she mutters, "Great bar."

We take the drinks over to the edge of Ryan's crew.

"These are Ryan's friends?" Jasmine asks, looking curiously at the group.

"Yeah, anyone you recognize?" I ask.

The gymnastics world is tiny—I wouldn't be surprised if she had crossed paths with anyone here.

"No, I'm just . . . interested, I guess. These are guys our own age," she comments.

"Don't get too excited," Sara warns.

I feel uneasy—not sure what to say to Ryan, too awkward to say hi to Goose or Melissa, and too nervous to strike up a conversation with any of his other friends. Maybe I shouldn't have come. But then, the high-pitched *ding* of a knife against glass cuts through the noise of the bar.

"Can I have everybody's attention for a minute, please?" Ryan asks.

He steps on a chair so he's high above the crowd. Conversations fade out, and people turn to face him.

"I wanted to thank you all for coming out tonight. As I've mentioned, all proceeds from the drinks go to a really great organization called the Elite Gymnastics Foundation, which supports elite gymnasts like the very talented athlete I'm hopefully taking to Tokyo this summer," he says.

"Whoop, whoop!" Goose calls out.

Ryan raises his glass. "So please, drink up, and don't worry about how you'll feel tomorrow morning. Okay? And while I have your attention, the *founders* of the foundation are here—let's give a round of applause to Avery Abrams and Jasmine Floyd."

He raises his drink in a toast, and everyone else follows suit.

It's a strange sensation, having people clap for me. It's happened before, of course, at plenty of competitions, but that was different. Back then, crowds cheered me on because of what I had been trained to do. Tonight, they're cheering me on for what I'm doing for others. This is new for me, but I like it.

Ryan hops down off of the chair and joins us.

"Hey there. Not a bad turnout, right?" he says.

"Pretty good," I say. "I really appreciate the effort."

"It's pretty cool that you did this," Jasmine says. She purses her lips. "Especially now that you've chosen to hang around better company."

He raises his hands in defense. "I know, I'm glad I turned down the job," he says. "You're going to Tokyo, right?"

"Yep. You haven't booked your flight yet?" she asks.

"Nah. It doesn't really make sense to book it until we know for sure if Hallie is going or not," he explains.

I'm in the same boat.

"Well, I'll be watching from home," Sara says.

"As long as you're watching NBC, that's fine by me," Jasmine says. "Gotta keep those ratings up."

"I'm jealous. Visiting Japan sounds amazing," Sara says.

"Are you planning to stick around after the Games?" I ask Ryan.

Ryan runs a hand through his hair. "Yeah, my plan is to travel around Asia."

"Ooh, fun," Sara says. "Where? I've always wanted to visit Thailand. Amazing food, gorgeous water, not crazy expensive compared to other destinations, you know?"

"Well, since I'll be starting off in Tokyo, it makes sense to explore more of Japan first," he says. "But it all really depends on what happens with Trials."

"Fingers crossed," Sara says.

Later, after Ryan moves on to chat with other people, we get another round of drinks. When they're finished, Sara says she has to get going to her friend's housewarming party. She invites Jasmine and me along. Jasmine, sorely in need of a real girls' night out, gladly accepts, and so I do, too. I don't want to put a damper on her night. We all say goodbye and thank Ryan for throwing the fund-raiser. Sara and Jasmine move ahead while I hang back.

"One sec, guys, I'll meet you outside," I tell Jasmine and Sara. Then, to Ryan, I add, "I just wanted to say thank you again for doing all of this. It really means so much to me that you care enough to bring your friends out for our cause."

"It's the least I could do, really," he says sheepishly.

"How much money do you think you've raised so far?" I ask.

He scans the room. "Let's say twenty people, an average of two drinks each, maybe . . ." He pauses to do the mental math. "Three hundred and fifty–ish?"

That pays for two therapy sessions, maybe three, tops. But I'm still grateful.

"That's awesome," I say—and I mean it.

"I'm really glad you came," he says. "I'd completely understand if you didn't want to, but it's cool that you got a chance to see this."

The emotions I've been feeling all day crest. All at once, I'm grateful and bittersweet and nostalgic for what we had together. I have to leave; I know if I stay any longer, I'll only be keeping myself in a situation primed to make me miss him.

"I think the Uber's coming," I say. "Gotta go—have a great night."

Before I can overthink it, I throw my arms around him in a quick hug. The wave of comfort I get from my body flush against his feels like a shock. It's overwhelming.

"Good night!" he calls as I hurry toward the door.

I join Sara and Jasmine outside, and soon we're on our way to the housewarming party. It's a get-together at a condo in Coolidge Corner in Brookline with a sliding glass door that opens the terrace up to a pretty, starry night. Sara introduces me proudly to her friends, and they all go slack-jawed when they hear I'm possibly on my way to the Olympics. A lanky guy in a chambray button-down brings me plastic cups of beer—apparently, the real glasses haven't even been unpacked yet—and shyly asks for my phone number at the end of the night. He's so not my type that the request catches me off guard, and even though the prospect of dating someone new still feels too strange right now, I give it to him. Maybe what I need is a distraction that will take my mind off Ryan for good.

It's only hours later, when I wake in the middle of the night to get a glass of water to soothe my parched mouth, that I see the text from Ryan. I must have missed it while I was sleeping. I rub at my eyes, not sure if I'm awake enough to read the message properly. But I read it three times in a row, and it seems solid. I can't believe it's real.

It was really great to see you tonight! The fund-raiser was a huge success. We raised $410. But I know that's not enough to make the kind of difference this cause deserves, and so I'm also donating the money I would've spent on my travels after the Olympics. Total, it'll be nearly $3,000. I know you're probably going to protest, but I've been thinking about this for days. I saved up the money for something important, and there's nothing more important than this.

• CHAPTER 31 •

Team Hallie Conway flies to the Olympic Trials in St. Louis on separate flights: Hallie and her parents in the morning, Ryan in the afternoon, and me and Sara on an evening flight so she didn't have to call out of work. Hallie insisted that Sara fly halfway across the country with us because she wanted a private yoga session before the big day. Paying for Sara's round-trip flight, hotel room, and meals probably costs the Conway family nearly two thousand bucks, but they don't seem to flinch. They've already sunk hundreds of thousands of dollars into this dream so far—it's not worth risking everything and winging it the morning of Olympic Trials by insisting that Hallie practice yoga on her own.

Sara and I are sharing a hotel room, so at seven thirty in the morning we walk together from our room to Hallie's, where we pick her up and continue on to the hotel's fitness center. Sara called ahead and confirmed that the fitness center's yoga studio would be available for them to use. She has a yoga mat strapped to her back and totes a bag full of supplies: a foam block, a speaker, a bottle of lavender essential oil. Hallie emerges from her hotel room in leggings and a stretchy tank top; she'll get ready and put on an actual leotard for Trials after yoga and a light breakfast.

"Morning," I say. "Ready for the big day?"

"Ha, no, but it's here," she says honestly.

Sara nudges her down the hall toward the elevator. "*Oh*-kay, let's go chill out for an hour and find a more positive attitude."

The yoga studio is located at the back of the fitness center, through a door along the far wall of the gym. As we walk past a row of treadmills and ellipticals, through a crew of sweaty dudes working out on weight machines, we cross paths with Ryan, who's bench-pressing weights. He grunts, sets the bar back on the holder, and removes one headphone.

"Hey," he breathes. "Morning."

"Morning," we chime.

"We won't distract you from your workout," Sara says.

Sara leads Hallie into the yoga studio and closes the door. I've never joined one of their sessions, and I wouldn't dare interrupt now. It's good for Hallie to have some solo time with Sara to focus on relaxing for the day ahead.

"So, I, uh, I'm not sure I ever properly thanked you for your text," I say to Ryan.

He removes his other headphone and sits up, grinning. "Yeah?"

"It's an absurdly extravagant donation," I point out. "Just, like, way above and beyond. You know that, right?"

He shrugs. "Eh."

"I just want to make sure you're really sure you want to do this," I say.

"Of course I'm sure," he says seriously.

I can't help it—I cover my face with my hands. "Okay!" I say brightly. "I'm gonna take your money and run, I guess, before you change your mind."

He laughs. "I'm not going to change my mind."

"When I told Jasmine, you know what she said?" I ask.

"What?" he asks.

"That the donation is enough for her to forgive you for almost working with Dimitri," I say.

His mouth twitches nervously. "Well, that's good. And . . . you?"

"It's one thing to apologize, but it's another thing to make a situation right again. And you did both," I explain. "So, yeah, I forgive you."

"Really?" he asks, almost like he can't believe what he's hearing.

"Yeah, we're cool," I say. "Obviously, I know things have been kind of . . . weird? Between us? For a while now. But I miss how easily we used to get along, and I'd like to go back to that."

I can feel my heart pounding as I tell him how I really feel; vulnerability is fucking scary. But then, a smile spreads across his face, and I'm flooded with relief. It's the exact same exhilarating sensation you get when you're flying upside down above the high bar on a release move and catch it solidly. It's a dangerous thrill, but then you know you're safe.

"Avery, you have no idea how much I feel the same way," he says. He looks down apologetically at his sweat-drenched T-shirt. "I'd want to hug you right now, but . . ."

"Yeah, no, I'm good without it," I tease.

"Your loss. I smell . . ." He sniffs his shirt and makes a sour face. ". . . *amazing* right now."

"Please just promise to shower before I have to spend the rest of the day with you today, okay?" I ask.

"I promise," he says earnestly.

"Now, back to work. Don't slack on those biceps, okay?" I joke.

He flexes one arm, and the muscle swells. I resist my instinct to look impressed, and instead say goodbye and walk out of the gym with my head held high.

• • •

I get some coffee, fruit, and yogurt at a café near the hotel, and then return to my hotel room to make myself look a little more presentable for the day. I know the cameras will catch at least a few glimpses of me, and some concealer and mascara will go a long way. I'm blending the makeup under my eyes when I see my phone light up with an incoming text. My stomach drops when I catch the name on the screen—it's Tyler. We haven't spoken once since I left LA.

Hey. I just wanted to say that I heard you're doing really well now, coaching and launching that organization. It all sounds really impressive. Congratulations!

I laugh, dumbfounded. I can't believe he reached out at all, especially to praise my accomplishments. He never expected me to make anything of myself again; he didn't think I had the drive to dream, achieve, or succeed anymore. It's deliciously satisfying to see him recognize how wrong he was. I wish I could travel back in time to that fight, the one a few months before our breakup, when he found me sitting on the kitchen floor with my wineglass in the middle of the afternoon and criticized what looked like a lack of ambition. If only that version of myself could see my life now.

I dash off the briefest, politest text I can muster. It's funny: for years, I cared more about him than anyone or anything—where he was, how he was doing, what he was up to. But now I don't even care to know what his life looks like.

Thanks! Hope everything's going well.

I've got more important things to do.

• • •

At nine, I meet Hallie in her suite. She invited me to sit with her as she gets ready, and when she opens the door, she looks visibly more relaxed than she did just ninety minutes earlier.

"I sent my parents out for breakfast," she explains, welcoming me inside. "They get even more nervous than I do on days like this. Stressful vibes."

"Mine were like that, too," I say. "Actually, they still are."

"Maybe they could all learn to meditate," she suggests. "Sit with me while I do my hair and makeup?"

We head into the bathroom, where I flip down the toilet seat and sit, and she plugs in a hair straightener. When it's hot, she irons each section of hair until it's perfectly smooth, then brushes it all into a high, tight ponytail and blasts the crown of her head with extra-strength hair spray. I never wore much makeup when I was her age—not even to competitions—but this generation of gymnasts grew up watching beauty tutorials on YouTube and spending their allowances on Urban Decay Naked palettes and Kylie Jenner lip kits. They're so much savvier and sophisticated than I ever was; during competitions, they look like Hollywood starlets on the red carpet.

"I'm going to skip foundation because it'll just sweat off," she explains, digging through her makeup bag.

"Not that you need it anyway," I point out.

She shrugs. "But I'll do concealer, highlighter, and a little blush and bronzer."

She expertly applies those, then moves on to eye shadow primer, three different shades of sparkly eye shadow, black eyeliner, and several swipes of mascara. I feel like I could learn a thing or two from her.

"Good?" she asks, seeking approval.

"Let's just say that if you ever get bored of gymnastics, you could have a backup career as a makeup artist," I say.

"So, I have two leotard options for today, and I wanted to get your opinion," she says.

She opens the closet door and pulls out two hangers.

"I didn't hang them—that's nuts—but my mom spent, like, a half hour steaming them so they wouldn't wrinkle," she explains. "Like I said, she's stressed."

Hallie holds up one leotard in front of her, then the other. The first is bright purple, with an ombré effect on the bodice, mesh cut-outs on the sleeves, and a spray of rhinestones over the chest. It's like the sporty version of a beauty pageant gown—what Miss America might wear for her talent portion. The second one is much simpler: entirely red and flecked with silver shimmer.

"You'd look great in both," I say.

"But if you *had* to pick one," she implores.

It truly doesn't matter what she wears; the most important thing is that she feels confident. I don't want to accidentally pick the one she's leaning against and trigger her to second-guess her instincts.

"I really like both," I insist.

She purses her lips. "You know why I like the red one?" she says shyly.

"It's more comfortable?" I guess.

"This doesn't look familiar?" she asks.

I try to remember if she's worn it before, but I can't recall.

"You wore one just like this," she says, blushing a little. "I saw you on TV when I was little, and I was so starstruck."

Suddenly, I know exactly what she's talking about.

"Olympic Trials, 2012," I say.

She nods. "I wanted to be just like you. I still do."

"That was my very last competition, you know," I say carefully.

"But this won't be mine, because you've coached me so well," she says. "I wouldn't even be here at Trials without you."

A hard lump forms in the back of my throat. For so many years now, I've felt like a failure: I failed to make the Olympics; I literally failed out of college; I floundered through a failing relationship. I squandered my fresh start in California, and I neglected to take care of myself the way I deserved. But none of that matters to Hallie. In her eyes, it seems as if I'm an inspiration. I'm a role model. And most important, I'm a coach who has helped to give her a fair shot at achieving her lifelong dream.

"Oh, Hallie," I say, wrapping her in a hug. "Being your coach is truly the best thing I've ever done. I mean it. I don't know what I would've done without this job."

"Thank you for everything," she says, squeezing me back.

I blink hard twice and shake my head to keep the tears at bay. Now is not the time. Hallie puts the purple leotard back in the closet, then takes the red one into the bathroom to change. When she opens the door again a minute later, she twirls in a circle to show off the look.

Now that she's pointed out the connection, it's impossible to ignore. Clad in red, she looks an awful lot like I did eight years ago. Except now, Hallie looks confident. Self-assured. Happy. I desperately hope she has better luck today than I did.

• CHAPTER 32 •

The competition arena looks the same. It always does. No matter where you are in the country or the world, regardless of who's winning or what the year is. The familiar, standard-issue apparatus and mats and chalk bowls are arranged on a basketball floor under fluorescent lighting, surrounded by bleachers, with frenzied energy pulsing through the air. Ryan and I flank Hallie as we arrive, looking like a real team in our matching Summit tracksuits. For the first time in months, I truly *feel* like the three of us are in sync again. I'm glad Ryan and I got the chance to talk this morning.

Hallie takes in the view of the arena with a curious expression.

"This is it," she says, sounding stunned.

"Nothing you haven't seen before," I remind her.

"That's kind of chill," she says.

"Good," Ryan says. "I like that attitude. Go warm up."

She nods, slips out of her tracksuit, and jogs to the floor to run a few laps. Ryan slides closer to me on the bench, bridging the empty space Hallie left behind.

"You know, no matter what happens today, whether she makes it or not, I'm proud of us," he says. "I think we did a killer job."

"We made a pretty good team," I say.

"We did, didn't we?" He lets out a short laugh. "It's crazy to think of how much has happened this year. You moving back to Greenwood, joining me at Summit, the Kaminsky scandal, the Powerhouse offer, your foundation . . ."

He trails off. He doesn't need to say the rest. I know what he's thinking: we got together, broke up . . . and yet, we're still here. So is Dimitri, across the arena. He won't even look at me.

"Hey, the schedule's up," I say, nudging him, glad to have a safe talking point emerge.

It's a crowded roster: fifteen gymnasts competing for just four real spots on the Olympic team. Technically speaking, two other gymnasts are named as alternates, just in case anyone gets seriously injured during the Olympic Games—they can swap in and compete as backups. But obviously, nobody aspires to be an alternate. That means that after barely missing the chance of a lifetime, probably by a fraction of a point, you have to sit on the sidelines and cheer for your teammates to achieve your dream. It sounds like torture. As terrible as my experience was, at least I could choose not to watch the competition from the comfort of my own home.

Hallie is up against several gymnasts I know—Emma Perry, Delia Cruz, Maggie Farber, Kiki McCloud, Skylar Hayashi, and Brit Almeda—and also several that I don't: Olivia Walsh, Madison Salazar, Riley Robinson, Jocelyn Snyder, Ayanna Clayton, Taylor O'Connor, Charlotte Chan, Lucy Shapiro. It's dizzying and heart-breaking to consider that the majority of these girls will have their careers end today. The next few hours will change all of their lives.

Once again, Hallie has been assigned to start on bars, which means she'll cycle through vault, beam, and then floor. Apparently having finished her cardio warm-up, she trots back to where Ryan and I are sitting to stretch. She rolls her wrists, bends over her feet, and occasionally waves at cameras passing by.

Before the first rotation starts, Ryan squats down next to her and waves me over to join.

"Look, I'm not going to make a big speech to psych you up, because I know you've got this," he says simply. "All I want you to do is go out there and perform just as beautifully as you've been doing every day. Don't worry about anything beyond the actual work. Because that's all you can control."

She nods heavily, then hugs each of us.

"Got it. Thank you for everything. Let's do this," she declares.

I'm secretly glad that she's up first on bars, because that will get her started on the right foot. She puts on her grips and warms up for the allotted few minutes, and then waits for her turn. When the announcer booms her name over the loudspeaker, she waves to a girl in the stands holding a poster with her name on it as she strides toward the bars. This is her moment to shine, and she knows it.

"Let's go, Hallie, let's go!" I cheer.

She centers herself in front of the low bar, lifts her chin, and with just a hint of a smug smirk, jumps forward into her mount. Across the arena, another gymnast's floor music begins to play, but it's clear that Hallie has tuned out everything except the bar under her hands. Her body rockets cleanly to the high bar, where she swings up into a handstand, pirouettes, and flings herself into the series she's been drilling all year with Ryan: a Tkatchev into a Pak Salto. It's gorgeous. She finishes strong with two giants and her breathtaking dismount, a double-twisting double back tuck. Hallie sticks the landing solidly with her fingers splayed out in an elegant flourish. The audience cheers as she straightens up into a proud salute for the judges, then waves to the crowd. That was a goddamn perfect routine.

Ryan, who was spotting her release moves, high-fives her with both hands. They look triumphant as they make their way back to where I'm sitting.

"That was epic!" I say.

"Let's see what the judges have to say," she says modestly.

The judges barely need to deliberate. They award her routine with a well-deserved 15.150.

Hallie squeals, smooshing a hand over her mouth to muffle her excitement.

"See? Nothing to worry about. You're doing an amazing job," Ryan tells her.

By the end of the first rotation, she reigns in second place. The only person who scored even a sliver higher than her for the first round was Dimitri's gymnast Emma, with a 15.250 on beam. That doesn't faze me. Emma is freakishly, supernaturally, horrifyingly talented. Hallie's second-place showing is still fantastic. With a strong start like that, she could be a real contender for one of the four Olympic-bound spots.

Thanks to her excellent bars routine, Hallie's sure-footed confidence carries over to vault. The event goes by in such a flash, I don't even have time to get nervous. She sticks clean landings on both her first run, an Amanar, and her second, a Mustafina. After her final salute, she glides back to the bench serenely. The judges reveal her score as she settles down: 14.975.

Vault is the shortest event, which means there's a bit of wait before the second rotation ends and we can see where Hallie will fall in the rankings. As she sucks down the contents of her water bottle, I watch the competition. Delia polishes off a glorious floor routine. Ayanna completes an impressive series of release moves on bars. On beam, Charlotte sways off balance when trying to land a front aerial and loses her footing. The crowd lets out a somber "Ooooh" when she falls to the ground. I cringe; I feel so terrible for her. She climbs back up on beam and finishes her routine with a disappointed grimace.

When the second rotation ends, Hallie has dropped into fourth place. That's still a very good spot to be in—if the competition were over right this second, she'd make the Olympic team—but it also means there's no more room for error or bad luck. If she doesn't perform the hell out of her next two routines, or if anyone *else* happens to have a startlingly successful showing, it's game over.

I've always known, of course, that making the Olympic team is a long shot. I knew there were no guarantees of Hallie's success when I signed on to coach her. But somehow, I've never thought through exactly what to say or do to console her if it turns out that she doesn't make the team, despite our best efforts. There's no good way to comfort a person whose sole dream has just slipped away. I hope it doesn't come to that.

Hallie heads off to warm up for beam.

"You okay, Avery?" Ryan asks, once she's gone.

"Ha. Hanging in there," I say.

"You look stressed," he says.

He knows me well enough to see through the calm act I'm putting on for Hallie.

"I didn't realize this would bother me until I got here, but being at Trials again? It's just kind of a lot," I confess.

"Because of what happened to you?" he asks.

"I know *I'm* fine, and it's not that I expect Hallie to have a freak accident the way I did, but today's major, even if we're pretending it's not. No matter what happens today, a few people's lives change for the better, and everyone else's lives will really suck," I explain. "I know that sounds really stupid and obvious, but I just . . . I feel for these girls."

"It's high stakes," he says, nodding.

He reaches for my hand and runs his thumb soothingly across my palm. The gesture is comforting.

"I hope Hallie makes it," I say glumly.

He heaves a giant sigh. "Me, too."

I barely breathe when it's Hallie's turn on beam. The problem with this apparatus is that you can't get cocky: it doesn't matter how talented you are or how hard you've worked to prepare—you can still fall, and then you're screwed. "Come on, come on, come on," I whisper, watching her execute the back handspring, whip back, back layout step-out combo we've drilled so many times. It's solid, but I still can't relax. Every muscle in my body tightens as she winds up to perform the wolf turn. I'm relieved when she stays on the beam without a wobble. There's a brief glint of surprise on her face, too. Her dismount goes smoothly, too, and it's only when she salutes the judges that I can finally exhale. The routine was good, but not great: I can imagine one tiny deduction for not seamlessly connecting two jumps, and another one for a leg that could've been a little bit straighter. But overall, it was a fine showing.

She barrels back to the bench, where I wrap her in a hug and stroke her hair.

"You're amazing," I say. "You're doing a really beautiful job."

She shudders. "At least beam is over."

The judges give her a 13.500, and by the time the rotation ends, that lands her in sixth place—barely in Olympic contention, but only as an alternate. She's fallen behind Emma, Kiki, Delia, Taylor, and Ayanna. From what I can tell, the problem wasn't that her beam routine was terrible, but rather that everyone else had an unusually great rotation. I wish I could calculate what score she'll need in order to guarantee a full spot on the Olympic team, but I don't know how to even begin figuring that out. My stomach cramps with nerves.

Hallie presses her lips together like she's trying not to wince or groan. I kneel down in front of her, gripping both of her hands in mine. I have to go off script.

"Look, I know that we've been saying all day that you should just pretend like this is a normal day, and that you should just chill out and not sweat the competition, but that isn't going to work for floor," I tell her bluntly.

"What do you mean?" she asks.

"This is the most important performance you've ever had," I tell her honestly. "You need to pour every ounce of energy, every ounce of passion into this routine. Go out there and enjoy every single second of it, because this is what you've been training for your entire life."

The hairs on my arms stand up on end. Hallie locks her eyes with mine and nods seriously.

"This is it," she says.

"This is it," I repeat. "No matter what the outcome is, I'll always be so proud of you. But I want you to feel proud of yourself, too, and that means giving it your all."

"I can do that," she says.

She gives me a hug and heads to floor to warm up.

"That was a solid pep talk," Ryan says.

I groan. "I just hope it was enough."

I'm almost too antsy to watch Hallie practice her tumbling passes, but I know I have to pay attention in case there's any last-minute practical advice I should offer her. I wish we could just fast-forward through the fourth rotation.

Finally, enough time creaks by and it's Hallie's turn to compete on floor. Ryan and I stand fifteen feet to the left of the judges' table, which is just about as close as we can get without causing a distraction. Adrenaline rushes through me as her name is announced over the loudspeaker one more time.

Hallie composes herself at the edge of the floor. She smiles warmly at the judges as she salutes, then gracefully walks to her starting spot. She settles into position and waits for her music to begin. For a moment, everything is still and quiet—or as quiet as a bustling arena like this can be. She's a vision in sparkling red. As the jazzy opening notes play, she blossoms into a swirl of motion. The flick of her wrist is precise and delicate; the swing of her hips is flashy and flirty. She's always been a gymnast, but here, after months of hard work, she's developed the grace of a dancer, too.

On her first tumbling pass, she bounds cleanly across the floor, rocketing skyward in an elegant stag jump to channel her extra energy. It works beautifully: she looks powerful, strong, and in control of every movement. She dances toward another corner of the floor, polishes off two precise leaps, then dives straight into a second excellent tumbling pass. As I watch her prance, pirouette, and flip, I get a chilling sense of excitement. This is one of the most gorgeous routines I've ever seen from her. Something genuinely special is unfolding here—this is a determined athlete at her peak.

After Hallie executes her third tumbling pass seamlessly, something in her posture shifts. By this point in a floor routine, even the fittest gymnasts can start to look a little sluggish or out of breath. But Hallie looks even lighter and more buoyant than ever. With fifteen seconds left in the routine, she bursts forward into a triumphant fourth tumbling pass, landing easily on her feet. As she sinks into her final dramatic pose, her face crumples with joy, She holds the position just long enough to give the end of her routine a real sense of gravitas, and then bounces to her feet to salute the judges. The minute she's done, I see her eyes glistening with tears of joy. She claps one hand over her mouth and waves to the crowd with the other. The audience roars in applause.

She lingers on the floor for a few seconds longer than necessary, soaking up this once-in-a-lifetime moment. The judges are still deliberating over her score, so for the next few precious seconds, *this* is all that matters—she delivered the hell out of a routine that challenged her, scared her, and forced her to grow into a better athlete. Soon, her fate will be sealed, but for now, I can tell that she's happy with herself. That's a rare feat in this sport.

She bounds off the floor into my waiting arms.

"I'm so damn proud of you," I repeat over and over.

Ryan joins us for a group hug. "You were phenomenal. Incredible. The best I've ever seen," he says.

"I can't believe I just did that," she says, breathing hard.

Suddenly, she freezes. Her score appears on the scoreboard: 15.100, pushing her into second place. Even though there's one more gymnast left to perform on floor, it doesn't matter what score she'll receive—she won't knock Hallie out of the top four slots.

"I made it, I made it, oh my god, I made it," Hallie sobs.

Ryan and I break away to look at the scoreboard, then turn back to her in awe.

"Oh my god, Hallie!" I say, voice breaking.

Watching her recognize that her lifelong dream is coming true is one of the most beautiful things I've ever had the privilege of seeing. I can't help the tears coming. I don't mind. We've all worked hard enough to justify them.

"I knew it," Ryan says. Even his voice is shaking. "You're going to be an Olympian."

"We did it," Hallie says, sounding stunned. "I can't believe we did it."

Not her. Not Hallie and Ryan. *Us.* All of us.

In my own time as a gymnast, there were so many ecstatic moments, like when a gold medal was draped around my neck or the day I qualified for Olympic Trials. But truthfully, nothing quite compared to this victory. I feel as if I could burst from bliss.

● ● ●

The medal ceremony is a happy blur. In the end, Emma takes the top spot, as everyone knew she would. Hallie is the surprise dark horse in second place, followed by Olympic veteran Delia, with Kiki rounding out the team in fourth. The girls confer for seconds before they announce their team name: the Fantastic Four, superhero reference very much intended. Madison Salazar and Taylor O'Connor are named alternates.

There's no avoiding it—I feel terribly sad for the girls who didn't make the cut. But if I can come back to this sport years later as a coach and make a real difference, they can, too. There's life for all of us after our gymnastics careers end. It just might take some time to figure out exactly what that means.

Hallie's parents have stumbled, dazed and overjoyed, from the bleachers into the main part of the arena, where they shower their daughter with hugs.

"Let's give them some space," I whisper to Ryan.

It's crowded in the center of the arena, anyway—gymnasts, families, judges, photographers, reporters.

"Good idea," he says. "Come with me to get something to drink? I'm thirsty."

"Sure," I say.

We walk by the bench with our bags so Ryan can grab his wallet, then wander down a maze of hallways until we find a vending machine, chattering the entire way about the highlights of Hallie's performances.

"I don't think I'll ever get over that floor routine," Ryan says with a note of awe in his voice. "I mean, it was *perfect* from start to finish. She's never been better."

"I can't believe we pulled that off," I say, feeling giddy.

"We? No, that was you," he insists. "I'll take full credit for hiring the best floor coach on the planet, but that whole routine was all you."

The vending machine is stocked with Gatorade bottles lined up in bright, color-coded rows. Ryan tilts his head.

"Berry or Fruit Punch?" he asks.

"Berry all the way," I say.

"I'll get two, then," he says.

He feeds dollar bills into the slot and presses the right buttons. I lean against the side of the machine as it whirs to life, retrieving the plastic bottles and dropping them down with two solid *thunks*. It's cool and quiet here. After today's whirlwind, there's nowhere else I'd rather be. Tonight, I'll sleep easily in the luxe hotel bed, and tomorrow we'll all book our flights to Tokyo. This doesn't feel real. It's unbelievable, somehow, that after all these years, I'm finally going to the Olympics. Everything is falling into place. Or, rather, almost everything.

Ryan bends down to pick up the drinks and hands me one, interrupting my train of thought.

"Thanks," I say.

He starts to open his bottle, but I stop him.

"Wait," I say, reaching for his hand.

"Yeah?" he asks.

I kiss him before I can lose my nerve, sliding my arms over his shoulders and pulling him toward me. I can feel the muscles in his shoulders tense for a split second, and I lean back, but then I see a dimpled smile spreading across his face.

"Come here," he says softly. "I like that."

We find our way back to each other tenderly. His hands brace my hips, and soon, our lips fall into rhythm together. I've spent so many months aching to be close to him, and from the way his mouth moves against mine, it's clear that he's felt the same way. He kisses me deeply, and it just feels so right.

"I didn't expect that," he mumbles into my hair.

"I didn't plan on that," I explain.

"I'm glad it happened, though," he says earnestly.

"Me, too," I say.

I didn't know it was humanly possible to feel more relief and happiness than I've already felt today, but I'm so glad that my gut instinct was right—he wanted that kiss as much as I did. Ryan takes the Gatorade out of my hand and places both bottles on the linoleum floor by our feet so that he can kiss me again. It's perfect.

"Look, I know I messed up—" Ryan starts, but I shush him with another kiss.

"There's no need to keep apologizing," I say, wrapping my hands around his waist.

"No, hear me out," he insists. "I never stopped caring about you."

He speaks slowly and fiercely, giving each word the weight it deserves.

"I didn't say it before because I was an idiot, but the past few months have made me realize exactly how I feel," he continues.

I go very still, even as my heart races. His dark eyes search mine.

"Avery, I love you," he says.

I feel a rush of pure joy and a ballooning sense that everything is right in the world. This moment? It's better than a perfectly stuck landing. It's sweeter than the view from the top of the medal podium.

"I love you, too," I say.

I know I've never stopped. This time, I'm not self-conscious to voice how I really feel. Suddenly, the significance of where we happen to be standing hits me, and I can't help but laugh.

"What?" he asks.

"Do you remember our first conversation?" I ask.

"The night I called you about coaching at Summit?" he guesses.

"No, think—the very first time we ever spoke," I prompt.

His eyes light up. "It was Nationals. I asked if you knew where the vending machine was."

I smirk and lean back against this current vending machine, fingers dancing over his chest.

"Here we are," he marvels.

JULY

2020

• EPILOGUE •

It's competition day in Tokyo. I gasp when I enter the arena for the first time; the space is larger and flashier than anywhere I've ever competed, and handmade signs written in multiple languages wave in the crowd. Cameras capture every angle.

Hallie and the rest of the Fantastic Four warm up for the competition's first rotation. They're resplendent in matching royal blue leotards, and they work with an efficient, upbeat energy. Even though the stakes are higher today than ever before, everyone seems just so plain happy to be here. Hallie's on floor first.

While the gymnasts get ready to compete, I stand on the sidelines with Ryan. We flew to Tokyo a few days early so Hallie could prep for the competition while adjusting to the fourteen-hour time difference, and though we've been working a lot, there's also been just enough downtime to sneak out together on dates. The sushi dinner, sumo match, and Zen garden visit were amazing, but truthfully, we could've had just as much fun sitting in the supply closet at Summit. Since we got back together at Trials, I've felt so at peace. We've decided to keep our relationship private until after the Olympics.

A competition official signals to Hallie that she has time for one more tumbling pass, and then the warm-up will be over. Hallie nods, and I watch as she launches into a high-powered, tight double Arabian with a cleanly stuck landing. I shake my head in awe.

"Today's going to be a good day," I predict. "I can feel it."

"Me, too," Ryan says. He watches me studying Hallie on floor, then asks quietly, "Do you wish it were you out there?"

The question catches me off guard. For so long, I so desperately wanted to be in Hallie's exact position. Losing out on the chance to compete in the Olympics was the single most devastating experience of my life—worse than surviving Dimitri's rage, worse than watching my relationship with Tyler fall apart, worse than the time I thought I lost Ryan for good.

But the funny thing about your dream coming true is that it never quite happens the way you think it will. There's always a twist. When I walked into the Olympic stadium for the first time, nobody cheered for me or waved signs with my name. My heart didn't race with anticipation for my upcoming routines. Sports reporters didn't hound me for interviews. And even stranger than all that? I didn't care. I'm overjoyed to be here as Hallie's coach. I've let go of my old dreams. My new life has replaced them.

Before I can tell him any of that, though, Hallie joins us on the sidelines for a slurp from her water bottle.

"We were just talking about how strong your tumbling looks today," I tell her. "You're gonna kill it out there."

She grins and throws her arms around me. "Thank you so much for everything. I wouldn't have made it here without you."

She hugs Ryan, too, takes a deep breath, and walks proudly to the side of the floor with her head held high. An official booms out her name over a loudspeaker, and a hush falls over the arena. She waits patiently for the judges to indicate that she can begin. When it's time, she salutes them and arranges herself into the starting pose I choreographed for her all those months ago. From where I'm sitting, I can glimpse the confident expression on her face. There's a real poise to her today that she didn't quite have when we met.

My eyes well up with tears as the first notes of her music ring out through the arena.

"No, Ryan," I tell him. "I'm happy to be right here."

• ACKNOWLEDGMENTS •

First, I'd like to thank you, reader, for picking up this novel. I'm honored that you chose to spend your time immersed in the world of this book. Thank you for reading!

I'm so grateful for the thoughtful, whip-smart guidance of my editor, Kaitlin Olson. This book is better in countless ways because of her creative instincts, attention to detail, and belief in these characters. From catching plot holes to sharpening dialogue, Kaitlin made this project shine.

I'm incredibly lucky to work with the same wonderful team at Atria Books yet again: many thanks to Megan Rudloff and Isabel DaSilva for ensuring this book falls into all the right hands, Tamara Arellano for her tireless copyedits, and Lindsay Sagnette, Suzanne Donahue, Jimmy Iacobelli, and Libby McGuire.

My agent, Allison Hunter, championed this idea from the moment my half-baked email landed in her inbox. Her vision for my career, faith in my abilities, and true friendship make her the best teammate an author could ask for. At Janklow & Nesbit, Clare Mao and Natalie Edwards made this process so seamless.

This book was born of my lifelong love of gymnastics. I will forever be awestruck by athletes, including Shannon Miller, Carly Patterson, Nastia Liukin, Shawn Johnson, Alicia Sacramone, Gabby Douglas, McKayla Maroney, Simone Biles, and more. Most important, thank you to my own hometown hero Aly Raisman, whose work ethic, talent, and bravery has been a source of inspiration to me since childhood.

I'm thankful for the support of all my colleagues at *Elite Daily* and Bustle Digital Group, including Kylie McConville, Veronica Lopez, Iman Hariri-Kia, Emma Rosenblum, and Bryan Goldberg. I always feel fortunate that I don't have to choose between my work as an editor and as an author.

My friends were the ultimate cheerleading squad. They gave me plenty of positivity during tough writing days and celebrated with me every step of the way! Many thanks to Annie Kehoe, Morgan Boyer, Roshan Berentes, Kelsey Mulvey, Elyssa Goodman, Alexia LaFata, Dayna Troisi, Emily Raleigh, Emma Albert-Stone, and Devon Albert-Stone.

Thanks to Jerry and Eleanor Hart; Karen, Bob, and Jake Sykes; Bruce, Heather, Xander, Nathan, and Zoe Orenstein; and Jamie, Karin, Dani, and Rosie Orenstein for all their love.

To properly thank Mom, Dad, and Julia, I have to borrow my favorite word from Yiddish: when I think about how fully they've supported me with encouragement, enthusiasm, and so much love, I'm *verklempt* (that roughly translates to "overcome with emotion"). I can't imagine a better family in the world.

HANNAH ORENSTEIN is the author of *Playing with Matches* and *Love at First Like*, and is the senior dating editor at *Elite Daily*. Previously, she was a writer and editor at Seventeen.com. She lives in New York.